THE VIRGIN OF THE SUN

THE VIRGIN OF THE SUN

BY

H. RIDER HAGGARD

GYAN

Published by

GYAN

Gyan Publishing House
5, Ansari Road
Daryaganj, New Delhi-110002
Phone: 011-47034999, 9811692060
E-mail: books@gyanbooks.com

Distribution Network
gyanbooks.com
India, USA, Canada, UK, Australia

ISBN: 978-81-212-7559-0 (PB)
First Published, 1922

2nd Impression 2024

Printed at: Gyan Press, Delhi.

THE VIRGIN OF THE SUN
Author: H. RIDER HAGGARD

THE VIRGIN OF THE SUN

THE VIRGIN OF THE SUN

BY

H. RIDER HAGGARD

CASSELL AND COMPANY, LIMITED
London, New York, Toronto and Melbourne

First published 1922.

Ditchingham,
Oct. 24, 1921.

My dear Little,

Some five-and-thirty years ago it was our custom to discuss many matters, among them, I think, the history and romance of the vanished Empires of Central America.

In memory of those far-off days will you accept a tale that deals with one of them, that of the marvellous Incas of Peru; with the legend also that, long before the Spanish Conquerors entered on their mission of robbery and ruin, there in that undiscovered land, lived and died a White God risen from the sea?

Ever sincerely yours,
H. Rider Haggard.

James Stanley Little, Esq.

CONTENTS

THE VIRGIN OF THE SUN

INTRODUCTORY

THERE are some who find great interest, and even consolation, amid the worries and anxieties of life in the collection of relics of the past, drift or long-sunk treasures that the sea of time has washed up upon our modern shore.

The great collectors are not of this class. Having large sums at their disposal, these acquire any rarity that comes upon the market and add it to their store which in due course, perhaps immediately upon their deaths, also will be put upon the market and pass to the possession of other connoisseurs. Nor are the dealers who buy to sell again and thus grow wealthy. Nor are the agents of museums in many lands, who purchase for the national benefit priceless things that are gathered together in certain great public buildings which perhaps, some day, though the thought makes one shiver, will be looted or given to the flames by enemies or by furious, thieving mobs.

Those that this Editor has in mind, from one of whom indeed he obtained the history printed in these pages, belong to a quite different category, men of small means often, who collect old things, for the most part at out-of-the-way sales or privately, because they love them, and sometimes sell them again because they must. Frequently these old things appeal, not because of any intrinsic value that they may have, not even for their beauty, since they may be quite unattractive even to the cultivated eye, but rather for their associations. Such folk love to reflect upon and to speculate about the long dead individuals who have owned the relics, who have supped their soup from the worn Elizabethan spoon, who have sat at the rickety oak table found in a kitchen or an out-house, or upon the broken, ancient chair. They love to think of the little children whose skilful, tired hands wrought the faded sampler and whose bright eyes smarted over its innumerable stitches.

Who, for instance, was the May Shore ("Fairy," broidered in a bracket underneath, was her pet name), who finished yonder elaborate example on her tenth birthday, the 1st of May—doubtless that is where she got her name—in the year 1702, and on what far shore does she keep her birthdays now? None will ever know. She has vanished into the great sea of mystery whence she came, and there she lives and has her being, forgotten upon earth, or sleeps and sleeps and sleeps. Did she die young or old, married or single? Did she ever set *her* children to work other samplers, or had she none? Was she happy or unhappy, was she homely or beautiful? Was she a sinner or a saint? Again none will ever know. She was born on the 1st of May, 1692, and certainly she died on some date unrecorded. So far as human knowledge goes that is all her history, just as much or as little as will be left of most of us who breathe to-day when this earth has completed two hundred and eighteen more revolutions round the sun.

But the kind of collector alluded to can best be exemplified in the individual instance of him from whom the manuscript was obtained, of which a somewhat modernized version is printed on these pages. He has been dead some years, leaving no kin; and under his will, such of his motley treasures as it cared to accept went to a local museum, while the rest and his other property were sold for the benefit of a mystical brotherhood, for the old fellow was a kind of spiritualist. Therefore, there is no harm in giving his plebeian name, which was Potts. Mr. Potts had a small draper's shop in an undistinguished and rarely-visited country town in the east of England, which shop he ran with the help of an assistant almost as old and peculiar as himself. Whether he made anything out of it or whether he lived upon private means is now unknown and does not matter. Anyway, when there was something of antiquarian interest or value to be bought, generally he had the money to pay for it, though at times, in order to do so, he was forced to sell something else. Indeed these were the only occasions when it was possible to purchase anything, indifferent hosiery excepted, from Mr. Potts.

Now I, the Editor, who also love old things, and to whom therefore Mr. Potts was a sympathetic soul, was aware of this fact and entered into an arrangement with the peculiar assistant to whom I have alluded, to advise me of such crises which arose whenever the local bank called Mr. Potts's attention to the state of his account. Thus it came about that one day I received the following letter :—

Sir,

The Guv'nor has gone a bust upon some cracked china, the ugliest that ever I saw though no judge. So if you want to get that old tall clock at the first price or any other of his rubbish, I think now is your chance. Anyhow, keep this dark as per agreement.

Your obedient,

TOM.

(He always signed himself Tom, I suppose to mystify, although I believe his real name was Betterly.)

The result of this epistle was a long and disagreeable bicycle ride in wet, autumn weather, and a visit to the shop of Mr. Potts. Tom, alias Betterly, who was trying to sell some mysterious undergarments to a fat old woman, caught sight of me, the Editor aforesaid, and winked. In a shadowed corner of the shop sat Mr. Potts himself upon a high stool, a wizened little old man with a bent back, a bald head and a hooked nose upon which were set a pair of enormous horn-rimmed spectacles that accentuated his general resemblance to an owl perched upon the edge of its nest-hole. He was busily engaged in doing nothing and in staring at nothingness as, according to Tom, was his habit when communing with what he, Tom, called his " dratted speerits."

" Customer ! " said Tom in a harsh voice. " Sorry to disturb you at your prayers, Guv'nor, but not having two pair of hands I can't serve a crowd," meaning the old woman of the undergarments and myself.

Mr. Potts slid off his stool and prepared for action. When he saw, however, who the customer was he bristled—that is the only word for it. The truth is that although between us there was an inward and spiritual sympathy, there was also an outward and visible hostility. Twice I had outbid Mr. Potts at a local auction for articles which he desired. Moreover, after the fashion of every good collector he felt it to be his duty to hate me as another collector. Lastly, several times I had offered him smaller sums for antiques upon which he set a certain monetary value. It is true that long ago I had given up this bargaining for the reason that Mr. Potts would never take less than he asked. Indeed he followed the example of the Vendor of the Sibylline books in ancient Rome. He did not destroy the goods indeed after the fashion of that person and demand the price of all of them for the one that remained, but invariably he put up his figure by ten per cent. and nothing would induce him to take off one farthing.

"What do *you* want, Sir?" he said grumpily. "Vests, hose, collars or socks?"

"Oh, socks, I think," I replied at hazard, thinking that they would be easiest to carry, whereupon Mr. Potts produced some peculiarly objectionable and shapeless woollen articles which he almost threw at me, saying that they were all he had in stock. Now I detest woollen socks and never wear them. Still, I made a purchase, thinking with sympathy of my old gardener whose feet they would soon be scratching, and while the parcel was being tied up, said in an insinuating voice, "Anything fresh upstairs, Mr. Potts?"

"No, Sir," he answered shortly, "at least, not much, and if there were what's the use of showing them to you after the business about that clock?"

"It was £15 you wanted for it, Mr. Potts?" I asked

"No, Sir, it was £17 and now it's ten per cent. on to that; you can work out the sum for yourself."

"Well, let's have another look at it, Mr. Potts," I replied humbly, whereon with a grunt and a muttered injunction to Tom to mind the shop, he led the way upstairs.

Now the house in which Mr. Potts dwelt had once been of considerable pretensions and was very, very old, Elizabethan, I should think, although it had been re-fronted with a horrible stucco to suit modern tastes. The oak staircase was good though narrow, and led to numerous small rooms upon two floors above, some of which rooms were panelled and had oak beams, now white-washed like the panelling—at least they had once been white-washed, probably in the last generation.

These rooms were literally crammed with every sort of old furniture, most of it decrepit, though for many of the articles dealers would have given a good price. But at dealers Mr. Potts drew the line; not one of them had ever set a foot upon that oaken stair. To the attics the place was filled with this furniture and other articles such as books, china, samplers with the glass broken, and I know not what besides, piled in heaps upon the floor. Indeed where Mr. Potts slept was a mystery; either it must have been under the counter in his shop, or perhaps at nights he inhabited a worm-eaten Jacobean bedstead which stood in an attic, for I observed a kind of pathway to it running through a number of legless chairs, also some dirty blankets between the moth-riddled curtains.

Not far from this bedstead, propped in an intoxicated way against the sloping wall of the old house, stood the clock which I desired. It was one of the first "regulator" clocks with a wooden pendulum, used by the maker himself to check the time-keeping of all his other clocks, and enclosed in a chaste and perfect mahogany case of the very best style of its period. So beautiful was it, indeed, that it had been an instance of "love at first sight" between us, and although there was an estrangement on the matter of settlements, or in other words over the question of price, now I felt that never more could that clock and I be parted.

So I agreed to give old Potts the £20 or, to be accurate, £18 14s. which he asked on the ten per cent. rise principle, thankful in my heart that he had not made it more, and prepared to go. As I turned, however, my eye fell upon a large chest of the almost indestructible yellow cypress wood of which were made, it is said, the doors of St. Peter's at Rome that stood for eight hundred years and, for aught I know, are still standing, as good as on the day when they were put up.

"Marriage coffer," said Potts, answering my unspoken question.

"Italian, about 1600?" I suggested.

"May be so, or perhaps Dutch made by Italian artists; but older than that, for somebody has burnt 1597 on the lid with a hot iron. Not for sale, not for sale at all, much too good to sell. Just you look inside it, the old key is tied to the spring lock. Never saw such poker-work in my life. Gods and goddesses and I don't know what; and Venus sitting in the middle in a wreath of flowers with nothing on, and holding two hearts in her hands, which shows that it was a marriage chest. Once it was full of some bride's outfit, sheets and linen and clothes, and God knows what. I wonder where she has got to to-day. Some place where the moth don't eat clothes, I hope. Bought it at the break-up of an ancient family who fled to Norfolk on the revocation of the Edict of Nantes—Huguenot, of course. Years ago, years ago! Haven't looked into it for many years indeed, but think there's nothing there but rubbish now."

Thus he mumbled on while he found and untied the old key. The spring lock had grown stiff from disuse and want of oil, but at length it turned and we opened the chest, revealing the poker-work glories on the inner side of the lid and elsewhere. Glories they were indeed; never had I seen such artistry of the sort.

"Can't see it properly," muttered Potts, "windows want washing, haven't been done since my wife died, and that's twenty years ago. Miss her very much, of course, but thank God there's no spring-cleaning now. The things I've seen broken in spring-cleaning! yes, and lost too. It was after one of them that I told my wife that now I understood why the Mahomedans declare that women have no souls. When she came to understand what I meant, which it took her a long time to do, we had a row, a regular row, and she threw a Dresden figure at my head. Luckily I caught it, having been a cricketer when young. Well, she's gone now, and no doubt heaven's a tidier place than it used to be—that is, if they will stand her rummagings there, which I doubt. Look at that Venus, ain't she a beauty? Might have been done by Titian when his paints ran out, and he had to take to a hot iron to express his art. What, you can't see her well? Wait a bit and I'll get a lantern. Can't have a naked candle here—things too valuable; no money could buy them again. My wife and I had another row about naked candles, or it may have been a paraffin lamp. You sit on that old prayer-stool and look at the work."

Off he went crawling down the dusky stairs and leaving me wondering what Mrs. Potts, of whom now I heard for the first time, could have been like. An aggravating woman, I felt sure, for upon whatever points men differ, as to "spring-cleaning" they are all of one mind. No doubt he was better without her, for what did that dried-up old artist want with a wife?

Dismissing Mrs. Potts from my mind, which to tell the truth, seemed to have no room for her shadowy and hypothetical entity, I fell to examining the chest. Oh! it was lovely. In two minutes the clock was deposed and that chest became the sultana in my seraglio of beauteous things. The clock had only been the light love of an hour. Here was the eternal queen, that is, unless there existed a still better chest somewhere else, and I should happen to find it. Meanwhile whatever price that old slave-dealer Potts wanted for it, must be paid to him, even if I had to overdraw my somewhat slender account. Seraglios, of whatever sort, it must be remembered are expensive, luxuries of the rich indeed, though, if of antiques, they can be sold again which cannot be said of the human kind for who wants to buy a lot of antique frumps?

There were plenty of things in the chest, such as

some odds and ends of tapestry and old clothes of a Queen Anne character, put here no doubt, for preservation, as moth does not like this cypress wood. Also there were some books and a mysterious bundle tied up in a curious shawl with stripes of colour running through it. That bundle excited me, and I drew the fringes of the shawl apart and looked in. So far as I could see it contained another dress of rich colours, also a thick packet of what looked like parchment, badly prepared and much rotted upon one side as though by damp, which parchment appeared to be covered with faint black-letter writing, done by some careless scribe with poor ink that had faded very much.

There were other things too within the shawl, such as a box made of some red foreign wood, but I had not time to investigate further for just then I heard old Potts's foot upon the stair, and thought it best to replace the bundle. He arrived with the lantern and by its light we examined the chest and the poker-work.

"Very nice," I said, "very nice, though a good deal knocked about."

"Yes, Sir," he replied with sarcasm, "I suppose you'd like to see it neat and new after four hundred years of wear, and if so, I think I can tell you where you can get one to your liking. I made the designs for it myself five years ago for a fellow who wanted to learn how to manufacture antiques. He's in quod now and his 'antiques' are for sale cheap. I helped to put him there to get him out of the way as a danger to Society."

"What's the price?" I asked with airy detachment.

"Haven't I told you it ain't for sale? Wait till I'm dead and come and buy it at my auction. No, you won't though, for it's going somewhere else."

I made no answer but continued my examination while Potts took his seat on the prayer-stool and seemed to go off into one of his fits of abstraction.

"Well," I said at length when decency told me that I could remain no longer, "if you won't sell it's no use my looking. No doubt you want to keep it for a richer man, and of course you are quite right. Will you arrange with the carrier about sending the clock, Mr. Potts, and I will let you have a cheque. Now I must be off, as I've ten miles to ride and it will be dark in an hour."

"Stop where you are," said Potts in a hollow voice. "What's a ride in the dark compared with a matter like this, even if you haven't a lamp and get hauled before your own bench? Stop where you are, I'm listening to something."

So I stopped and began to fill my pipe.

"Put that pipe away," said Potts, coming out of his reverie, "pipes mean matches; no matches here."

I obeyed and he went on thinking till at last what between the chest and the worm-eaten Jacobean bed and old Potts on the prayer-stool, I began to feel as if I were being mesmerized. At length he rose and said in the same hollow voice,

"Young man, you may have that chest and the price is £50. Now for heaven's sake don't offer me £40, or it will be £100 before you leave this room."

"With the contents?" I said casually.

"Yes, with the contents. It's the contents I'm told you are to have."

"Look here, Potts," I said exasperated, "what the devil do you mean? There's no one in this room except you and me, so who can have told you anything unless it was old Tom downstairs."

"Tom," he said with unutterable sarcasm, "Tom! Perhaps you mean the mawkin that was put up to scare birds from the peas in the garden, for it has more in its head than Tom. No one here? Oh! what fools some men are Why the place is thick with them"

"Thick with whom?"

"Who? why ghosts of course, as you would call them in your ignorance. Spirits of the dead I name them. Beautiful enough too, some of them. Look at that one there." and he lifted the lantern and pointed to a pile of old bed posts of Chippendale design.

"Good day, Potts," I said hastily.

"Stop where you are," repeated Potts. "You don't believe me yet, but when you are as old as I am you will remember my words and believe—more than I do and see—clearer than I do, because it's in your soul, yes, the seed is in your soul, though as yet it is choked by the world, the flesh and the devil. Wait till your sins have brought you trouble; wait till the fires of trouble have burned the flesh away; wait till you have sought Light and found Light and live in Light, then you will believe; *then* you will see."

All this he said very solemnly, and standing there in that dusky room surrounded by the wreck of things that once had been dear to dead men and women, waving the lantern in his hand and staring—at what was he staring?—really old Potts looked most impressive. His twisted shape and ugly countenance became spiritual; he was as one who had "found Light and lived in Light."

"You won't believe me yet," he went on, "but I pass on to you what a woman has been telling me. She's a queer sort of woman; I never saw her like before, a foreigner and dark-hued with strange rich garments and something on her head. There, that, *that*" and he pointed through the dirty window-place to the crescent of a young moon which had appeared in the sky. "A fine figure of a woman," he went on, "and oh! heaven, what eyes—I never saw such eyes before. Big and tender, something like those of the deer in the park yonder. Proud too, she is, one who has ruled, and a lady, though foreign. Well, I never fell in love before, but I feel like it now, and so would you, young man, if you could see her, and so I think did someone else in his day."

"What did she say to you?" I asked, for by now I was interested enough. Who wouldn't be when old Potts took to describing beautiful women?

"It's a little difficult to tell you for she spoke in a strange tongue, and I had to translate it in my head, as it were. But this is the gist of it. That you were to have that chest and what was in it. There's a writing there, she says, or part of a writing for some has gone—rotted away. You are to read that writing or to get it read and to print it so that the world may read it also. She said that 'Hubert' wishes you to do so. I am sure the name was Hubert, though she also spoke of him with some other title which I do not understand. That's all I can remember, except something about a city, yes, a City of Gold and a last great battle in which Hubert fell, covered with glory and conquering. I understood that she wanted to talk about that because it isn't in the writing, but you interrupted and of course she's gone. Yes, the price is £50 and not a farthing less, but you can pay it when you like for I know you're as honest as most, and whether you pay it or not, you must have that chest and what's in it and no one else."

"All right," I said, "but don't trust it to the carrier, I'll send a cart for it to-morrow morning. Lock it now and give me the key."

In due course the chest arrived and I examined the bundle for the other contents do not matter, although some of them were interesting. Pinned inside the shawl I found a paper, undated and unsigned, but which from the character and style of the writing was, I should say, penned by a lady about sixty years ago. It ran thus :—

"My late father, who was such a great traveller in his young days and so fond of exploring strange places, brought these things home from one of his journeys before his marriage, I think from South America. He told me once that the dress was found upon the body of a woman in a tomb and that she must have been a great lady, for she was surrounded by a number of other women, perhaps her servants who were brought to be buried with her here when they died. They were all seated about a stone table at the end of which were the remains of a man. My father saw the bodies near the ruins of some forest city, in the tomb over which was heaped a great mound of earth. That of the lady, which had a kind of shroud made of the skins of long-wooled sheep wrapped about it as though to preserve the dress beneath, had been embalmed in some way, which the natives of the place, wherever it was, told him showed that she was royal. The others were mere skeletons, held together by the skin, but the man had a long fair beard and hair still hanging to his skull, and by his side was a great cross-hilted sword that crumbled to fragments when it was touched, except the hilt and the knob of amber upon it which had turned almost black with age. I think my father said that the packet of skins or parchment of which the underside is badly rotted with damp, was set under the feet of the man. He told me that he gave those who found the tomb a great deal of money for the dress, gold ornaments and emerald necklace, as nothing so perfect had been found before, and the cloth is all worked with gold thread. My father told me too that he did not wish the things to be sold."

This was the end of the writing.

Having read it I examined the dress. It was of a

sort that I had never seen before, though experts to whom I have shown it say that it is certainly South American of a very early date, and like the ornaments, probably pre-Inca Peruvian. It is full of rich colours such as I have seen in old Indian shawls which give a general effect of crimson. This crimson robe clearly was worn over a skirt of linen that had a purple border. In the box that I have spoken of were the ornaments, all of plain dull gold; a waist-band; a circlet of gold for the head from which rose the crescent of the young moon and a necklace of emeralds, uncut stones now much flawed, for what reason I do not know, but polished and set rather roughly in red gold. Also there were two rings. Round one of these a bit of paper was wrapped upon which was written, in another hand, probably that of the father of the writer of the memorandum:—

"Taken from the first finger of the right hand of a lady's mummy which I am sorry, in our circumstances, it was quite impossible to carry away."

This ring is a broad band of gold with a flat bezel upon which something was once engraved that, owing to long and hard wear, now cannot be distinguished. In short, it appears to be a signet of old European make but of what age and from what country, it is impossible to determine. The other ring was in a small leather pouch, elaborately embroidered in gold thread or very thin wire, which I suppose was part of the lady's costume. It is like a very massive wedding ring, but six or eight times as thick, and engraved all over with an embossed conventional design, of what look like stars with rays round them, or possibly petalled flowers. Lastly there was the sword-hilt, of which presently.

Such were the trinkets, if so they may be called. They are of little value intrinsically except for their weight in gold, because, as I have said, the emeralds are flawed as though they have been through a fire or from some other unknown cause. Moreover, there is about them nothing of the grace and charm of ancient Egyptian jewellery; evidently they belonged to a ruder age and civilization. Yet they had, and still have, to my imagining, a certain dignity of their own.

Also—here I became infected with the spirit of the peculiar Potts—without doubt these things were rich in human associations. Who had worn that dress of crimson with the crosses worked on it in gold wire (they cannot have been Christian crosses), and the purple-bordered skirt underneath, and the emerald necklace and the golden circlet from which rose the crescent of the young moon? Apparently a mummy in a tomb, the mummy of some long-dead lady of a strange and alien race. Was she such a one as that old lunatic Potts had dreamed he saw standing before him in the filthy, cumbered upper-chamber of a ruinous house in an English market town, I wondered, one with great eyes like to those of a doe and a regal bearing?

No, that was nonsense. Potts had lived with shadows until he believed in shadows that came out of his own imagination and into it returned again. Still she was a woman of some sort, and apparently she had a lover or a husband, a man with a great fair beard. How at this date, which must have been remote, did a golden-bearded man come to foregather with a woman who wore such robes and ornaments as these? And that sword hilt, worn smooth by handling and with an amber knob? Whence came it? To my mind—this was before expert examination confirmed my view—it looked very Norse. I had read the Sagas and I remembered a tale recorded in them of some bold Norsemen who about the years eight or nine hundred, had wandered to the coast of what is known now to be America—I think a certain Eric was their captain. Could the fair-haired man in the grave have been one of these?

Thus I speculated before I looked at the pile of parchments so evidently prepared from sheep skins by one who had only a very rudimentary knowledge of how to work such stuff, not knowing that in those parchments was hid the answer to many of my questions. To these I turned last of all, for we all shrink from parchments; their contents are generally so dull. There was a great bundle of them that had been lashed together with a kind of straw rope, fine straw that reminded me of that used to make Panama hats. But this had rotted underneath together with all the bottom part of the parchments, many sheets of them, of which only fragments remained, covered with dry mould and crumbling. Therefore the rope was easy to remove and beneath it, holding the sheets in place, was only some stout and comparatively modern string—it had a red thread in it that marked it as navy cord of an old pattern.

I slipped these fastenings off and lifted a blank piece of skin set upon the top. Beneath appeared the first sheet of parchment, closely, very closely covered with small "black-letter" writing, so faint and faded that even if I were able to read black-letter, which I cannot, of it I could have made nothing at all. The thing was hopeless. Doubtless in that writing lay the key to the mystery, but it could never be deciphered by me or anyone else. The lady with the eyes like a deer had appeared to old Potts in vain; in vain had she bidden him to hand over this manuscript to me.

So I thought at the time, not knowing the resources of science. Afterwards, however, I took that huge bundle to a friend, a learned friend whose business in life it was and is, to deal with and to decipher old manuscripts.

"Looks pretty hopeless," he said, after staring at these. "Still, let's have a try; one never knows till one tries."

Then he went to a cupboard in his muniment room and produced a bottle full of some straw-coloured fluid into which he dipped an ordinary painting brush. This charged brush he rubbed backwards and forwards over the first lines of the writing and waited. Within a minute before my astonished eyes, that faint indistinguishable script turned coal-black, as black as though it had been written with the best modern ink yesterday.

"It's all right," he said triumphantly, "it's vegetable ink, and this stuff has the power to bring it up as it was on the day when it was used. It will stay like that for a fortnight and then fade away again. Your manuscript is pretty ancient, my friend, time of Richard II., I should say, but I can read it easily enough. Look, it begins, 'I, Hubert de Hastings, write this in the land of Tavantinsuyu, far from England where I was born, whither I shall never more return, being a wanderer as the rune upon the sword of my ancestor, Thorgrimmer, foretold that I should be, which sword my mother gave me on the day of the burning of Hastings by the French,' and so on." Here he stopped.

"Then for heaven's sake, do read it," I said.

"My dear friend," he answered, "it looks to me as though it would mean several months' work, and forgive me for saying that I am paid a salary for my time. Now I'll tell you what you have to do. All this stuff must be treated, sheet by sheet, and when it turns black it must be photographed before the writing fades once more. Then a skilled person—so-and-so, or so-and-so, are two names that occur to me—must be employed to decipher it, again, sheet by sheet. It will cost you money, but I should say that it was worth while. Where the devil is, or was, the land of Tavantinsuyu?"

"I know," I answered, glad to be able to show myself superior to my learned friend in one humble instance. "Tavantinsuyu was the native name for the Empire of Peru before the Spanish Invasion. But, how did this Hubert get there in the time of Richard II.? That is some centuries earlier than Pizarro set foot upon its shores."

"Go and find out," he answered. "It will amuse you for quite a long while and perhaps the results may meet the expenses of decipherment, if they are worth publishing. I expect they are not, but then, I have read so many old manuscripts and found most of them so jolly dull."

Well, that business was accomplished at a cost that I do not like to record, and here are the results, more or less modernized, since often Hubert of Hastings expressed himself in a queer and archaic fashion. Also sometimes he used Indian words as though he had talked the tongue of these Peruvians, or rather the Chanca variety of it, so long that he had begun to forget his own language. Myself I have found his story very romantic and interesting, and I hope that some others will be of the same opinion. Let them judge.

But oh, I do wonder what was the end of it, some of which doubtless was recorded on the rotted sheets, though of course there can have been no account of the great battle in which he fell, since Quilla could not write at all, least of all in English, though I suppose she survived it and him.

The only hint of that end is to be found in old Potts's dream or vision, and what is the worth of dreams and visions?

BOOK I

CHAPTER I

The Sword and the Ring

I, Hubert of Hastings, write this in the land of Tavantinsuyu, far from England, where I was born, whither I shall never more return, being a wanderer as the rune upon the sword of my ancestor, Thorgrimmer, foretold that I should be, which sword my mother gave me on the day of the burning of Hastings by the French. I write it with a pen that I have shaped from a wing feather of the great eagle of the mountains, with ink that I have made from the juices of certain herbs which I discovered, and on parchment that I have split from the skins of native sheep, with my own hands, but badly I fear, though I have seen that art practised when I was a merchant of the Cheap in London Town.

I will begin at the beginning.

I am the son of a fishing-boat owner and was a trader in the ancient town of Hastings and my father was drowned while following his trade at sea. Afterwards, being the only child left of his, I took on his business, and on a certain day went out to sea to net fish with two of my serving men. I was then a young man of about three and twenty years of age and not uncomely. My hair, which I wore long, was fair in colour and curled. My eyes, set wide apart, were and still are large and blue, although they have darkened somewhat and sunk into the head in this land of heat and sunshine. My nose was wide-nostrilled and large, my mouth also was over-large, although my mother and some others used to think it well-shaped. In truth, I was large all over though not so tall, being burly, with a great breadth of chest and uncommon thickness through the body, and very strong; so strong that there were few who could throw me when I was young.

For the rest, like King David, I, who am now so tanned and weather worn, that at a little distance were my hair and beard hidden, I might almost be taken for one of the Indian Chiefs about me, was of a ruddy and a pleasant countenance, perhaps because of my wonderful health, who had never known a day of sickness, and of an easy nature that often goes with health. I will add this, for why should I not—that I was no fool, but one of those who succeed in that upon which they set their minds. Had I been a fool I should not to-day be the king of a great people, and the husband of their queen; indeed, I should not be alive.

But enough of myself and my appearance in those years that seem as far off as though they had never been save in the land of dreams.

Now I and my two serving men, sailors both of them, like myself and the most of the folk of Hastings, set out upon a summer eve, purposing to fish all night and return at dawn. We came to our chosen ground and cast out the net, meeting with wonderful fortune since by three in the morning the big boat was full of every kind of fish. Never before, indeed, had we made so large a haul.

Looking back at that great catch as here in this far land it is my habit to do upon everything, however small, that happened to me in my youth before I became a wanderer and an exile, I seem to see in it an omen. For has it not always been my lot in life to be kissed of fortune and to gather great store, and then of a sudden, to lose it all as I was to lose that rich multitude of fishes?

To-day, when I write this, once more I have great wealth of pomp and love and power, of gold also, more than I can count. When I go forth, my armies, who still look on me as half a god, shout their welcome and kiss the air after their heathen fashion. My beauteous queen bows down to me and the women of my household abase themselves into the dust. The people of the ancient City of Gold turn their faces to the wall and the children cover their eyes with their hands that they may not look upon my splendour as I pass, while maidens throw flowers for my feet to tread. Upon my judgment hangs life or death, and my lightest word is as though it were spoken from heaven. These and many other things are mine, the trappings of power, the prerogative of the Lord-from-the-Sea who brought victory to the Chanca people and led them back to their ancient home where they might live safe, far from the Inca's rage.

And yet often, as I sit alone in my splendour upon the roof of the ancient halls or wander through the starlit palace gardens, I call to mind that great catch of fishes in the English sea and of what followed after. I call to mind also my prosperity and wealth as one of the first merchants of London Town and what followed after. I call to mind too, the winning of Blanche Aleys, the lady so far above me in rank and station and what followed after. Then it is that I grow afraid of what may follow after this present hour of peace and love and plenty.

Certainly one thing will follow, and that is death. It may come late or it may come soon. But yesterday a rumour reached me through my spies that Kari

Upanqui, the Inca of Tavantinsuyu, he who once was as my brother, but who now hates me because of his superstitions, and because I took a Virgin of the Sun to be my wife, gathers a great host to follow on the path we trod many years ago when the Chancas fled from the Inca tyranny back to their home in the ancient City of Gold, and to smite us here. That host, said the rumours, cannot march till next year, and then will be another year upon its journey. Still, knowing Kari, I am sure that it will march, yes, and arrive, after which must befall the great battle in the mountain passes wherein, as of old, I shall lead the Chanca armies.

Perchance I am doomed to fall in that battle. Does not the rune upon Wave-Flame, the sword of Thorgrimmer my ancestor, say of him that holds it that,

> *"Conquering, conquered shall he be,*
> *And far away shall sleep with me"?*

Well, if the Chancas conquer, what care I if I am conquered? 'Twould be a good death and a clean, to fall by Kari's spear, if I knew that Kari and his host fell also, as I swear that fall they shall, St. Hubert helping me. Then at least Quilla and her children would live on in peace and greatness since they can have no other foe to fear.

Death, what is death? I say that it is the hope of every one of us and most of all of the exile and the wanderer. At the best it may be glory; at the worst it must be sleep. Moreover am I so happy that I should fear to die? Quilla cannot read this writing, and therefore I will answer, No. I am a Christian, but she and those about her, aye, my own children with them, worship the moon and the host of heaven. I am white-skinned, they are the hue of copper, though it is true that my little daughter, Gudruda, whom I named so after my mother, is almost white. There are secrets in their hearts that I shall never learn and there are secrets in mine from which they cannot draw the veil, because our bloods are different. Yet God knows, I love them well enough, and most of all that greatest of women, Quilla.

Oh! the truth is that here on earth there is no happiness for man.

It is because of this rumour of the coming of Kari with his host, that I set myself to this task, that I have long had in my mind, to write down something of my history, both in England and in this land which, at any rate for hundreds of years, mine is the first white foot to press. It seems a foolish thing to do since when I have written who will read, and what will chance to that which I have written? I shall leave orders that it be placed beneath my feet in the tomb, but who will ever find that tomb again? Still I write because something in my heart urges me to the task.

I return to the far-off days. Our boat being full, with merry hearts we set sail before a faint wind for Hastings beach. As yet there was little light and much fog, still the landward breeze was enough to draw us forward. Then of a sudden we heard sounds as of men talking upon ships and the clank of spars and blocks. Presently came a puff of air lifting the fog for a little and we saw that we were in the midst of a great fleet, a French fleet, for the Lilies of France flew at their mast-heads, saw too that their prows were set for Hastings, though for the while they were becalmed, since the wind that was enough for our light, large-sailed fishing-boat could not stir their bulk. Moreover they saw us, for the men-at-arms on the nearest ship shouted threats and curses at us and followed the shouts with arrows that almost hit us.

Then the fog closed down again, and in it we slipped through the French fleet.

It may have been the best part of an hour later that we reached Hastings. Before the boat was made fast to the jetty, I sprang to it shouting:

"Stir! stir! the French are upon you! To arms! We have slipped through a whole fleet of them in the mist."

Instantly the sleepy quay seemed to awaken. From the neighbouring fish market, from everywhere sailormen and others came running, followed by children with gaping mouths, while from the doors of houses far away shot women with scared faces, like ferreted rabbits from their burrows. In a minute the crowd had surrounded me, all asking questions at once in such a fashion that I could only answer them with my cry of:

"Stir! the French are upon you. To arms, I say. To arms!"

Presently through the throng advanced an old white-bearded man who wore a badge of office, crying as he came, "Make way for the bailiff!"

The crowd obeyed, opening a path and soon we were face to face.

"What is it, Hubert of Hastings?" he asked. "Is there fire that you shout so loudly?"

"Aye Worship," I answered. "Fire and murder and all the gifts that the French have for England. The Fleet of France is beating up for Hastings, fifty sail of them or more. We crept through them in the fog, for the wind which would scarce move them, served our turn and beyond an arrow or two, they took no note of a fishing-boat."

"Whence come they?" asked the bailiff, bewildered.

"I know not, but those in another boat we passed in the mist, shouted that these French were ravaging the coast and heading for Hastings to put it to fire and sword. Then that boat vanished away, I know not where, and that is all I have to tell save that the French will be here within an hour."

Without staying to ask more questions, the bailiff turned and ran towards the town, and presently the alarm bells rang out from the towers of All Saints and St. Clement's, while criers summoned all men to the market-place. Meanwhile I, not without a sad look at my boat and the rich catch within, made my way into the town, followed by my two men.

Presently I reached an ancient, timbered house, long, low and rambling, with a yard by its side full of barrels, anchors and other marine stores such as rope, that had to do with the trade I carried on at this place.

I, Hubert, with a mind full of fears, though not for myself, and a stirring of the blood such as was natural to my age at the approach of my first taste of battle, ran fast up to that house which I have described, and paused for a moment by the big elm tree that grew in front of the door, of which the lower boughs were sawn off because they shut out the light from the windows. I remember that elm tree very well, first because when I was a child starlings nested in a hole in the trunk, and I reared one of their young in a wicker cage and made a talking bird of it which I kept for several years. It was so tame that it used to go about sitting on my shoulder, till at last, outside the town a cat frightened it thence, and before I could recapture it, it was taken by a hawk, which hawk I shot afterwards with an arrow out of revenge.

Also this elm is impressed upon me by the fact that on that morning when I halted by it, I noted how green and full of leaf it was. Next morning, after the fire, I saw it again, all charred and blackened, with its beautiful foliage withered by the heat. This contrast remained upon my memory and whenever I see any great change of fortune from prosperity to ruin, or from life to death, always I bethink me of that elm. For it is by little things which we ourselves have seen and not by those written of or told by others, that we measure and compare events.

The reason that I ran so hard and then paused by the elm, was because my widowed mother lived in that house. Knowing that the French meant mischief, for a good reason, because one of their arrows, or perhaps a quarrel from a cross-bow, whistled just past the back of my head out there upon the sea, my first thought was to get her away to some place of safety, no easy task seeing that she was infirm with age. My second, that which caused me to pause by the tree, was how I should break the news to her in such a fashion that she would not be over-frightened. Having thought this over I went on into the house.

The door opened into the sitting-room that had a low roof of plaster and big oak beams. There I found my mother kneeling by the table upon which food was set for breakfast ; fried herrings, cold meat and a jug of ale. She was saying her prayers after her custom, being very religious though in a new fashion, since she was a follower of a preacher called Wycliffe, who troubled the Church in those days. She seemed to have gone to sleep at her prayers, and I watched her for a moment, hesitating to waken her. My mother, as even then I noted, was a very handsome woman, though old, for I was born when she had been married twenty years or more, with white hair and well-cut features that showed the good blood of which she came, for she was better bred than my father and quarrelled with her kin to marry him.

At the sound of my footsteps she woke up and saw me.

"Strange," she said. "I slept at my prayers who did so little last night, as has become a habit with me when you are out a-fishing, for which God forgive me, and dreamed that there was some trouble forward. Scold me not, Hubert, for when the sea has taken the father and two sons, it is scarcely wonderful that I should be fearful for the last of my blood. Help me to rise, Hubert, for this water seems to gather in my limbs and makes them heavy. One day, the leech says, it will get to the heart and then all will be over."

I obeyed, first kissing her on the brow, and when she was seated in her armed chair by the table, I said,

"You dream too well, Mother. There is trouble. Hark! St. Clement's bells are talking of it. The French come to visit Hastings. I know for I sailed through their fleet just after dawn."

"Is it so?" she asked quietly. "I feared worse. I feared lest the dream meant that you had gone to join your brothers in the deep. Well, the French are not here yet, as thank God you are. So eat and drink, for we of England fight best on full bellies."

Again I obeyed who was very hungry after that long night and needed food and ale, and as I swallowed them we heard the sound of folk shouting and running.

"You are in haste, Hubert, to join the others on the quay and send a Frenchman or two to hell with that big bow of yours?" she said inquiringly.

"Nay," I answered, "I am in haste to get you out of this town, which I fear me may be burnt. There is a certain cave up yonder by the Minnes Rock where I think you might lie safe, Mother."

"It has come down to me from my fathers, Hubert, that it was never the fashion of the women of the north to keep their men to shield them when duty called them otherwhere. I am helpless in my limbs and heavy, and cannot climb, or be borne up yonder hill to any cave. Here I stop where I have dwelt these five-and-forty years, to live or die as God pleases. Get you to your duty, man. Stay. Call those wenches and bid them fly inland to their folk, out Burwash way. They are young and fleet of foot, and no Frenchman will catch them."

I summoned the girls who were staring, white-faced, from the attic window place. In three minutes they were gone, though it is true that one of them, the braver, wished to bide with her mistress.

I watched them start up the street with other fugitives who were pouring out of Hastings, and came back to my mother. As I did so a great shout told me that the French fleet had been sighted.

"Hubert," she said, "take this key and go to the oak chest in my sleeping room, lift out the linen at the top and bring me that which lies wrapped in cloth beneath."

I did so, returning with a bundle that was long and thin. With a knife she cut the string that tied it. Within were a bag of money and a sword in an ancient scabbard covered with a rough skin which I took to be that of a shark, which scabbard in parts was inlaid with gold.

"Draw it," said my mother.

"I did so, and there came to light a two-edged blade of blue steel, such as I had never seen before, for on the blade were engraved strange characters whereof I could make nothing, although as it chanced I could read and write, having been taught by the monks in my childhood. The hilt, also, that was in the form of a cross, had gold inlaid upon it; at the top of it, a large knob or apple of amber, much worn by handling. For the rest it was a beauteous weapon and well balanced.

"What of this sword?" I asked.

"This, Son. With the black bow that you have," and she pointed to the case that leaned against the table, "it has come down in my family for many generations. My father told me that it was the sword of one Thorgrimmer, his ancestor, a Norseman, a Viking he called him, who came with those who took England before the Norman time; which I can well believe since my father's name like mine, till I married, was Grimmer. This sword, also, has a name and it is Wave-Flame. With it, the tale tells, Thorgrimmer did great deeds, slaying many after their heathen fashion in his battles by land and sea. For he was a wanderer, and it is said of him that once he sailed to a new land far across the ocean, and won home again after many strange adventures, to die at last here in England in some fray. That is all I know, save that a learned man from the north once told my father's father that the writing on the sword means :—

He who lifts Wave-Flame on high
In love shall live and in battle die;
Storm-tossed o'er wide seas shall roam
And in strange lands shall make his home.
Conquering, conquered shall he be,
And far away shall sleep with me.

Those were the words which I remember because of the jingle of them; also because such seems to have been the fate of Thorgrimmer and the sword that his grandson took from his tomb.

Here I would have asked about this grandson and the tomb, but having no time, held my peace.

"All my life have I kept that sword," went on my mother, "not giving it to your father or brothers, lest the fate written on it should befall them, for those old wizards of the north, who fashioned such weapons with toil and skill, could foresee the future—as at times

I can, for it is in my blood. Yet now I am moved to bid you take it, Hubert, and go where its flame leads you and dree your doom, whatever it may be, for I know you will use it like Thorgrimmer's self."

She paused for a moment, then went on.

"Hubert, perhaps we part for the last time, for I think that my hour is at hand. But let not that trouble you, since I am glad to go to join those who went before, and others with them, perchance Thorgrimmer's self. Hearken, Hubert. If aught befalls me, or this place, stay not here. Go to London town and seek out John Grimmer, my brother, the rich merchant and goldsmith who dwells in the place called Cheap. He knew you as a child and loved you, and lacking offspring of his own will welcome you for both our sakes. My father would not give John the sword lest its fate should be on him, but I say that John will be glad to welcome one of our race who holds it in his hand. Take it then, and with it that bag of gold, which may prove of service ere all be done.

"Aye, and there is one more thing—this ring which, so says the tale, came down with the sword and the bow, and once had writing on it like the sword, though that is long since rubbed away. Take it and wear it till perchance, in some day to come, you give it to another as I did."

Wondering at all this tale which, after her secret fashion, my mother had kept from me till that hour, I set the ring upon my finger.

"I gave yonder ring to your father on the day that we were betrothed," went on my mother, "and I took it back again from his corpse after he had been found floating in the sea. Now I pass it on to you who soon will be all that is left of both of us."

"Hark!" she continued, "the crier summons all men with their arms to the market-place to fight

England's foes. Therefore one word more while I buckle the sword Wave-Flame on to you, as doubtless his women folk did on to Thorgrimmer, your ancestor. My blessing on you, Hubert. Be you such an one as Thorgrimmer was, for we of the Norse blood desire that our loves and sons should prove not backward when swords are aloft and the arrows fly. But be you more than he, be you a Christian also, remembering that however long you live, and the Battle-maidens have not marked you yet, at last you must die and give account.

"Hubert, you are such a one as women will love; one too who, I fear me, will be a lover of women, for that weakness goes with strength and manhood by Nature's laws. Be careful of women, Hubert, and if you may, choose those who are not false and cling to her who is most true. Oh, you will wander far; I read it in your eyes that you will wander far, yet shall your heart stay English. Kiss me and begone! Lad, are you forgetting your spare arrows and the bull-hide jerkin that was your father's? You will want them both to-day. Farewell, farewell! God and His Christ be with you—and shoot you straight and smite you hard. Nay, no tears, lest my eyes should be dimmed, for I'll climb to the attic and watch you fight."

CHAPTER II

The Lady Blanche

So I went, with a sore heart, for I remembered that when my father and brothers were drowned, although I was then but a little one, my mother had foreseen it, and I feared much lest it might be thus in her own case also. I loved my mother. She was a stern woman, it was true, with little softness about her, which I think came with her blood, but she had a high heart, and oh! her last words were noble. Yet through it all I was pleased, as any young man would have been, with the gift of the wonderful sword which once had been that of Thorgrimmer, the sea-rover whose blood ran in my body against which it lay, and I hoped that this day I might have chance to use it worthily as Thorgrimmer did in forgotten battles. Having imagination, I wondered also whether the sword knew that after its long sleep it had come forth again to drink the blood of foes.

Also I was pleased with another thing, namely that my mother had told me that I should live my life and not die that day by the hand of Frenchmen; and that in my life I should find love, of which to tell truth already I knew a little of a humble sort, for I was a comely youth, and women did not run away from me, or if they did, soon they stopped. I wanted to live my life, I wanted to see great adventures and to win great love. The only part of the business which was not to my taste was that command of my mother's, that I should go to London to sit in a goldsmith's shop.

Still, I had heard that there was much to be seen in London, and at least it would be different from Hastings.

The street outside our doors was crowded with folk, some of the men making their way to the market-place, about whom hung women and children weeping; others, old people, wives and girls and little ones fleeing from the town. I found the two sailormen who had been with me on the boat, waiting for me. They were brawny fellows named Jack Grieves and William Bull, who had been in our service since my childhood, good fishermen and fighters both; indeed one of them, William Bull, had served in the French wars.

"We knew that you were coming, Master, so we bided here for you," said William, who having once been an archer was armed with a bow and a short sword, whereas Jack had only an axe, also a knife such as we used on the smacks for cleaning fish.

I nodded, and we went on to the market-place and joined the throng of men, a vast number of them, who were gathered there to defend Hastings and their homes. Nor were we too soon, for the French ships were already beaching within a few yards of the shore or on it, their draught being but small, while the sailors and men-at-arms were pushing off in small boats or wading to the strand.

There was great confusion in the market-place, for as is common in England, no preparation had been made against attack though such was always to be feared.

The bailiff ran about shouting orders, as did others, but proper officers were lacking, so that in the end men acted as the fancy took them. Some went down towards the beach and shot with arrows at the Frenchmen. Others took refuge in houses, others stood irresolute, waiting, knowing not which way to turn. I and my two men were with those who went on to the beach where I loosed some arrows from my big black bow, and saw a man fall before one of them.

But we could do little or nothing, for these Frenchmen were trained soldiers under proper command. They formed themselves into companies and advanced, and we were driven back. I stopped as long as I dared, and drawing the sword, Wave-Flame, fought with a Frenchman who was in advance of the others. What is more, making a great blow at his head which I missed, I struck him on the arm and cut it off, for I saw it fall to the ground. Then others rushed up at me and I fled to save my life.

Somehow I found myself being pressed up the steep Castle Hill with a number of Hastings folk, followed by the French. We reached the Castle and got into it, but the old portcullis would not close, and in sundry places the walls were broken down. Here we found a number of women who had climbed for refuge, thinking that the place would be safe. Among these was a beautiful and high-born maiden whom I knew by sight. Her father was Sir Robert Aleys who, I believe, was then the Warden of the Castle of Pevensey, and she was named the Lady Blanche. Once indeed I had spoken with her on an occasion too long to tell. Then her large blue eyes, which she knew well how to use, had left me with a swimming head, for she was very fair and very sweet and gracious, with a most soft voice, and quite unlike any other woman I had ever seen, nor did she seem at all proud. Soon her father, an old knight, who had no name for gentleness in the country-side, but was said to be a great lover of gold, had come up and swept her away, asking her what she did, talking with a common fishing churl. This had happened some months before.

Well, there I found her in the Castle, alone it seemed,

and knowing me again, which I thought strange, she ran to me, praying me to protect her. More, she began to tell me some long tale, to which I had not time to listen, of how she had come to Hastings with her father, Sir Robert, and a young lord named Deleroy, who I understood was some kinsman of hers, and slept there. How, too, she had been separated from them in the throng when they were attempting to return to Pevensey which her father must go to guard, because her horse was frightened and ran away, and of how finally men took her by the arm and brought her to this castle, saying that it was the safest place.

"Then here you must bide, Lady Blanche," I answered, cutting her short. "Cling to me and I will save you if I can, even if it costs me my life."

Certainly she did cling to me for all the rest of that terrible day, as will be seen.

From this height we saw Hastings beginning to burn, for the Frenchmen had fired the town in sundry places, and being built of wood, it flamed furiously. Also we saw and heard horrible scenes and sounds of rapine, such as chance in this Christian world of ours where a savage foe finds peaceful folk of another race at his mercy. In the houses people were burnt; in the streets they were being murdered, or worse. Yes, even children were murdered, for afterwards I saw the bodies of some of them.

A while later through the wreaths of smoke we perceived companies of the French advancing to attack the Castle. There may have been three hundred of them in all, and we did not count more than fifty men, some of us ill-armed, together with a mob of aged people and many women and children. What had become of the other men I do not know, but orders had been shouted from all quarters, and some had gone this way and some that. Some, too, I think had fled, lacking leaders.

The French having climbed the hill, began to attack our ill-fenced gateways, bringing up beams of timber to force them in. Those of us who had bows shot some of them, though, their armour being good, for the most part the arrows glanced. But few had bows. Moreover whenever we showed ourselves they poured such a rain of quarrels and other shafts upon us that we could not face it, lacking mail as we did, and a number of us were killed or wounded. At last they forced the easternmost gate which was the weakest, and got in there and over a place in the wall where it was broken. We fought them as well as we could; myself I cut down two with the sword, Wave-Flame, hewing right through the helm of one, for the steel of that sword was good. Here, too, Jack Grieves was killed by my side by a pike thrust, and died calling to me to fight on for old England and Hastings town; after which he said something about beer and breathed his last.

The end of it was that those who were left were driven out of the Castle together with the women and children, the murdering French killing every man who fell wounded where he lay, and trying to make prisoner any women they thought young and fair enough. Especially did they seek to capture the Lady Blanche, because they saw that she was beautiful and of high station. But by good fortune more than aught else, I saved her from this fate.

As it chanced we were among the last to leave the Castle, whence to tell truth, I was loath to go, for by now my blood was up, and with a few others fought till I was driven out. I prayed the Lady Blanche to run forward with the other women. But she would not, answering that she trusted no one else, but would stay to die with me, as though that would help either of us.

Thus it came about that a tall French knight who had set his eyes on her, out-climbed his fellows upon the slope of the hill, for they were weary and gathering to re-form, and catching her round the middle, strove to drag her away. I fell on him and we fought. He had fine armour and a shield while I had none, but I held the long sword while he only wielded a battle-axe. I knew that if he could get in a blow with that battle-axe, I was sped, since the bull's hide of my jerkin would never stand against it. Therefore it was my business to keep out of his reach. This, being young and active, for the most part I made shift to do, especially as he could not move very quickly in his mail. The end of it was that I cut him on the arm through a joint in his harness, whereon he rushed at me, swearing French oaths.

I leapt on one side and as he passed, smote with all my strength. The blow fell between neck and shoulder, from behind as it were, and such was the temper of that sword named Wave-Flame that it shore through his mail deep into the flesh beneath, to the backbone as I believe. At least he went down in a heap—I remember the rattle of his armour as he fell, and there lay still. Then we fled on down the steep path, I holding the bloody sword with one hand and Lady Blanche with the other, while she thanked me with her eyes.

At length we were in the town again, running up my own street. On either side of us the houses burned, and behind us came another body of the French. The reek got into our eyes and we stumbled over dead or fainting people.

Looking to the left I caught sight of the elm tree of which I have spoken, that grew in front of our door and saw that behind it our house was burning. Yes, and I saw more, for at the attic window which was open, the flames making an arch round her, sat my mother. Moreover, she was singing for I heard her voice and the wild words she sang, though this was a strange thing for a woman to do in the hour of such a death. Further, she saw and knew me, for she waved her hands to me, then pointed towards the sea, why, I did not guess at the time. I stopped, purposing to try to rescue her though the front of the house was flaming, and the attempt must have ended in my death. But at that moment the roof fell in, causing the fire to spout upwards and outwards. This was the last that I saw of my mother, though afterwards we found her body and gave it burial with those of many other victims.

There was no time to stay, for the conquering French were pouring up the street behind us, shooting as they came and murdering any laggards whom they could catch. On we went up the steep slope of the Minnes Rock. I would have fled on into the open country, but the Lady Blanche had no strength left. Twice she sank to the ground, stricken with terror and weariness, and each time prayed me not to leave her; nor indeed did I wish to do so. The end of it was that William Bull and I between us half carried her with much toil to the cave of which I had spoken to my mother. The task was heavy and slow, since always we must scramble over sheer ground. What is more, a party of the French, seeing our plight, followed us. Perhaps some of them guessed who the lady was, for there were many spies in Hastings who might have told them, and desired to capture and hold her to ransom.

At the least they came on after us and a few others, women all of them, who had joined our company, being unable to travel further, or trusting to William Bull and myself to protect them.

We reached the cave, and thrusting the women along it, William and I stood in the mouth and waited. He had no bow and all my arrows were gone save three, but of these I, who was noted for my archery, determined to make the best use I could. So I drew them out, and having strung the bow, sat down to get my breath. On came the French, shouting and jabbering at us to the effect that they would cut our throats and carry off *la belle dame* to be their sport.

"She shall be mine!" yelled a big fellow with a flattened nose and a wide mouth who was ahead of the others, and not more than fifty yards away.

I rose, and praying my patron, good St. Hubert after whom I was named because first I saw light upon his day, the 23rd of November, to give me skill, I drew the great bow to my ear, aimed and loosed. Nor did St. Hubert, a lover of fine shooting, fail me in my need, for that arrow rushed out and found its home in the big mouth of the Frenchman, through which it passed, pinning his foul tongue to his neck bone.

Down he went, and cheered by the sight I refitted and loosed at the next. Him too, the arrow caught, so that he fell almost on the other.

I set the third and last arrow on the string and waited a space. Behind these two was a squat, broad man, a knight I suppose, for he wore armour, and had a shield with a cock painted on it. This man, frightened by the fate of his companions, yet not minded to give up the venture for those in rear of him urged him on, bent himself almost double, and holding the shield over his helm which was closed, so as to protect his head and body, came on at good pace.

I waited till he was within five-and-twenty yards or so, hoping that the roughness of the ground would cause him to stumble and the shield to shift so that I could get a chance at him behind it. But it did not, so at last, again praying to St. Hubert, I drew the big bow till the string touched my ear, and let drive. The shaft, pointed with tempered steel, struck the shield full in the centre, and by Heaven, pierced it, aye, and the mail behind, aye and the flesh it covered, so that he too got his death.

"A great shot, Master," said William, "that no other bow in Hastings could have sped."

"Not so ill," I answered, "but it is my last. Now we must fight as we can with sword and axe until we be sped."

William nodded, and the women in the cave began to wail while I unstrung my bow and set it in its case, from habit I think, seeing that I never hoped to look upon it again.

Just then from the French ships in the harbour there came a great blaring of trumpets giving some alarm, and the Frenchmen of a sudden, ceasing from their attack, turned and ran towards the shore. I stepped out of the cave with William and looked. There on the sea drawing near from the east before a good wind, I saw ships and saw, too, that from their masts flew the pennons of England, for the golden leopards gleamed in the sun.

"It is our fleet, William," I said, "come to talk with these French."

"Then I would that it had come sooner," answered William. "Still, better now than not at all."

Thus were we saved, through Hamo de Offyngton, the Abbot of Battle Abbey, or so I was told afterwards, who collected a force by land and sea and drove off the French after they had ravaged the Isle of Wight, attacked Winchelsea, and burned the greater part of

Hastings. So it came about that in the end these pirates took little benefit by their wickedness, since they lost sundry ships with all on board, and others left in such haste that their people remained on shore where they were slain by the mob that gathered as soon as it was seen that they were deserted, helped by a company of the Abbot's men who had marched from Battle. But with all this I had nothing to do who now that the fight was over, felt weak as a child and could think of little save that I had seen my mother burning.

Presently, however, that happened which woke me from my grief and caused my blood which had grown sluggish, to run again. For when she knew that she was safe the Lady Blanche came out of the cave and addressed me as I stood there leaning against the rock with the red sword Wave-Flame in my hand, as I had drawn it to make ready for the last fight to the death. All sorts of sweet names she called me—a hero, her deliverer, and I know not what besides.

In the end, as I made no answer, being dazed, also hurt by an axe blow on the breast which I had not felt before, dealt by that Frenchman whom I slew near the Castle, she did more. Throwing her arms about me she kissed me thrice, on either cheek and on the lips, doubtless because she was overwrought, and in her thankfulness forgot her maidenly reserve, though as William Bull said afterwards, this forgetfulness did not cause her to kiss him who had also helped her up the hill.

Those kisses were like wine to me, for it is strange how, if we love her, by the decree of Nature the touch of a beautiful woman's lips, felt for the first time, affects us in our youth. Whatever else we forget, that we always remember, however false those lips may afterwards be proved. For then the wax is soft and the die sinks deep, so deep that no after heats can melt its stamp and no fretting wear it out while we live beneath the sun.

Now my young blood being awakened, I was minded to return those kisses, and began to do so with a Jew's interest, when I heard a rough voice swearing many strange oaths, and heard also the other women who had sheltered with us in the cave, begin to titter, for the moment forgetting all their private woes, as those of their sex will do when there is kissing in the wind.

"God's blood!" said the rough voice, "who is this that handles my daughter as though they had been but an hour wed? Take those lips of yours from her, fellow, or I'll cut them from your chops."

I looked round astonished, to see Sir Robert Aleys mounted on a grey horse, and followed by a company of men-at-arms who appeared to be under the command of a well-favoured, dark-eyed young captain with long hair, and dressed more wondrously than any man I had ever seen before. Had he put on Joseph's coat over his mail, he could not have worn more colours, and I noted that the toes of his shoes curled up so high, that I wondered however he worked them through his stirrups, and what would happen to him if by chance he were unhorsed.

Being taken aback I made no answer, but William Bull, who, if a rough fellow, had a tongue in his head and a ready wit, spoke up for me.

"If you want to know," he said in his Sussex drawl, "I'll tell you who he is, Sir Robert Aleys. He is my worshipful master, Hubert of Hastings, ship-owner, householder and trader of this town. Or at least he was these things, but now it seems that his ships and house are burnt and his mother with them; also that there will be no trade in Hastings for many a day."

"Mayhap," answered Sir Robert, adding other oaths, "but why does he buss my daughter?"

"Perchance because he must give as good as he got, which is a law among honest merchants, noble Sir Robert. Or perchance because he has a better right to buss her than any man alive, seeing that but for him, by now she would be but stinking clay, or a Frenchman's leman."

Here the fine young captain cut in, saying,

"Whatever else this worshipful trader may need, he does not lack a trumpeter."

"That is so, my Lord Deleroy," replied William unmoved, "for when I find a good song I like to sing it. Go now and look at those three men who lie yonder on the slope, and see whether the arrows in them bear my master's mark. Go also and look upon the Castle Hill and find a knight with his head well-nigh hewn from his shoulders, and see whether yonder sword fits into the cut. Aye and at others that I could tell you of, slain, every one of them, to save this fair lady. Aye, go you whose garments are so fine and unstained, and then come back and talk of trumpeters."

"Pish!" said my Lord Deleroy with a shrug of his shoulders, "a lady who is overwrought and hangs to some common fellow, like one who kisses the feet of a wooden saint that she thinks has saved her from calamity!"

At these words I, who had been listening like a man in a dream, awoke as it were, for they stung me. Moreover, I had heard that this fine Deleroy was one of those who owed his place and rank to the King's favour, as he did his high name, being, it was reported, by birth but a prince's bastard sprung from some relative of Sir Robert whom therefore he called cousin.

"Sir," I said, "you know best whether I am more common than you are. Let that be. At least I hold in my hand the sword of one who begat my forefather hundreds of years ago, a certain Thorgrimmer who was great in his time. Now I have had my fill of fighting to-day, and you, doubtless through no fault of your own, have had none; you also are clad in mail and I, a common fellow, have none. Deign then to descend from that horse and take a turn with me though I be tired, and thus prove my commonness upon my body. Of your nobility do this, seeing that after all we are of one flesh."

Now, stung in his turn, he made as though he would do what I prayed, when for the first time, after glancing at her father who sat still—puzzled it would seem—the Lady Blanche spoke.

"Be not mad, Cousin," she said. "I tell you that this gentleman has saved my life and honour, twice at least to-day. Is it wonderful, then, if I thanked him in the best fashion that a woman can, and thus brought your insults on him?"

He hesitated, though one of his curled-up shoes was out of the stirrup, when suddenly Sir Robert broke in in his big voice, saying:

"God's truth, Cousin, I think that you will do well to leave this young cock alone, since I like not the look of that red spur of his," and he glanced at the sword Wave-Flame. "Though he be weary, he may have a kick or two in him yet."

Then he turned to me and added:

"Sir, you have fought well; many a man has earned knighthood for less, and if a fair maid thanked you in her own fashion, you are not to blame. I, her father, also thank you and wish you all good fortune till we meet again. Farewell. Daughter, make shift to share this horse with me, and let us away out of this stricken town to Pevensey, where perchance it will please those French to call to-morrow."

A minute later they were gone, and I noted with a pang that as they went the Lady Blanche, having waved her good-bye to me, talked fast to her cousin Deleroy and that he held her hand to steady her upon her father's horse.

CHAPTER III

Hubert Comes to London

When the Lady Blanche was out of sight, followed by the women who had sheltered with us in the cave, William and I went to a stream we knew of not far away and drank our fill. Then we walked to the three whom I had shot with my big bow, hoping to regain the arrows, for I had none left. This, however, could not be done though all the men were dead, for one of the shafts, the last, was broken, and the other two were so fixed in flesh and bone that only a surgeon's saw would loose them.

So we left them where they were, and before the men were buried many came to marvel at the sight, thinking it a wonderful thing that I should have killed these three with three arrows, and that any bow which arm might bend could have driven the last of them through an iron shield and a breastplate behind it.

This armour, I should tell, William took for himself, since it was of his size. Also on the morrow, returning to the Castle Hill, I stripped the knight whom I had slain with the sword, Wave-Flame, of his splendid Milan mail, whereof the *plastron*, or breast-plate, was inlaid with gold, having over it a *camail* of chain to cover the joints, through which my good sword had shorn into his neck. The cognizance on his shield strangely enough was three barbed arrows, but what was the name of the knight who bore it I never learned. This mail, which must have cost a great sum, the Bailiff of Hastings granted me to keep, since I had slain its wearer and borne myself well in the fight. Moreover, I took the three arrows for my own cognizance, though in truth I had no right to any, being in those days but a trader. (Little did I know then how well this mail was to serve me in the after years.)

By now night was coming on, and as we could see from the cave mouth that the part of Hastings which lies towards the village of St. Leonards seemed to have escaped the fire, thitherward we went by the beach to avoid the heat and falling timbers in the burning town. On our way we met others and from them heard all that had befallen. It would seem that the French loss in life was heavier than our own, since many of them were cut off when they tried to fly to their ships, and some of these could not be floated from the beach or were rammed and sunk with all aboard by the English vessels. But the damage done to Hastings was such as could scarcely be made good in a generation, for the most of it was burnt or burning. Also many, like my own mother, had perished in the fire, being sick or aged or in childbed, or for this reason and that forgotten and unable to move. Indeed on the beach were hundreds of folk in despair, nor was it only the women and children who wept that evening.

For my part, with William I went beyond the burning to the house of a certain old priest who was my confessor, and the friend of my father before me, and there we found food and slept, he returning thanks to God for my escape and offering me consolation for the loss of my mother and goods.

I rested but ill that night, as those do who are over weary. Moreover, this had been my first taste of battle, and again and again I saw those men falling before my sword and arrows. Very proud was I to have slain them, wicked ravishers as they were, and very glad that from my boyhood I had practised myself with sword and bow till I could fence with any, and was perhaps the most skilled marksman in Hastings, having won the silver arrow at the butts at the last meeting, and from archers of all ages. Yet the sight of their deaths haunted me who remembered how well their fate might have been my own, had they got in the first shot or blow.

Where had they gone to, I wondered? To the priest's Heaven or Hell? Were they now telling their sins to some hard-faced angel while he checked the count from his book, reminding them of many that they had forgotten? Or were they fast asleep for ever and ever as a shrewd thinker whom I knew had told me secretly he was sure would be the fate of all of us, whatever the priests might teach and believe? And where was my mother whom I had loved and who loved me well, although outwardly she was so stern a woman, my mother whom I had seen burned alive, singing as she burned? Oh! it was a vile world, and it seemed strange that God should cause men and women to be born that they might come to such cruel ends. Yet who were we to question His decrees of which we knew neither the beginning nor the finish?

Anyway, I was glad I was not dead, for now that all was over I trembled and felt afraid, which I had never done during the fighting, even when my hour seemed very near.

Lastly there was this high-born lady, Blanche Aleys, with whom fortune had thrown me so strangely that day. Those blue eyes of hers had pierced my heart like darts, and do what I would I might not rid my mind of the thought of her, or my ears of the sound of her soft voice, while her kisses seemed still to burn upon my lips. It wrung me to think that perhaps I should never see her again, or that if I did I might not speak with her, being so far beneath her in condition, and having already earned the wrath of her father, and, as I guessed, the jealousy of that scented cousin of hers whom they said the King loved like a brother.

What had my mother told me ? To leave this place and go to London, there to find my uncle, John Grimmer, goldsmith and merchant, who was my godfather, and to ask him to take me into his business. I remembered this uncle of mine, for some seven or eight years before, when I was a growing lad, because there was a plague in London he had come down to Hastings to visit us. He only stayed a week, however, because he said that the sea air tied up his stomach and that he would rather risk the plague with a good stomach than leave it behind him with a bad one—though I think it was his business he thought of, not his stomach.

He was a strange old man, not unlike my mother, but with a nose more hooked, small dark eyes, and a bald head on which he set a cap of velvet. Even in the heat of summer he was always cold and wore a frayed fur robe, complaining much if he came into a draught of air. Indeed he looked like a Jew, though a good Christian enough, and laughed about it, because he said that this appearance of his served him well in his trade, since Jews were always feared, and it was held to be impossible to overreach them.

For the rest I only recalled that he examined me as to my book learning which did not satisfy him, and went about valuing all our goods and fishing-boats, showing my mother how we were being cheated and might earn more than we did. When he departed he gave me a gold piece and said that Life was nothing but vanity, and that I must pray for his soul when he was dead as he was sure it would need such help, also that I ought to put the gold piece out to interest. This I did by buying with it a certain fierce mastiff dog I coveted that had been brought on a ship from Norway, which dog bit some great man in our town, who hauled my mother before the bailiff about it and caused the poor beast to be killed, to my great wrath.

Now that I came to think of it, I had liked my Uncle John well enough although he was so different from others. Why should I not go to him? Because I did not wish to sit in a shop in London, I who loved the sea and the open air; also because I feared he might ask me what I had done with that gold piece and make a mock of me about the dog. Yet my mother had bid me go, and it was her last command to me, her dying words which it would be unlucky to disobey. Moreover, our boats and house were burnt and I must work hard and long before these could be replaced. Lastly, in London I should see no more of the Lady Blanche Aleys, and there could learn to forget the lights in her blue eyes. So I determined that I would go and at last fell asleep.

Next morning I made my confession to the old priest that, amongst other matters, he might shrive me of the blood which I had shed, though this he said needed no forgiveness from God or man, being as I think, a stout Englishman at heart. Also I took counsel with him as to what I should do, and he told me it was my duty to obey my mother's wishes, since such last words were often inspired from on high and declared the will of Heaven. Further he pointed out that I should do well to avoid the Lady Blanche Aleys who was one far above me in degree, the following of whom might bring me to trouble, or even to death; moreover, that I might mend my broken fortunes through the help of my uncle, a very rich man as he had heard, to whom he would write a letter about me.

Thus this matter was settled.

Still some days went by before I left Hastings, since first I must wait until the ashes of our house were cool enough to search in them for my mother's body. Those who found her at length said that she was not so much burned as might have been expected, but as to this I am uncertain, since I could not bring myself to look upon her who desired to remember her as she had been in life. She was buried by the side of my father, who was drowned, in the churchyard of St. Clement's, and when all had gone away I wept a little on her grave.

The rest of that day I spent making ready for my journey. As it chanced when the house was burnt the outbuildings which lay on the farther side of the yard behind escaped the fire, and in the stable were two good horses, one a grey riding-gelding and the other a mare that used to drag the nets to the quay and bring back the fish, which horses, although frightened and wild, were unharmed. Also there was a quantity of stores, nets, salt, dried fish in barrels, and I know not what besides. The horses I kept, but all the rest of the gear together with the premises, the ground on which the house had stood, and the other property I made over to William, my man, who promised to pay me their value when he could earn it in better times.

Next morning I rode away for London upon the grey horse, loading the armour of the knight I had killed and such other possessions as remained to me, upon the mare which I led with a rope. Save William there was none to say me good-bye, for the misery in Hastings was so great that all were concerned with their own affairs or in mourning their dead. I was not sorry that it fell out thus, since I was so full of sadness at leaving the place where I was born and had lived all my life, that I think I should have shed tears if any who had been my friends had spoken kind words to me, which would have been unmanly. Never had I felt so lonely as when from the high ground I gazed back to the ruins of Hastings over which still hung a thin pall of smoke. My courage seemed to fail me altogether ; I looked forward to the future with fear, believing that I had been born unlucky, that it held no good for me who probably should end my days as a common soldier or a fisherman, or mayhap in prison or on the gallows. From childhood I had suffered these fits of gloom, but as yet this was the blackest of them that I had known.

At length, the sun that had been hidden, shone out and with its coming my temper changed. I remembered that I who might so easily have been dead, was sound, young and healthy, that I had sword, bow and armour of the best, also twenty or more of gold pieces, for I had not counted them, in the bag which my mother gave me with Wave-Flame. Further I hoped that my uncle would befriend me, and if he did not, there were plenty of captains engaged in the wars who might be glad of a squire, one who could shoot against any man and handle a sword as well as most.

So putting up a prayer to St. Hubert after my simple fashion, I pushed on blithely to the crest of the long rise and there came face to face with a gay company who, hawk on wrist and hound at heel, were, I guessed, on their way to hunt in the Pevensey marshes. While they were still a little way off I knew these to be no other than Sir Robert Aleys, his daughter Blanche, and the King's favourite, young Lord Deleroy, with their servants, and was minded to turn aside to avoid them. Then I remembered that I had as much right to the King's Highway as they, and my pride aiding me, determined to ride on taking no note of them, unless first they took note of me. Also they knew me, for my ears being very sharp, I heard Sir Robert say in his big voice,

"Here comes that young fisherman again. Pass him in silence, Daughter;" heard too Lord Deleroy drawl out, "It seems that he has been gathering gear from the slain, and like a good chapman bears it away for secret sale."

Only the Lady Blanche answered neither the one nor the other, but rode forward with her eyes fixed before her, pretending to talk to the hawk upon her wrist, and now that she was rested and at ease, looking even more beautiful than she had done on the day of the burning.

So we met and passed, I glancing at them idly and guiding my horses to the side of the road. When there were perhaps ten yards between us I heard Lady Blanche cry,

"Oh, my hawk!" I looked round to see that the falcon on her wrist had in some way loosed itself, or been loosed, and being hooded, had fallen to the ground where one of the dogs was trying to catch and kill it. Now there was great confusion, the eyes of all being fixed upon the hawk and the dog, in the midst of which the lady Blanche very quietly turned her head, and lifting her hand as though to see how the hawk had fallen from it, with a swift movement laid her fingers against her lips and threw a kiss to me.

As swiftly I bowed back and went on my way with a beating heart. For a few moments I was filled with joy since I could not mistake the meaning of this signalled kiss. Then came sorrow like an April cloud, since my wound which was in the way of healing was all re-opened. I had begun to forget the Lady Blanche, or rather by an effort of the will, to thrust her from my thought, as my confessor had bidden me. But now on the wings of that blown kiss thither she had flown back again, not to be frighted out for many a day.

That night I slept at an inn at Tonbridge, a comfortable place where the host stared at the gold piece from the bag which I tendered in payment, and at first would not take what was due to him out of it, because it bore the head of some ancient king. However in the end a merchant of Tonbridge who came in for his morning ale showed him that it was good, so that trouble passed.

About two that afternoon I came to Southwark, a town that to me seemed as big as Hastings before it was burned, where was a fine inn called the Tabard at which I stopped to bait my horses and to take a bite and a drink of ale. Then I rode on over the great Thames where floated a multitude of ships and boats, crossing it by London Bridge, a work so wonderful that I marvelled that it could be made by the hand of man, and so broad that it had shops on either side of the roadway, in which were sold all sorts of merchandise. Thence I inquired my way to Cheapside, and came there at last thrusting a path through a roaring multitude of people, or so it seemed to me who never before had seen so many men and women gathered together, all going on their way and, it would appear, ignorant of each other.

Here I found a long and crowded thoroughfare with gabled houses on either side in which all kinds of trades were carried on. Down this I wandered, being cursed at more than once because my pack mare, growing frightened, dragged away from me and crossed the path of carts which had to stop till I could pull her free. After the third of these tangles I halted by the side of the footway behind a wain with barrels on it, and looked about me bewildered.

To my left was a house somewhat set back from

the general line that had a little patch of garden ground in front of it in which grew some untended and thriftless-looking shrubs. This house seemed to be a place of business because from an iron fastened to the front of it hung a board on which was painted an open boat, high at the prow and stern, with a tall beak fashioned to the likeness of a dragon's head and round shields all down the rail.

While I was staring at this sign and wondering emptily what kind of a boat it was and of what nation were the folk who had sailed in her, a man came down the garden path and leaned upon the gate, staring in turn at me. He was old and strange-looking, being clad in a rusty gown with a hood to it that was pulled over his head, so that I could only see a white, peaked beard and a pair of brilliant black eyes which seemed to pierce me as a shoemaker's awl pierces leather.

"What do you, young man," he asked in a high thin voice, "cumbering my gate with those nags of yours? Would you sell that mail you have on the pack-horse? If so I do not deal in such stuff, though it seems good of its kind. So get on with it elsewhere."

"Nay, Sir," I answered, "I have naught to sell who in this hive of traders seek one bee and cannot find him."

"Hive of traders! Truly the great merchants of the Cheap would be honoured. Have they stung you, then, already, young bumpkin from the countryside, for such I write you down? But what bee do you seek? Stay now, let me guess. Is it a certain old knave named John Grimmer, who trades in gold and jewels and other precious things and who, if he had his deserts, should be in jail?"

"Aye, aye, that's the man," I said.

"Surely he also will be honoured," exclaimed the

old fellow with a cackle. " He's a friend of mine and I will tell him the jest."

" If you would tell me where to find him it would be more seasonable."

" All in good time. But first, young Sir, where did you get that fine armour ? If you stole it, it should be better hid."

" Stole it !—" I began in wrath. " Am I a London chapman—— ? "

" I think not, though you may be before all is done, for who knows what vile tricks Fortune will play us ? Well, if you did not steal it, mayhap you slew the wearer and are a murderer, for I see black blood on the steel."

" Murderer ! " I gasped.

" Aye, just as you say John Grimmer is a knave. But if not, then perchance you slew the French knight who wore it on Hastings Hill, ere you loosed the three arrows at the mouth of the cave near Minnes Rock."

Now I gaped at him.

" Shut your mouth, young man, lest those teeth of yours should fall out. You wonder how I know ? Well, my friend John Grimmer, the goldsmith knave, has a magic crystal which he purchased from one who brought it from the East, and I saw it in that crystal."

As he spoke, as though by chance he pushed back the hood that covered his head, revealing a wrinkled old face with a mocking mouth which drooped at one corner, a mouth that I knew again, although many years had passed since I looked upon it as a boy.

" You are John Grimmer ! " I muttered.

" Yes, Hubert of Hastings, I am that knave himself. And now tell me, what did you do with the gold piece I gave you some twelve summers gone ? "

Then I was minded to lie, for I feared this old man. But thinking better of it, I answered that I had spent it on a dog. He laughed outright and said,

"Pray that it is not an omen and that you may not follow the gold piece to the dogs. Well, I like you for speaking the truth when you are tempted to do otherwise. Will you be pleased to shelter for a while beneath the roof of John Grimmer, the merchant knave?"

"You mock me, Sir," I stammered.

"Perhaps, perhaps! But there's many a true word spoken in jest; for if you do not know it now you will learn afterwards that we are all knaves, each in his own fashion, who if we do not deceive others, at least deceive ourselves, and I perhaps more than most. Vanity of vanities! All is vanity."

Then, waiting for no reply, he drew a silver whistle from under his dusty robe and blew it, whereon—so swiftly that I marvelled whether he were waiting—a stout-built serving man appeared to whom he said,

"Take these horses to the stable and treat them as though they were my own. Unload the pack beast, and when it has been cleaned, set the mail and the other gear upon it in the room that has been made ready for this young master, Hubert of Hastings, my nephew."

Without a word the man led off the horses.

"Be not afraid," chuckled John Grimmer, "for though I am a knave, dog does not eat dog and what is yours is safe with me and those who serve me. Now enter," and he led the way into the house, opening the iron-studded oak door with a key from his pouch.

Within was a shop where I saw precious things such as furs and gold ornaments lying about.

"The crumbs to catch the birds, especially the ladybirds," he said with a sweep of his hand, then took me through the shop into a passage and thence to a room on the right. It was not a large room but more wonderfully furnished than any I had ever seen. In the centre was a table of black oak with cunningly carved legs, on which stood cups of silver and a noble centre piece that seemed to be of gold. From the ceiling, too, hung silver lamps that already had been lit, for the evening was closing in, and gave a sweet smell. There was a hearth also with what was rare, a chimney, upon which burned a little fire of logs, while the walls were hung with tapestries and broidered silks.

Whilst I stared about me, my uncle took off his cloak beneath which he was clothed in some rich but rather threadbare stuff, only retaining the velvet skullcap that he wore. Then he bade me do the same, and when I had laid my outer garment aside, looked me all over in the lamplight.

"A proper young man," he muttered to himself, "and I'd give all I have to be his age and like him. I suppose those limbs and sinews of his came from his father, for I was ever thin and spare, as was my father before me. Nephew Hubert, I have heard all the tale of your dealings with the Frenchmen, on whom be God's curse, at Hastings yonder; and I say that I am proud of you, though whether I shall stay so is another matter. Come hither."

I obeyed and taking me by my curling hair with his delicate hand, he drew down my head and kissed me on the brow, muttering, "Neither chick nor child for me and only this one left of the ancient blood. May he do it honour."

Then he motioned to me to be seated and rang a little silver bell that stood upon the table. As in the case of the man without, it was answered instantly from which I judged that Master Grimmer was well served. Before the echoes of the bell died away a door opened, the tapestry swung aside, and there appeared two most comely serving maids, tall and well-shaped both of them, bearing food.

"Pretty women, Nephew, no wonder that you look at them," he said when they had gone away to fetch other things, "such as I like to have about me although I am old. Women for within and men for without, that is Nature's law and ill will be the day when it is changed. Yet beware of pretty women, Nephew, and I pray you kiss not these as you did the Lady Blanche Aleys at Hastings, lest it should upset my household and turn servants into mistresses."

I made no answer, being confounded by the knowledge that my uncle showed of me and my affairs, which afterwards I discovered he had, in part at any rate, from the old priest, my confessor, who had written to commend me to him, telling my story and sending the letter by a King's messenger, who left for London on the morrow of the Burning. Nor did he wait for any, for he bade me sit down and eat, plying me with more meats than I could swallow, all most delicately dressed, also with rare wines such as I had never tasted, which he took from a cupboard where they were kept in curious flasks of glass. Yet as I noted, himself he ate but little, only picking at the breast of a fowl and drinking but the half of a small silver goblet filled with wine.

"Appetite, like all other good things, for the young," he said with a sigh as he watched my hearty feasting. "Yet remember, Nephew, that if you live to reach it, a day will come when yours will be as mine is. Vanity of vanities, saith the preacher, all is vanity!"

At length when I could eat no more, again he rang the silver bell and those fair waiting girls dressed alike in green, appeared and cleared away the broken meats. After they were gone he crouched over the fire rubbing his thin hands to warm them, and said suddenly,

"Now tell me of my sister's death and all the rest of your tale."

So as well as I was able I told him everything from the hour when I had sighted the French fleet on board my fishing boat to the end.

"You are no fool," he said when I had finished, "who can talk like any clerk and bring things that have happened clearly to the listener's eye, which I have noted few are able to do. So that's the story. Well, your mother had a great heart, and she made a great end, such an one as was loved of our northern race, and that even I, the old merchant knave, desire and shall not win, who doubtless am doomed to die a cow's death in the straw. Pray the All-Father Odin—nay, that is heresy for which I might burn if you or the wenches told it to the priests—pray God I mean, that He may grant you a better, as He did to old Thorgrimmer, if the tale be true, Thorgrimmer whose sword you wear and have wielded shrewdly, as that French knight knows in hell to-day."

"Who was Odin ?" I asked.

"The great god of the North. Did not your mother tell you of him ? Nay, doubtless she was too good a Christian. Yet he lives on, Nephew. I say that Odin lives in the blood of every fighting man, as Freya lives in the heart of every lad and girl who loves. The gods change their names, but hush ! hush ! talk not of Odin and of Freya, for I say that it is heresy, or pagan which is worse. What would you do now ? Why came you to London ?"

"Because my mother bade me and to seek my fortune."

"Fortune—what is fortune ? Youth and health are the best fortune, though, if they know how to use it, those who have wealth as well may go further than the rest. Also beauteous things are pleasant to the sight and there is joy in gathering them. Yet at the last they mean nothing, for naked we came out of the blackness and naked we return there. Vanity of vanities, all is vanity !"

CHAPTER IV

KARI

THUS began my life in London in the house of my uncle, John Grimmer, who was called the Goldsmith. In truth, however, he was more than this, since not only did he fashion and trade in costly things; he lent out moneys to interest upon security to great people who needed it, and even to the King Richard and his Court. Also he owned ships and did much commerce with Holland, France, yes, and with Spain and Italy. Indeed, although he appeared so humble, his wealth was very large and always increased, like a snowball rolling down a hill; moreover he owned much land, especially in the neighbourhood of London where it was likely to grow in value.

"Money melts," he would say, "furs corrupt with moth and time and thieves break in and steal. But land —if the title be good—remains. Therefore buy land which none can carry away, near to a market or a growing town if may be, and hire it out to fools to farm, or sell it to other fools who wish to build great houses and spend their goods in feeding a multitude of idle servants. Houses eat, Hubert, and the larger they are, the more they eat."

No word did he say to me as to my dwelling on with him, yet there I remained, by common consent as it were. Indeed on the morrow of my coming a tailor appeared to measure me for such garments as he thought I should wear, by his command I suppose, as I was never asked for payment, and he bade me furnish my chamber to my own liking, also another room at the back of the house that was much larger than it seemed, which he told me was to be mine to work in, though at what I was to work he did not say.

For a day or two I remained idle, staring at the sights of London and only meeting my uncle at meals which sometimes we ate alone and sometimes in the company of sea-captains and learned clerks or of other merchants, all of whom treated him with great deference and as I soon guessed, were in truth his servants. At night, however, we were always alone and then he would pour out his wisdom on me while I listened, saying little. On the sixth day, growing weary of this idleness, I made bold to ask him if there was aught that I could do.

"Aye, plenty if you have a mind to work," he answered. "Sit down now, and take pen and paper and write what I shall tell you."

Then he dictated a short letter to me as to shipping wine from Spain and when it was sanded, read it carefully.

"You have it right," he said, seeming pleased, "and your script is clear if boyish. They taught you none so ill yonder at Hastings where I thought you had only learned to handle ropes and arrows. Work? Yes, there is plenty of it of the more private sort which I do not give to this scribe or to that who might betray my secrets. For know," he went on in a stern voice, "there is one thing which I never pardon, and it is betrayal. Remember that, nephew Hubert, even in the arms of your loves, if you should be fool enough to seek them, or in your cups."

So he talked on and while he did so went to an iron chest that he unlocked, and thence drew out a parchment roll which he bade me take to my workroom and copy there. I did so and found that it was an inventory of his goods and estates, and oh! before I had done I wished that there were fewer of them. All the long day I laboured, only stopping for a bite at noon, till my head swam and my fingers ached. Yet as I did so I felt proud, for I guessed that my uncle had set me this task for two reasons ; first to show his trust in me and secondly to acquaint me with the state of his possessions, but as it were in the way of business. By nightfall I had finished and checked the copy which with the original I hid in my robe when the green-robed waiting maid summoned me to eat.

At our meal my uncle asked me what I had seen that day and I replied—naught but figures and crabbed writing—and handed him the parchments which he compared item by item.

"I am pleased with you," he said at last, "for here so far I find but a single error and that my fault, not yours ; also you have done two days' work in one. Still it is not fit that you who are accustomed to the open air, should bend continually over deeds and inventories. Therefore to-morrow I shall have another task for you, for like yourself your horse needs exercise."

And so he had, for with two stout servants riding with me and guiding me, he sent me out of London to view a fair estate of his upon the borders of the Thames and to visit his tenants and make report of their husbandry, also of certain woods where he proposed to fell oak for ship-building. This I did, for the servants made me known to the tenants, and got back at nightfall, able to tell him all which he was glad to learn, since it seemed that he had not seen this estate for five long years.

On another day he sent me to visit ships in which goods of his were being laden at the wharf, and on another took me with him to a sale of furs that came from the far north where I was told the snow never melts and there is always ice in the sea.

Also he made me known to merchants with whom he traded, and to his agents who were many, though for the most part secret, together with other goldsmiths who held moneys of his, and in a sense were partners, forming a kind of company so that they could find great sums in sudden need. Lastly his clerks and dependents were made to understand that if I gave an order it must be obeyed, though this did not happen until I had been with him for some time.

Thus it came about that within a year I knew all the threads of John Grimmer's great business, and within two it drifted more and more into my hands. The last part of it with which he made me acquainted was that of lending money to those in high places, and even to the State itself, but at length I was taught this also and came to know sundry of these men, who in private were humble borrowers, but if they met us in the street passed us with the nod that the great give to their inferiors. Then my uncle would bow low, keeping his eyes fixed upon the ground and bid me do the same. But when they were out of hearing he would chuckle and say,

"Fish in my net, goldfish in my net! See how they shine who presently must wriggle on the shore. Vanity of vanities! All is vanity and doubtless Solomon knew such in his day."

Hard I worked and ever harder, toiling at the mill of all these large affairs and keeping myself in health during such time as I could spare by shooting at the butts with my big bow where I found that none could beat me, or practising sword play in a school of arms that was kept by a master of the craft from Italy. Also on holidays and on Sundays after mass I rode out of London to visit my uncle's estates where sometimes I slept a night, and once or twice sailed to Holland or to Calais with his cargoes.

One day, it was when I had been with him about eighteen months, he said to me suddenly,

"You plough the field, Hubert, and do not tithe the crop, but live upon the bounty of the husbandman. Henceforward take as much of it as you will. I ask no account."

So I found myself rich, though in truth I spent but little, both because my tastes were simple and it was part of my uncle's policy to make no show which he said would bring envy on us. From this time forward he began to withdraw himself from business, the truth being that age took hold of him and he grew feeble. The highest of the affairs he left to me, only inquiring of them and giving his counsel from time to time. Still because he must do something, he busied himself in the shop which, as he said, he kept as a trap for the birds, chaffering in ornaments and furs as though his bread depended upon his earning a gold piece, and directing the manufacture of beautiful jewels and cups which he, who was an artist, designed to be made by his skilled and highly-paid workmen, some of whom were foreigners.

"We end where we began," he would say. "A smith was I from my childhood and a smith I shall die. What a fate for one of the blood of Thorgrimmer! Yet I am selling you into the same bondage, or so it would seem. But who knows? Who knows? We design, but God decrees."

It is to be noted that when old men cease from the occupations of their lives, often enough within a very little time they also cease from life itself. So it was with my uncle. Day by day he faded till at last at the beginning of the third winter after I came to him he took to his bed where he lay growing ever weaker till at length he died in the hour of the birth of the new year.

To the last his mind remained clear and strong and never more so than on the night of his death. That evening after I had eaten I went to his room as usual and found him reading a beautiful manuscript of the book of the Wisdom of Solomon that is called Ecclesiastes, a work which he preferred to all others, since its thoughts were his. "I gathered me also silver and gold and the peculiar treasure of kings," he read aloud, whether to himself or to me I knew not, and went on, "So I was great, and increased more than all that were before me. . . Then I looked on all the works that my hands had wrought, and on the labour that I had laboured to do; and behold all was vanity and vexation of spirit, and there was no profit under the sun."

He closed the book saying,

"So shall you find, nephew, you, and every man in the evil days of age when you shall say, 'I have no pleasure in them.' Hubert, I am going to my long home, nor do I grieve. In youth I met with sorrow for though I have never told you, I was married then and had one son, a bright boy, and oh! I loved him and his mother. Then came the plague and took them both. So having naught left and being by nature one of those who could wean himself from women, which I fear that you are not, Hubert, noting all the misery there is in the world and how those who are called noble whom I hate, grind down the humble and the poor, I turned myself to good works. Half of all my gains I have given and still give to those who minister to poverty and sickness; you will find a list of them when I am gone should you wish to continue the bounty, as to which I do not desire to bind you in any way. For know, Hubert, that I have left you all that is mine; the gold and the ships with the movables and chattels to be your own, but the lands which are the main wealth, for life and afterwards to be your children's, or if you should die childless, then to go to certain hospitals where the sick are tended."

Now I would have thanked him but he waved my words aside and went on,

"You will be a very rich man, Hubert, one of the richest in all London; yet set not your heart on wealth and above all do not ape nobility or strive to climb from the honest class of which you come into the ranks of those idle and dissolute cut-throats and pick-brains who are called the great. Lighten their pockets if you will, but do not seek to wear their silken, scented garments. That is my counsel to you."

He paused a while picking at the bedclothes as the dying do, and continued,

"You told me that your mother thought you would be a wanderer, and it is strange that now my mind should be as hers was in this matter. For I seem to see you far away amidst war and love and splendour, holding Wave-Flame aloft as did that Thorgrimmer who begat us. Well, go where you are called or as occasion drives, though you have much to keep you at home. I would that you were wed, since marriage is an anchor that few ships can drag. Yet I am not sure, for how know I whom you would wed, and once that anchor is down no windlass will wind it up and death alone can cut its chain. One word more. Though you are so young and strong remember that as I am, so shall you be. To-day for me, to-morrow for thee, said the wise old man, and thus it ever was and is."

"Hubert, I know not why we are born to struggle and to suffer and at last be noosed with the rope of Doom. Yet I hope the priests are right and that we live again, though Solomon thought not so; that is, if we live where there is neither sin nor sorrow nor fear of death. If so, be sure that in some new land we shall meet afresh, and there I shall ask account of you of the wealth I entrusted to your keeping. Think of me kindly at times, for I have learned to love you who are of my blood, and while we live on in the hearts of those we love, we are not truly dead. Come hither that I may bless you in your coming in and going out while you still look upon the sun."

So he blessed me in beautiful and tender words, and kissed me on the brow, after which he bade me leave him and send the woman to watch him, because he desired to sleep.

When she looked at him at midnight just as the bells rang in the new year, he was dead.

According to his wish John Grimmer, the last of that name, was buried by the bones of his forgotten wife and child, who had left the world over fifty years before, in the chancel of that church in the Cheap which was within a stone's throw of his dwelling house. By his desire also the funeral was without pomp, yet many came to it, some of them of high distinction, although the day was cold and snowy. I noted, moreover, the deference they showed to me who by now was known to be his heir, even if they had never spoken with me before, as was the case with certain of them, taking occasion to draw me aside and say that they trusted that their ancient friendship with my honoured uncle would be continued by myself.

Afterwards I looked up their names in his private book and found that one and all of those who had spoken thus owed moneys to his estate.

When the will was sworn and I found myself the master of many legions, or rather of more money, land and other wealth than I had ever dreamed of, at first I was minded to be rid of trade and to take up my abode upon one or other of my manors, where I might live in plenty for the rest of my days. In the end, however, I did not do so, partly because I shrank from new faces and surroundings, and partly because I was sure that such would not have been my uncle's wish.

Instead I set myself to play and outpass his game. He had died very rich; I determined that I would die five or ten times richer; the richest man in England if I could, not because I cared for money, of which indeed I spent but little upon myself, but because the getting of it and the power that it brought, seemed to me the highest kind of sport. So bending my mind to the matter I doubled and trebled his enterprises on this line and on that, and won and won again, for even where skill and foresight failed, Fortune stood my friend with a such strange persistence that at length I became superstitious and grew frightened of her gifts. Also I took pains to hide my great riches from the public eye, placing much of them in the names of others whom I could trust, and living most modestly in the same old house, lest I should become a man envied by the hungry and marked for plunder by the spendthrift great.

It was during the summer following my uncle's death that I went to the wharves to see to the unloading of a ship that came in from Venice, bearing many goods from the East on my account, such as ivory, silks, spices, glass, carpets and I know not what. Having finished my business and seen these precious things warehoused, I handed over the checking of a list of them to another and turned to seek my horse.

Then it was that I saw a number of half-grown lads and other idlers mobbing a man who stood among them wrapped in a robe of what looked like tattered sheep-skin, yet was not because the wool on it was of a reddish hue and very long and soft, which robe was thrown over his head almost hiding his face. At this man—a tall figure who stood there patiently like a martyr at the stake—these lewd fellows were hurling offal, such as fishes' heads and rotted fruits that lay in plenty on the quay, together with coarse words. "Blackamoor" was one I caught.

Such sights were common enough, but there was a quiet dignity of bearing about this victim which moved me, so that I went to the rabble commanding them to desist. One of them, a rough bumpkin, not knowing who I was, pushed me aside, bidding me mind my own business, whereon, being very strong, I dealt him such a blow between the eyes that he went down like a felled ox and lay there half stunned. His companions beginning to threaten me, I blew upon my whistle, whereon two of my serving-men, without whom I seldom rode in those troublous times, ran up from behind a shed, laying hands upon their short swords, on seeing which the idlers took to their heels.

When they had gone I turned to look at the stranger, whose hood had fallen back in the hustling, and saw that he was about thirty years of age, and of a dark and noble countenance, beardless, but with straight black hair, black flashing eyes, and an aquiline nose. Another thing I noted about him was that the lobe of his ear was pierced and in a strange fashion, since the gristle was stretched to such a size that a small apple could have been placed within its ring. For the rest the man's limbs were so thin as though from hunger, that everywhere his bones showed, while his skin was scarred with cuts and scratches, and on his forehead was a large bruise. He seemed bewildered also and very weak, yet I think he understood that I was playing a friend's part to him, for he bowed towards me in a stately courteous way and kissed the air thrice, but what this meant at the time I did not know.

I spoke to him in English, but he shook his head

gently to show that he did not understand. Then, as though by an afterthought, he touched his breast several times, and after each touch, said in a voice of strange softness, "Kari," which I took it he meant was his name. At any rate from that time forward I called him Kari.

Now the question was how to deal with him. Leave him there to be mocked or to perish I could not, nor was there anywhere whither I could send him. Therefore it seemed the only thing to do was to take him home with me. So grasping his arm gently I led him off the quay where our horses were and motioned to him to mount one that had been ridden by a servant whom I bade to walk. At the sight of these horses, however, a great terror took hold of him for he trembled all over, a sweat bursting out upon his face, and clung to me as though for protection, making it evident that he had never seen such an animal before. Indeed, nothing would persuade him to go near them, for he shook his head and pointed to his feet, thus showing me that he preferred to walk, however weak his state.

The end of it was that walk he did and I with him from Thames side to the Cheap, since I dared not leave him alone for fear lest he should run away. A strange sight we presented, I leading this dusky wanderer through the streets, and glad was I that night was falling so that few saw us and those who did thought, I believe, that I was bringing some foreign thief to jail.

At length we reached the Boat House as my dwelling was called, from the image of the old Viking vessel that my uncle had carved and set above the door, and I led him in staring about him with all his eyes, which in his thin face looked large as those of an owl, taking him up the stairs, which seemed to puzzle him much, for at every step he lifted his leg high into the air, to an empty guest room.

Here besides the bed and other furniture was a silver basin with its jug, one of the beautiful things that John Grimmer had brought I know not whence. On these Kari fixed his eyes at once, staring at them in the light of the candles that I had lit, as though they were familiar objects to him. Indeed, after glancing at me as though for permission, he went to the jug that was kept full of water in case of visitors of whom I had many on business, lifted it, and after pouring a few drops of the water on to the floor as though he made some offering, drank deeply, thus showing that he was parched with thirst.

Then without more ado he filled the basin and throwing off his tattered robe began to wash himself to the waist, round which he wore another garment, of dirty cotton I thought, which looked like a woman's petticoat. Watching him I noted two things, that his poor body was as scratched and scarred as though by old thorn wounds, as were his face and hands, also marked with great bruises as though from kicks and blows, and secondly that hung about his neck was a wondrous golden image about four inches in length. It was of rude workmanship with knees bent up under the chin, but the face, in which little emeralds were set for eyes, was of a great and solemn dignity.

This image Kari washed before he touched himself with water, bowing to it the while, and when he saw me observing him, looked upwards to the sky and said a word that sounded like *Pachacamac*, from which I took it to be some idol that the poor man worshipped. Lastly, tied about his middle was a hide bag half filled with I knew not what.

Now I found a washball made of oil of olives mixed with beech ash and showed him the use of it. At first he shrank from this strange thing, but coming to understand its office, served himself of it readily, smiling when he saw how well it cleansed his flesh. Further, I fetched a shirt of silk with a pair of easy shoes and a fur-lined robe that had belonged to my uncle, also hosen, and showed him how to put them on, which he learned quickly enough. A comb and a brush that were on the table he seemed to understand already, for with them he dressed his tangled hair.

When all was finished in a fashion, I led him down the stairs again to the eating-room where supper was waiting, and offered him food, at the sight of which his eyes glistened, for clearly he was wellnigh starving. The chair I gave him he would not sit on, whether from respect for me or because it was strange to him, I do not know, but seeing a low stool of tapestry which my uncle had used to rest his feet, he crouched upon this, and thus ate of whatever I gave him, very delicately although he was so hungry. Then I poured wine from Portugal into a goblet and drank some myself to show him that it was harmless, which, after tasting it, he swallowed to the last drop.

The meal being finished which I thought it well to shorten lest he should eat too much who was so weak, again he lifted up his eyes as though in gratitude, and as a sign of thankfulness, or so I suppose, knelt before me, took my hand and pressed it against his forehead, thereby, although I did not know it at the time, vowing himself to my service. Then seeing how weary he was I conducted him back to the chamber and pointed out the bed to him, shutting my eyes to show that he should sleep there. But this he would not do until he had dragged the bedding on to the floor, from which I gathered that his people, whoever they might be, had the habit of sleeping on the ground.

Greatly did I wonder who this man was and from what race he sprang, since never had I seen any human being who resembled him at all. Of one thing only was

I certain, namely that his rank was high, since no noble of the countries that I knew had a bearing so gentle or manners so fine. Of black men I had seen several, who were called negroes, and others of a higher sort called Moors; gross, vulgar fellows for the most part and cut-throats if in an ill-humour, but never a one of them like this Kari.

It was long before my curiosity was satisfied and even then I did not gather much. By slow degrees Kari learned English, or something of it, though never enough to talk fluently in that tongue into which he always seemed to translate in his mind from another full of strange figures of thought and speech. When after many months he had mastered sufficient of our language, I asked him to tell me his story which he tried to do. All I could make of it, however, came to this.

He was, he said, the son of a king who ruled over a mighty empire far far away, across thousands of miles of sea towards that part of the sky where the sun sank. He declared that he was the eldest lawful son, born of the King's sister, which seemed dreadful to my ideas though perhaps he meant cousin or relative, but that there were scores of other children of his father, which if true, showed that this King must be a very loose-living man who resembled in his domesticities the wise Solomon of whom my uncle was so fond.

It appeared further, according to the tale that this king, his father, had another son born of a different mother, and that of this son he was fonder than of my guest, Kari. His name was Urco, and he was jealous of and hated Kari the lawful heir. Moreover, as is common, a woman came into the business, since Kari had a wife, the loveliest lady in all the land, though as I understood, not of the same tribe or blood as himself, and with this wife of his Urco fell in love. So greatly did he desire her, although he had plenty of wives of his own, that being the general of the King's troops, he sent Kari, with the consent of their father, to command an army that was to fight a distant savage nation, hoping that he would be killed, much as David did in the matter of Uriah and Bathsheba, of whom the Bible tells the story. But as it happened, instead of being killed like Uriah, Kari conquered the distant nation, and after two years returned to the King's court, where he found that his brother Urco had led astray his wife whom he had taken into his household. Being very angry, Kari recovered his wife by command of the King, and put her to death because of her faithlessness.

Thereon the King, his father, a stern man, ordered him into banishment because he had broken the laws of the land, which did not permit of private vengeance over a matter of a woman who was not even of the blood-royal, however fair as she might be. Before he went, however, Urco, who was mad at the loss of his love, caused some kind of poison to be given to Kari, which although it does not kill, for he dared not kill him because of his station, deprives him who takes it of his reason, sometimes for ever and sometimes for a year or more. After this, said Kari, he remembered little or nothing, save long travellings in boats and through forests, and then again upon a raft or boat on to which he was driven alone, for many, many days, drinking of a jar of water which he had with him, and eating some dried flesh and with it a marvellous drug of his people, some of which remained to him in the leathern bag that has power to keep the life in a man for weeks, even if he is labouring hard.

At last, he declared, he was picked up by a great ship such as he had never seen before, though of this ship he recalled little. Indeed he remembered nothing more until he found himself upon the quay where I discovered him, and of a sudden his mind seemed to return, but he said he believed that he had come ashore in a boat in which were fishermen, having been thrown into it by people on the ship which went on elsewhere, and that he had walked up the shores of a river. This story the bruises on his forehead and body seemed to bear out, but it was far from clear, and by the time I learned it months afterwards of course no traces of the fishermen or their boat could be found. I asked him the name of the country from which he came. He answered that it was called *Tavantinsuyu.* He added that it was a wonderful country in which were cities and churches and great snow-clad mountains and fertile valleys and high plains, and hot forests through which ran wide rivers.

From all the learned men whom I could meet, especially those who had travelled far, I made inquiries concerning this country called Tavantinsuyu, but none of them had so much as heard its name. Indeed they declared that my brown man must have come from Africa, and that his mind being disordered, he had invented this wondrous land which he said lay far away to the west where the sun sank.

So there I must leave the matter, though for my part I was sure that Kari was not mad, whatever he might have been in the past. A great dreamer he was, it is true, who declared that the poison which his brother had given him had "eaten a hole in his mind," through which he could see and hear things which others could not. Thus he was able to read the secret motives of men and women with wonderful clearness, so much so that sometimes I asked him laughing, if he could not give me some of that poison that I might see into the hearts of those with whom I dealt. Of another thing, too, he was always certain, namely that he would return to his country Tavantinsuyu of which he thought day and night, and that *I should accompany him.* At this I laughed again and said that if so it would be after we were both dead.

By degrees he learned English quite well and even how to read and write it, teaching me in return much of his own language which he called *Quichua*, a soft and beautiful tongue, though he said that there were also many others in his country, including one that was secret to the King and his family, which he was not allowed to reveal although he knew it. In time I mastered enough of this Quichua to be able to talk to Kari in brief sentences of it when I did not wish others to understand what I said.

To tell the truth while I studied thus and listened to his marvellous tales, a great desire arose in me to see this land of his and to open up a trade with it, since there he declared gold was as plentiful as was iron with us. I thought even of making a voyage of discovery to the west, but when I spoke of it to certain sea-captains, even the most venturesome mocked at me and said that they would wait for that journey until they "went west" themselves, by which in their sea parlance that they had learned in the Mediterranean, they meant until they died.* When I told Kari this he smiled in his mysterious way and answered that all the same, I and he should make that journey together and this before we died, a thing that came about indeed, though not by my own will or his.

For the rest when Kari saw my workmen fashioning gold and setting jewels in it for sale to the nobles and ladies of the Court, he was much interested and asked if he might be allowed to follow this craft, of which he

* Of late there has been much dispute as to the origin of the phrase "to go west," or in other words, to die. Surely it arises from the custom of the Ancient Egyptians who, after death, were ferried across the Nile and entombed upon its western shore.—Ed.

said he understood something, and thus earn the bread he ate. I answered, yes, for I knew that it irked his proud nature to be dependent on me, and gave him gold and silver with a little room having a furnace in it where he could labour. The first thing he made was an object about two inches across, round and with a groove at the back of it, on the front of which he fashioned an image of the sun having a human face and rays of light projecting all about. I asked him what was its purpose, whereon he took the piece and thrust it into the lobe of his ear where the gristle had been stretched in the fashion that I have described, which it fitted exactly. Then he told me that in his country all the nobles wore such ornaments and that those who did so were called "ear-men" to distinguish them from the common people. Also he told me many other things too long to set out, which made me desire more than ever to see this empire with my eyes, for an empire and no less he declared it to be.

Afterwards Kari made many such ornaments which I sold for brooches with a pin set at the back of them. Also he shaped other things for his skill as a goldsmith was wonderful, such as cups and platters of strange design and rich ornamentation which commanded a great price. But on every one of them, in the centre or some other part of the embossment, appeared this image of the sun. I asked him why. He answered because the sun was his god as his people were Sun-worshippers. I reminded him that he had said that a certain Pachacamac whose image he wore about his neck, was his god. To this he replied:

"Yes, Pachacamac is the god above gods, the Creator, the Spirit of the World, but the Sun is his visible house and raiment that all may see and worship," a saying that I thought had truth in it, seeing that all Nature is the raiment of God.

I tried to instruct him in our faith, but although he listened patiently and I think understood, he would not become a Christian, making it very plain to me that he thought that a man should live and die in the religion in which he was born and that from what he saw in London he did not hold that Christians were any better than those who worshipped the sun and the great spirit, Pachacamac. So I abandoned this attempt, although there was danger to him while he remained a heathen. Indeed twice or thrice the priests made inquiry concerning his faith, being curious as to all that had to do with him. However I silenced them by pretending that I was instructing him as well as I was able and that as yet he did not know enough English to hearken to their holy expositions. Also when they became persistent I made gifts to the monasteries to which they belonged, or if they were parish priests, then to their cures or churches.

Still I was troubled about this matter, for some of these priests were very fierce and intolerant, and I was sure that in time they would push the business further.

One more thing I noticed about Kari, namely that he shrank from women and indeed seemed to hate them. The maids who had remained with me since my uncle's death, noticed this, by nature as it were, and in revenge would not serve him. The end of it was that, fearing lest they should do him some evil turn with the priests or otherwise, I sent them away and hired men to take their place. This distaste of Kari for women I set down to all that he had suffered at the hands of his false and beautiful wife, not wrongly as I think.

CHAPTER V

THE COMING OF BLANCHE

ONE day, it was the last of the year, the anniversary of the death of my uncle whose goodness and wisdom I pondered on more and more as time went by, having a little time to spare from larger affairs, I chanced to be in the shop in the front of the house, which as John Grimmer had said, he kept as a trap to "snare the ladybirds," and I continued, because I knew that he would not wish that anything should be changed. Here I was pleasing myself by looking over such pieces as we had to sell which the head craftsman was showing to me, since myself I knew little of them, except as a matter of account.

Whilst I was thus engaged there entered the shop a very fine lady accompanied by a still finer lordling arrayed so similarly that, at first sight, in their hooded ermine-lined cloaks it was difficult to know which was man and which was woman. When they threw these aside, however, for the shop was warm after the open air, I knew more than that, since with a sudden stoppage of the heart I saw before me none other than the lady Blanche Aleys and her relative, the lord Deleroy.

She, who in the old days of the Hastings burning had been but a lily bud, was now an open flower and beautiful exceedingly ; indeed in her own fashion the most beautiful woman that ever I beheld. Tall she was and stately as a lily bloom, white as a lily also, save for those wondrous blue eyes over which curled the dark lashes. In shape, too, she was perfect, full-breasted, yet not too full, small-waisted and with delicate limbs, a very Venus, such an one as I had seen in ancient marble brought in a ship from Italy and given, as I believe, to the King, who loved such things, to be set up in his palace.

My lord also was yet handsomer than he had been, more set and manly, though still he affected his cox-comb party-coloured dress with the turned-up shoes of which the points were fastened by little golden chains beneath the knee. Still he was a fine man with his roving black eyes, his loose mouth and little pointed beard from which, as from his hair, came an odour of scents. Seeing me in my merchant's gown, for I remained mindful of my uncle's advice as regards attire, he spoke to me as great men do to shop-keepers.

"Well met, Goldsmith," he said in his round, well-trained voice, "I would make a new-year gift to the lady here and I am told that you have plate-wares of the best; gold cups and jewels of rich and rare design, stamped all of them with the image of the sun which one would wish to remember on such a day as this. But hearken, let John Grimmer himself come to serve me for I would treat with no underlings, or take me to him where he is."

Now I bowed before him, rubbing my hands, and answered, for so the humour led me: "Then I fear that I must take my lord farther than my lord would wish to travel just at present, though who knows? Perchance like the rest of us, he may take that journey sooner than he thinks."

Now at the sound of my voice I saw the lady Blanche stare at me, trying to catch sight of my face beneath the hood which I wore on this cold day, while Deleroy started and said briefly,

"Your meaning?"

"It is plain, my lord. John Grimmer is dead and I know not where he dwells at present since he took that secret with him. But I, who unworthily carry on his trade, am at your lordship's service."

Then I turned and bade the shopman command Kari to come hither and bring with him the choicest of our cups and jewels.

He went and I busied myself in setting stools for these noble customers to rest on before the fire. As I did so by chance my hand touched that of the lady Blanche, whereat once more she strove to peer beneath my hood. It was as though the nature in her knew that touch again, as by some instinct every woman does, if once the toucher's lips have been near her own, though it be long ago. But I only turned my head away and drew that hood the closer.

Now Kari came and with him the shopman bearing the precious wares. Kari wore a wool-lined robe, very plain, which yet became him so well that with his fine-cut face and flashing eyes he looked like an Eastern prince disguised. At him this fine pair stared for never had they seen such a man, but taking no note, with many bows he showed the jewels one by one. Among these was a gem of great value, a large, heartshaped ruby that Kari had set in a surround of twisted golden serpents with heads raised to strike and little eyes of diamonds. Upon this brooch the lady Blanche fixed her gaze and discarding all others, began to play with it, till at length the lord Deleroy asked the price. I consulted with Kari, explaining that myself I did not handle this branch of my business, then named it carelessly ; it was a great sum.

"God's truth! Blanche," said Deleroy, "this merchant thinks I am made of gold. You must choose a cheaper ornament for your new year's gift, or he will have to wait for payment."

" Which mayhap I should be willing to do from one of your quality, my lord," I interrupted, bowing.

He looked at me and said,

" Can I have a word apart with you, merchant ? "

Again I bowed and led him to the eating room where he gazed about him amazed at the richness of the furnishings. He sat him down upon a carven chair while I stood before him humbly and waited.

" I am told," he said at length," that John Grimmer did other business besides that of selling jewels."

" Yes, my lord, some foreign trade."

" And some home trade also. I mean that he lent money."

" At times, my lord, on good security, if he chanced to have any at command, and at a certain interest. Perhaps my lord will come to his point."

" It is short and clear. Those of us who are at Court always want money where it is needful if we would have advancement and earn the royal favour of one who does not pay, at least in gold."

" Be pleased to state the amount and the security offered, my lord."

He did so. The sum was high and the security was bad.

" Are there any who would stand surety for my lord ? "

" Yes, one of great estate, Sir Robert Aleys who has wide lands in Sussex."

" I have heard the name and if my lord will bid his lawyers put the matter in writing, I will cause the lands to be valued and give an answer as quickly as may be."

" For a young man you are careful, merchant."

" Alas ! such as I need to be who must guard our small earnings in these troublous times of war and tumult. Such a sum as you speak of would take all that John Grimmer and I have laid by after years of toil."

Again he looked at the furnishings of the room and shrugged his shoulders, then said,

"Good, it shall be done for the need is urgent. To whom is the letter to be sent?"

"To John Grimmer, at the Boat House, Cheapside."

"But you told me John Grimmer was dead."

"And so he is, my lord, but his name remains."

Then we returned to the shop and as we went I said,

"If your lordship's lady should set her heart upon the ruby the cost of it can stand over for a while, since I know that it is hard for a husband to disappoint a wife of what she desires."

"Man, she is my distant cousin, not my wife. I would she were, but how can two high-placed paupers wed?"

"Perhaps it is for this reason that my lord wishes to borrow money."

Again he shrugged his shoulders, and as we entered the shop I threw back the hood from off my head upon which I wore a merchant's cap of velvet. The lady Blanche caught sight of me and started.

"Surely, surely —" she began, "you are he who shot the three arrows at the cave's mouth at Hastings."

"Yes, my lady, and did your hawk escape the dogs upon the London road?"

"Nay, it was crippled and died, which was the first of many troubles, for I think my luck rode away with you that day, Master Hubert of Hastings," she added with a sigh."

"There are other hawks and luck returns," I replied, bowing. "Perhaps this trinket will bring it back to you, my lady," and taking the snake-surrounded ruby heart, I proffered it to her with another bow.

"Oh!" she said, her blue eyes shining with pleasure, "oh! it is beautiful, but whence is the price to come for so costly a thing?"

"I think the matter is one that can wait."

At that moment the lord Deleroy broke in, saying,

"So you are the man who slew the French knight with an ancient sword, and afterwards shot three other Frenchmen with three shafts, sending one of them through shield and mail and body, a tale that was spoken of afterwards, even in London. God's truth! you should be serving the King in the wars, not yourself behind the counter."

"There are many ways of serving, my lord," I answered, "by pen and merchandise as well as by steel and shafts. Now with me it is the turn of the former, though perhaps the ancient sword and the great black bow wait till their time comes again."

He stared at me and muttered, half to himself,

"A strange merchant and a grim, as those dead Frenchmen may have thought. I tell you, Sir Trader, that your talk and the eyes of that tall Moor of yours turn my back cold; it is as though someone walked over my grave. Come, Blanche, let us begone ere our horses be chilled as I am. Master Grimmer, or Hastings, you shall hear from me, unless I can do my business otherwise, and for the trinket send me a note at your leisure."

Then they went, but as the lady Blanche left the shop she caught her robe and turned to free it, while she did so flashing at me one of her sweet looks such as I remembered well.

Kari followed to the door and watched them mount their horses at the gate, then he searched the ground with his eyes.

"What was it hooked her cloak?" I asked.

"A dream, or the air, Master, for there is nothing

else to which it could have hung. Those who would throw spears behind them must first turn round."

"What think you of those two, Kari?"

"I think that they will not pay for your jewel, but perhaps this was but a bait upon the hook."

"And what more, Kari?"

"I think that the lady is very fair and false, and that the great lord's heart is as black as are his eyes. Also I think that they are dear to each other and well-matched. But it seems that you have met them both both before, Master, so you will know better about them than your slave."

"Yes, I have met them," I answered sharply, for his words about Blanche angered me, adding, "I have noted, Kari, that you have never a good word for anyone whom I favour. You are jealous-natured, Kari, especially of women."

"You ask, I answer," he replied humbly, falling into broken English, as was his fashion when moved, "and it is true that those who have much love, are much jealous. That is a fault in my people. Also I love not women. Now I go make another piece for that which Master give the lady. Only this time it all snake and no heart."

He went, taking the tray of jewels with him, and I too went to the eating-room to think.

How strange was this meeting. I had never forgotten the lady Blanche, but in a sense I had lived her memory down and mindful of my uncle's counsel, had not sought to look upon her again, for which reason I kept away from Hastings where I thought that I should find her. And now here she was in London and in my house, brought thither by fate. Nor was that all, since those blue eyes of hers had re-lighted the dead fires in my heart and, seated there alone, I knew that I loved her; indeed had never ceased to love her. She was more to me than all my wealth, more than anything, and alas! between us there was still a great gulf fixed.

She was not wed, it was true, but she was a highly-placed lady and I but a merchant who could not even call myself a squire, or by law wear garments made of certain stuffs which I handled daily in my trade. How might that gulf be crossed?

Then as I mused there rose in my mind a memory of certain sayings of my wise old uncle, and with it an answer to the question. Gold would bridge the widest streams of human difference. These fine folk for all their flauntings were poor. They came to me to borrow money wherewith to gild their coronets and satisfy the importunate creditors at their door, lest they should be pulled from their high places and forced back into the number of the common herd as those who could no longer either give or pay.

And after all was this difference between them and me so wide? The grandsire of Sir Robert Aleys, I had been told, gathered his wealth by trade and usury in the old wars; indeed it was said that he was one who dealt in cattle, while Lord Deleroy was reported to be a bastard, if of the bluest blood, so blue that it ran nigh to the royal purple. Well, what was mine? On the father's side Saxon descended from that of Thanes who went down before the Normans and thereafter became humble landed folk of the lesser sort. On the mother's, of the race of the old sea-kings who slew and conquered through all the world they knew. Was I then so far beneath these others? Nay, but like my father and my uncle I was one who bought and sold and the hand of the dyer was stained to the colour of his vat.

Thus stood the business. I, a stubborn man, not ill-favoured, to whom Fortune had given wealth, was determined to win this woman who, it seemed to me, looked upon me with no unkind eye since I had saved her from certain perils. To myself then and there I swore I would win her. The question was—how could it be done? I might enter the service of the King and fight his battles and doubtless win myself a knighthood, or more, which would open the closed gate.

Nay, it would take too long and something warned me that time pressed. That strange foreign man, Kari, said that Blanche was enamoured of this Deleroy, and although I was wroth with him, setting his words down to jealousy of any on whom I looked with kindness, I knew well that Kari saw far. If I tarried, this rare white bird would slip from my hand into another's cage. I must stir at once or let the matter be. Well, I had wealth, so let wealth be my friend. Time enough to try war when it failed me.

On the third day of the new year, which at this time of Court revelry showed that the matter must indeed be pressing, I received those particulars for which I had asked, together with a list of the lands and tenements that Sir Robert Aleys was ready to put in pawn on behalf of his friend and relative, the lord Deleroy. Why should he do this, I wondered? There could only be one answer; because he and not Deleroy was to receive the money, or most of it.

Nay, another came into my mind as probable. Because he looked upon Deleroy as his heir, which, should he marry the lady Blanche, he would become. If this were so I must act, and quickly, that is, if I would ever see more of the lady Blanche, as perchance I might do by treading this gold-paved road, but not otherwise. I studied the lists of lands. As it chanced I knew most of them, for they lay about Pevensey and Hastings, and saw that they were scarcely worth the moneys which were asked of me. Well, what of it? This matter was not one of trade, and large as the sum might be, I would risk it for the chance of winning Blanche.

The end of it was that waiting for no valuings I wrote that on proof of title clean and unencumbered and completion of all deeds, I would pay over the gold to whoever might be appointed to receive it.

This letter of mine proved to be but the beginning of a long business whereof the details may be left untold. On the very next day indeed I was summoned to the house of Sir Robert Aleys which was near to the palace and abbey of Westminster. Here I found the gruff old knight grown greyer and having, as it seemed to me, a hunted air, and with him the lord Deleroy and two foxy lawyers of whom I did not like the look. Indeed, from the first, I suspected that I was being tricked and had it not been for the lady Blanche, would have broken off the loan. Because of her, however, this I did not do, but having stated my terms anew, and the rate and dates of interest, sat for a long while saying as little as possible, while the others unfolded parchments and talked and talked, telling tales that often contradicted each other, till at length the lord Deleroy, who seemed ill at ease, grew weary and left the chamber. At last all was done that could be done at that sitting and it being past the hour of dinner, I was taken in to eat, consenting, because I hoped that I should see the lady Blanche.

A butler, or chamber-groom, led me to the dining-hall and sat me with the lawyers at a table beneath the dais. Presently on this dais appeared Sir Robert Aleys, his daughter Blanche, the lord Deleroy and perhaps eight or ten other fine folk whom I had never seen. She, looking about her, saw me seated at the lower table, and spoke to her father and Deleroy, reasoning with the latter, as it would appear. Indeed, in a sudden hush I caught some of her words. They were, "If you are not ashamed to take his money, you should not be ashamed to sit at meat with him."

Deleroy stamped his foot, but the end of it was that I was summoned to the high table where the lady Blanche made place for me beside her, while Deleroy sat himself down between two splendid dames at the other end of the board.

Here then I stayed by Blanche who, I noted, wore the ruby heart encircled by serpents. Indeed, this was the first thing of which she spoke to me, saying,

"It looks well upon my robe, does it not, and I thank you for it, Master Hubert, who know surely that it is not my cousin Deleroy's gift, but yours, since for it you will never see your money."

By way of answer I looked at the sumptuous plate and furnishings, the profusion of the viands and the number of the serving-men. Reading my thought, she replied,

"Aye, but pledged, all of it. I tell you, Master Hubert, that we are starved hounds, though we live in a kennel with golden bars. And now they would pawn you that kennel also."

Then, while I wondered what to say, she began to talk of our great adventure in bygone years, recalling every tiny thing that had happened and every word that had been spoken between us, some of which I had forgotten. Of one thing only she said nothing—the kisses with which we had parted. Amongst much else, she spoke of how the ancient sword had shorn through the armour of the French knight, and I told her that the sword was named Wave-Flame and that it had come down to me from my ancestor, Thorgrimmer the Viking, and of what was written on its blade, to all of which she listened greedily.

"And they thought you not fit to sit at meat with them, you whose race is so old and who are so great a warrior, as you showed that day. And it is to you that I owe my life and more than life, to you and not to them."

So saying she shot a glance at me that pierced me through and through, as my arrows had pierced the Frenchmen, and what is more beneath the cover of the board for a moment let her slim hand rest upon my own.

After this for a while we were silent, for indeed I could not speak. Then we talked on as we could do well enough, since there was no one on my left where the board ended, and on Blanche's right was a fat old lord who seemed to be deaf and occupied himself in drinking more than he should have done. I told her much about myself, also what my mother had said to me on the day of the Burning, and of how she had prophesied that I should be a wanderer, words at which Blanche sighed and answered:

"Yet you seem to be well planted in London and in rich soil, Master Hubert."

"Aye, Lady, but it is not my native soil and for the rest we go where Fate leads us."

"Fate! What does that word bring to my mind? I have it; yonder Moor of yours who makes those jewels. He has the very eyes of Fate and I fear him."

"That is strange, Lady, and yet not so strange for about this man there is something fateful. Ever he swears to me that I shall accompany him to some dim land where he was born, of which land he is a prince."

Then I told her all the story of Kari, to which she listened open-eyed and wondering, saying when I had finished,

"So you saved this poor wanderer also, and doubtless he loves you well."

"Yes, Lady, almost too well, seeing that at times he is jealous of me, though God knows I did little for him save pick him from a crowd upon the quay."

"Ah! I guessed it, who saw him watching you the other day. Yet it is strange, for I thought that only women could be jealous of men, and men of women. Hush! they are mocking us because we talk so friendly."

I looked up, following her glance, and saw that Deleroy and the two fine ladies between whom he sat, all of whom appeared to have had enough of wine, were pointing at us. Indeed, in a silence, such as now and again happens at feasts, I heard one of them say,

"You had best beware lest that fair white dove of yours does not slip your hand and begin to coo in another's ear, my Lord Deleroy," and heard his answer,

"Nay, I have her too fast, and who cares for a pinioned dove whereof the feathers adorn another's cap?"

Whilst I was wondering what this dark talk might mean the company broke up, the lady Blanche gliding away through a door at the back of the dais, followed, as I noted, by Deleroy who seemed flushed and angry.

Many times I visited that prodigal house which seemed to me to be the haunt of folk who, however highly placed and greatly favoured at Court, were as loose in their lives as they were in their talk. Indeed, although I was no saint, I liked them not at all, especially the men with their scented hair, turned up shoes and party-coloured clothes. Nor as I thought, did Sir Robert Aleys like them, who, whatever his faults, was a bluff knight of the older sort, who had fought with credit in the French wars. Yet I noted that he seemed to be helpless in their hands, or rather in those of Deleroy, the King's favourite, who was the chief of all the gang. It was as though that gay and handsome young man had some hold over the old soldier, yes, and over his daughter also, though what this might be I could not guess.

Now I will move on with the tale. In due course the parchments were signed and delivered, and the money in good gold was paid over on my behalf, after which the great household at Westminster became more prodigal than before. But when the time came for the discharge of the interest due not a groat was forthcoming. Then afterwards there was talk of my taking over certain of the pledged lands in lieu of this interest. Sir Robert suggested this and I assented, because Blanche had told me that it would help her father. Only when the matter was set on foot by my lawyers it was found that these lands were not his to transfer, inasmuch as they had been already mortgaged to their value.

Then there was a fierce quarrel between Sir Robert Aleys and the lord Deleroy, at which I was present. Sir Robert with many oaths accused his cousin of having forged his name when he was absent in France, while Deleroy declared that what he did was done with due authority. Almost they drew swords on each other, till at length Deleroy took Aleys aside and with a fierce grin, whispered something into his ear which caused the old knight to sink down on a stool and call out,

"Get you gone, you false rogue! Get out of this house, aye, and out of England. If I meet you again, by God's Blood I swear that King's favourite or no King's favourite, I'll throat you like a hog!"

To which Deleroy mocked in answer,

"Good! I'll go, my gentle cousin, which it suits me well to do who have certain business of the King's awaiting me in France. Aye, I'll go and leave you to settle with this worthy trader who may hold that you have duped him. Do it as you will, except in one fashion, of which you know. Now a word with my cousin Blanche and another at the Palace and I ride for Dover. Farewell, Cousin Aleys. Farewell, worthy merchant for whose loss I should grieve, did I not know that soon you will recoup youself out of gentle pockets. Mourn not over me over much either of you, since doubtless ere so very long I shall return."

Now my blood flamed up and I answered,

"I pray you do not hurry, my lord, lest you should find me waiting for you with a shield and a sword in place of a warrant and a pen."

He heard and called out, "Fore God, this chapman thinks himself a knight!"

Then with a mocking laugh he went.

CHAPTER VI

Marriage—and After

Sir Robert and I stood facing each other, speechless with rage, both of us. At length he said in a hoarse voice:

"Your pardon, Master Hastings, for the affronts that this bastard lordling has put upon you, an honest man. I tell you that he is a loose-living knave, as you would agree if you knew all his story, a cockatrice that for my sins I have nurtured in my bosom. 'Tis he that has wasted all my substance; 'tis he that has made free of my name, so that I fear me you are defrauded. 'Tis he that uses my house as though it were his own, bringing into it vile women of the Court, and men that are viler still, however high their names and gaudy their attire," and he choked in his wrath and stopped.

"Why do you suffer these things, Sir?" I asked.

"Forsooth because I must," he answered sullenly, "for he has me and mine by the throat. This Deleroy is very powerful, Master Hastings. At a word from him whispered in the King's ear, I, or you, or any man might find ourselves in the Tower accused of treason, whence we should appear no more."

Then, as though he wished to get away from the subject of Deleroy and his hold upon him, he went on:

"I fear me that your money, or much of it, is in danger for Deleroy's bond is worthless, and since the land is already pledged without my knowledge, I have nowhere to turn for gold. I tell you that I am an honest man if one who has fallen into ill company, and this wickedness cuts me deep, for I know not how you will be repaid."

Now a thought came to me and as was my bold fashion in all business, I acted on it instantly.

"Sir Robert Aleys," I said, "should it be pleasing to you and another, I can see a way in which this debt may be cancelled without shame to you and yet to my profit."

"Then in God's name speak it! For I see none."

"Sir, in bygone time, as it chanced I was able yonder at Hastings to do some service to your daughter and in that hour she took my heart."

He started but motioned to me to continue.

"Sir, I love her truly and desire more than anything to make her my wife. I know she is far above me in station, still although but a merchant, I am of good descent as I can prove to you. Moreover, I am rich, for this money that I have advanced to you, or to the Lord Deleroy, or to both of you, is but a small part of my wealth which grows day by day through honest trade. Sir, if my suit were accepted I should be ready, not only to help you further on certain terms, but by deed and will to settle most of it upon the Lady Blanche and upon our children. Sir, what say you?"

Sir Robert tugged at his red beard and stared down at the floor. Presently he lifted his head and I saw that his face was troubled, the face of a man indeed, who is struggling with himself, or as I thought, with his pride.

"A fair offer fairly put," he said, "but the question is, not what I say, but what says Blanche."

"Sir, I do not know who have never asked her. Yet at times I have thought that her mind towards me is not unkind."

"Is it so? Well, perhaps now that he—well, let that lie. Master Hastings, you have my leave to try your fortune and I tell you straight that I hope it will be good. With your wealth your rank may be soon mended and you are an honest man whom I should be glad to welcome as a son, for I have had enough of these Court knaves and painted Jezebels. But, if such is your fancy towards Blanche, my counsel to you is that you put it quickly to the proof—aye, man, at once. Mark my words, for such a swan as she is many snares are set beneath the dirty waters of this Court."

"The sooner the better, Sir."

"Good. I'll send her to you and, one word more —be not over shy, or ready to take the first 'no' for an answer, or to listen to the tale of bygone fancies, such as all women have."

Then suddenly he went, leaving me there wondering at his words, and manner, which I did not understand. This I understood, however, that he desired that I should marry Blanche, which considering all things I held somewhat strange, although I had the wealth she lacked. Doubtless, I thought, it must be because his honour had been touched on the matter of the trick that had been played upon him without his knowledge. Then I ceased from these wonderings and gave my thought to what I should say to Blanche.

I waited a long while and still she did not come, till at last I believed that she was away from the house, or guessing my business, had refused to see me. At length, however, she entered the room, so silently that I who was staring at the great abbey through a window place, never heard the door open or close. I think that some sense of her presence must have drawn me, since suddenly I turned to see her standing before me. She was clad all in white, having a round cap or coronet upon her head beneath which her shining fair hair was looped in braids. Her little coat, trimmed with ermine, was fastened with a single jewel, that ruby heart embraced by serpents, which I had given her. She wore no other ornament. Thus seen she looked most lovely and most sweet and all my heart went out in yearning for her.

"My father tells me that you wish to speak with me, so I have come," she said in her low clear voice, searching my face curiously with her large eyes.

I bowed my head and paused, not knowing how to begin.

"How can I serve you, who, I fear, have been ill served?" she went on with a little smile as though she found amusement in my confusion.

"In one way only," I exclaimed, "by giving yourself in marriage to me. For that I seek, no less."

Now her fair face that had been pale, became stained with red and she let her eyes fall as though she were searching for something among the rushes that strewed the floor.

"Hearken before you answer," I continued. "When first I spoke with you on that bloody day at Hastings and you had but just come to womanhood, I loved you and swore to myself that I would die to save you. I saved you and we kissed and were parted. Afterwards I tried to put you out of my heart, knowing that you were set far above me and no meat for such as I, though still for your sake I wooed no other woman in marriage. The years went by and fortune brought us together again, and lo! the old love was stronger than before. I know that I am not worthy of you who are so high and good and pure. Still——" and I stopped, lacking words.

She moved uneasily and the red colour left her cheeks as though she had been suddenly pained.

"Bethink you," she said with a touch of hardness in her voice, "can one who lives the life I live and keeps my company, remain as holy and unstained as you believe? If you would gather such a lily, surely you should seek it in a country garden, not in the reek of London."

"I neither know nor care," I answered, whose blood was all afire. "I know only that wherever you grow and from whatever soil, you are the flower I would pluck."

"Bethink you again; an ugly slug might have smeared my whiteness."

"If so the honest sun and rain will recover and wash it and I am a gardener who scatters lime to shrivel slugs."

"If to this one you will not listen, then hear another argument. Perchance I do not love you. Would you win a loveless bride?"

"Perchance you can learn of love, or if not, I have enough to serve for two."

"By my faith! it should not be difficult with a man so honest and so well favoured. And yet—a further plea. My cousin Deleroy has cheated you" (here her face hardened), "and I think I am offered to you by my father in satisfaction of his honour, as men who have no gold, offer a house or a horse to close a debt."

"It is not so. I prayed you of your father. The loss, if loss there be, is but a chance of trade, such as I face every day. Still, I will be plain and tell you that I risked it with open eyes, expecting nothing less, that I might come near to you."

Now she sat herself down upon a chair, covering her face with her hands, and I saw from the trembling of her body that she was sobbing. While I wondered what to do, for the sight wrung me, she let fall her hands and there were tears upon her face.

"Shall I tell you all my story, you good, simple gentleman?" she asked.

"Nay, only two things. Are you the wife of some other man?"

"Not so, though perhaps—once I went near to it. What is the other question?"

"Do you love some other man so that your heart tells you it is not possible that you should ever love me."

"No, I do not," she answered almost fiercely, "but by the Rood! I hate one."

"Which is no affair of mine," I said laughing. "For the rest, let it sleep. Few are they that know life's wars who have no scar to hide and I am not one of them, though in truth your lips made the deepest yonder by the cave at Hastings."

When she heard this she coloured to her brow and forgetting her tears, laughed outright, while I went on:

"Therefore let the past be and if it is your will, let us set our eyes upon the future. Only one promise would I ask of you, that never again will you be alone with the Lord Deleroy, since one so light-fingered with a pen would, I think, steal other things."

"By my soul! the last thing I desire is to be alone with my cousin Deleroy."

Now she rose from the chair and for a little while we stood facing each other. Then very slightly she opened her arms and lifted her face towards me.

Thus did Blanche Aleys and I become affianced, though afterwards, when I thought the business over, I remembered that never once did she say that she would marry me. This, however, troubled me little, since in such matters it is what women do that weighs, not what they say. For the rest I was mad with love of her, also both then and as the days went by, more and more did she seem to be travelling on this same road of Love. If not, indeed she acted well.

Within a month we were wed on a certain October day in the church of St. Margaret's at Westminster. Once it was agreed all desired to push on this marriage, and not least Blanche herself. Sir Robert Aleys said that he wished to be gone from London to his estates in Sussex, having had enough of the Court and its ways, desiring there to live quietly till the end; I, being so much in love, was on fire for my bride and Blanche herself vowed that she was eager to become my wife, saying that our courtship, which began on Hastings hill, had lasted long enough. For the rest, there was nothing to cause delay. I cancelled Sir Robert's debt to me and signed a deed in favour of his daughter and her offspring, whereof I gave a copy to his lawyer and there was nought else to be done except to prepare my house for her which, with money at command, was easy.

No great business was made of this marriage, since neither his kin nor Sir Robert himself wished to noise it about that his only child, the last of his House, was taking a merchant for her husband to save her and him from wreck. Nor did I, the merchant, wish to provoke talk amongst those of my own station, especially as it was known that I had advanced moneys to these fine folk of the Court. So it came about that few were asked to the ceremony that was fixed for an early hour, and of these not many came, because on that day although it was but October, a great gale with storms of rain began to blow, the greatest indeed that I had known in my life.

Thus it chanced that we were wed in an almost empty church while the fierce wind, thundering against the windows, overcame the feeble voice of the old priest, so that he looked like one acting in a show without words. The darkness caused by the thick rain was so deep, also, that scarce could I see my bride's lovely face or find the finger upon which I must set the ring.

At length it was done and we went down the aisle to find our horses whereon we must ride to my house in Cheapside, where there was to be a feast for my dependents and such of my few friends as cared to come, among whom were not numbered any grand folk from Westminster. As we drew near the church door I noted among those who were present those two gaudy ladies between whom Deleroy had sat at that meal after the business of the loan was settled. Moreover I heard one of them say:

"What will Deleroy do when he comes back to find his darling gone?" and the other answer with a high laugh:

"Seek another doubtless, or borrow more money from the merchant and——" here I lost their talk in the rush of the wind through the opened door.

In the porch was old Sir Robert Aleys:

"Mother of God!" he shouted, "may the rest of the lives of you two be smoother than your nuptials. No Cheapside feast for me, I'm for home in such fiend's weather. Farewell, son Hubert and all joy to you. Farewell, Blanche. Learn to be obedient as a wife and keep your eyes for your husband's face, that is my counsel to you. Till we meet again at Christmastide in Sussex, whither I ride to-morrow, farewell to both of you."

Farewell, it was indeed, for never did either of us look on him again.

Wrapped close in our cloaks we battled through the storm and at length, somewhat breathless, reached my house in the Cheap where the garlands of autumn flowers and greenery that I had caused to be wreathed from posts before the door, were all torn away by the gale. Here I welcomed my wife as best I could, kissing her as she crossed the threshold and saying certain sweet words that I had prepared, to which she smiled an answer. Then the women took her to her chamber to make herself ready and afterwards came the feast, which was sumptuous of its sort, though the evil weather kept some of the guests away.

Scarcely had it begun when Kari who of late had been sad-faced and brooding, and who did not eat with us, entered and whispered to me that my Master of Lading from the docks prayed to see me at once on a matter which would brook no delay. Making excuse to Blanche and the company, I went out to see him in the shop and found the man much disturbed. It seemed that a certain vessel of mine that I had re-christened *Blanche* in honour of my wife, which lay in the stream ready to sail, was in great danger because of the tempest. Indeed, she was dragging at her anchor and it was feared that unless more anchors could be let down she would come ashore and be wrecked against the jetty-heads or otherwise. The reason why this had not been done, was that only the master and one sailor were on board the vessel; the rest were feasting ashore in honour of my marriage, and refused to row out to her, saying that the boat would be swamped in the gale.

Now this ship, although not very large, was the best and staunchest that I owned, being almost new; moreover the cargo on board of her, laden for the Mediterranean, was of great value, so great indeed that its loss would have been very grievous to me. Therefore it was plain that I must see to the matter without delay, since from my servant's account there was no hope that these rebellious sailors would listen to any lesser man than myself. So, if I would save the ship and her cargo, I must ride for the docks at once.

Going back to the eating-chamber, in a few words I told my wife and the guests how the matter stood, praying the oldest man among the latter to take my place by the bride, which he did unwillingly, muttering that this was an unlucky marriage feast.

Then it was that Blanche rose, beseeching me earnestly and almost with tears that I would take her with me to the docks. I laughed at her, as did the company, but still she besought with much persistence, till I began to believe that she must be afraid of something, though the others cried that it was but love and fear lest I should come to harm.

In the end I made her drink a cup of wine with me, but her hand shook so much that she spilled the cup and the rich red wine ran down her breast, staining the whiteness of her robe, whereat some women among the company murmured, thinking it a bad omen. At length with a kiss I tore myself away, for I could bide no longer and the horses were waiting. So presently I was riding for the docks as fast as the storm would suffer, with tiles from the roofs, and when we were clear of these, the torn-off limbs of trees hurtling round me. Kari, I should say, would have accompanied me, but I took a serving-man, bidding Kari bide where he was in the house in case he might be of service.

At last we came safely to the docks where I found all as my Cargo-master had described. The ship *Blanche* was in great peril and dragging every minute towards a pierhead which, if she struck, would stave her in and make an end of her. The men, too, were still feasting in the inn with their wharfside trollops, and, some of them, half drunk. I spoke to them, showing them their shame, and saying that if they would not come, I and my man would take a boat and get aboard alone and this upon my wedding day. Then they hung their heads and came.

We won to the ship safely though with much toil and danger, and there found the master almost crazed with fear and doubt of the issue, and the man with him injured by a falling block. Indeed, this poor captain clung to the rail, watching the cable as it dragged the anchor and fearing every moment lest it should part.

The rest is soon told. We got out two more anchors and did other things such as sailors know, to help in such a case. When all was as safe as it could be made, I and my man and four sailors started for the quay, telling the master that I would return upon the morrow. The wind and current aiding us, we landed safe and sound and at once I rode back to Cheapside.

Now, though it is short to tell, all this had taken a long while, also the way was far to ride in such a storm. Thus it came about that it was nigh to ten o'clock at night when, thanking God, I dismounted at the gate of my house and bade the servant take the horses to the stable. As I drew near the door, it opened, which astonished me and, as the light within showed, there stood Kari. What astonished me still more, he had the great sword, Wave-Flame, in his hand, though not drawn, which sword he must have fetched from where it was kept with the French knight's armour and the shield that bore three arrows as a cognizance.

Laying his finger on his lips he shut the door softly, then said in a low voice:

"Master, there is a man up yonder with the lady."

"What man?" I asked.

"That same lord, Master, who came here with her once before to buy jewels and borrow gold. Hearken. The feast being finished the guests went away at fall of night, but the wife-lady withdrew herself into the chamber that is called sun-room (the solar), that up the stairs, which looks out on the street. About one hour gone there came a knock at the door. I who was watching, opened, thinking it was you returned, and there stood that lord. He spoke to me saying:

"Moor-man, I know that your master is from home, but that the lady is here. I would speak with her."

Now I would have turned him away, but at that moment the lady herself, who it seemed was watching, came down the stairs, looking very white, and said:

"Kari, let the lord come in. I have matters of your master's business about which I must talk with him. So, Master, knowing that you had lent money to this lord, I obeyed, though I liked it not, and having fetched the sword which I thought perchance might be needed, I waited."

This was the substance of what he said, though his talk was more broken since he never learned to speak English well and helped it out with words in his own tongue, of which, as I have told, he had taught me something.

"I do not understand," I exclaimed when he had finished. "Doubtless it is little or nothing. Yet, give me the sword, for who knows? and come with me."

Kari obeyed and as I went up the stairs I buckled Wave-Flame about me. Also Kari brought two candles of Italian wax lighted upon their stands. Coming to the door of the solar I tried to open it, but it was bolted.

"God's truth!" I said, "this is strange," and hammered on the panel with my fist.

Presently it opened, but before entering, for I feared some trick, I stood without and looked in. The room was lit by a hanging lamp and a fire burned brightly on the hearth, for the night was cold. In an oak chair by the fire and staring into it, sat Blanche still as any statue. She glanced round and saw me in the light of the candles that Kari held, and again stared into the fire. Half-way between her and the door stood Deleroy, dressed as ever in fine clothes, though I noted that his cape was off and hung over a stool near the fire as though to dry. I noted also that he wore a sword and a dagger. I entered the room, followed by Kari, shut the door behind me and shot the bolt. Then I spoke, asking:

"Why are you here with my wife, Lord Deleroy?"

"It is strange, Master merchant," he answered, "but I was about to put much the same question to you; namely, why is *my* wife in your house?"

Now, while I reeled beneath these words, without turning her head, Blanche by the fire said:

"He lies, Hubert. I am not his wife."

"Why are you here, my Lord Deleroy?" I repeated.

"Well, if you would know, Master merchant, I bring a paper for you, or rather a copy of it, for the writ itself will be served on you to-morrow by the King's officers. It commits you to the Tower under the royal seal for trading with the King's enemies, a treason that can be proved against you, of which as you know, or will shortly learn, the punishment is death," and as he spoke he threw a writing down upon a side table.

"I see the plot," I answered coldly. "The King's unworthy favourite, forger and thief, uses the King's authority to try to bring the King's honest subject to bonds and death by a false accusation. It is a common trick in these days. But let that be. For the third time I ask you—why are you here with my new-wed wife and at this hour of the night?"

"So courteous a question demands a courteous

answer, Master merchant, but to give it I must trouble you to listen to a tale."

"Then let it be like my patience, brief," I replied.

"It shall," he said with a mocking bow.

Then very clearly and quietly he set out a dreadful story, giving dates and circumstances. Let that story be. The substance of it was that he had married Blanche soon after she reached womanhood and that she had borne him a child which died.

"Blanche," I said when he had done, "you have heard. Is this true?"

"Much of it is true," she answered in that strange cold voice, still staring at the fire. "Only the marriage was a false one by which I was deceived. He who celebrated it was a companion of the Lord Deleroy tricked out as a priest."

"Do not let us wrangle of this matter," said Deleroy. "A man who mixes with the world like yourself, Master merchant, will know that women in a trap rarely lack excuses. Still if it be admitted that this marriage did not fulfil all formalities, then so much the better for Blanche and for myself. If she be your lawful wife and not mine, you, I learn, have signed a writing in her favour under which she will inherit your great wealth. That indenture, I think you can find no opportunity to dispute, and if you do I have a promise that the property of a certain traitor shall pass to me the revealer of his treachery. Let it console you in your last moments, Master merchant, to remember that the lady whom you have honoured with your fancy, will pass her days in wealth and comfort in the company of him whom she has honoured with her love."

"Draw!" I said briefly as I unsheathed my word.

"Why should I fight with a base, trading usurer?"

he asked still mocking me, though I thought that there was doubt in his voice.

"Answer your own question, thief. Fight if you will, or die without fighting if you will not. For know that until I am dead you do not leave this room living."

"Until I dead too, O lord," broke in Kari in his gentle voice, bowing in his courteous, foreign fashion.

As he did so with a sudden motion Kari shook the cloak back from his body and for the first time I saw that thrust through his leathern belt was a long weapon, half sword and half dagger, also that its sharpened steel was bare.

"Oh!" exclaimed Deleroy, "now I understand that I am trapped and that when you told me, Blanche, that this man would not return to-night and that therefore we were safe together, you lied. Well, my Lady Blanche, you shall pay for this trick later."

Whilst he spoke thus, slowly, as though to gain time, he was looking about him and as the last word left his lips, knowing that the door was locked, he dashed for the window, hoping I suppose, to leap through the casement, or if that failed, to shout for help. But Kari, who had set the candles he bore on a side table, that where the writing lay, read his mind. With a movement more swift than that of a polecat leaping on its prey, the swiftest indeed that ever I saw, he sprang between him and the casement, so that Deleroy scarce escaped pinning himself upon the steel that he held in his long outstretched arm. Indeed, I think it pricked his throat, for he checked himself with an oath and drew his sword, a double-edged weapon with a sharp point, as long as mine perhaps, but not so heavy.

"I see that I must finish the pair of you. Perchance, Blanche, you will protect my back as a loving wife should do, until this lout is done with," he said, swaggering to the last.

"Kari," I commanded, "hold the candles aloft that the light may be good, and leave this man to me."

Kari bowed and took the copper taper stands, one in either hand, and held them aloft. But first he placed his long dagger, not back in his belt, but between his teeth with the handle towards his right hand. Even then in some strange fashion I noted how terrible looked this grim dark man holding the candles high with the knife gripped between his white teeth.

Deleroy and I faced each other in the open space between the fire and the door. Blanche turned round upon her stool and watched, uttering no sound. But I laughed aloud for of the end I had no doubt. Had there been ten Deleroys I would have slain them all. Still presently I found there was cause to doubt, for when, parrying his first thrust, I drove at him with all my strength, instead of piercing him through and through the ancient sword, Wave-Flame, bent in my hand like a bow as it is strung, telling me that beneath his Joseph's coat of silk, Deleroy wore a shirt of mail.

Then I cried: "*A-hoi!*" as Thorgrimmer my ancestor may have done when he wielded this same sword, and while Deleroy still staggered beneath my thrust, I grasped Wave-Flame with both hands, wheeled it aloft and smote. He lifted his left arm round which he had wound his cloak, to protect his head, but the sword shore through cloak and arm, so that his hand with the glittering rings upon it fell to the floor.

Again I smote for, as both of us knew, this business was to the death, and Deleroy fell down dead, smitten through the brain.

Kari smiled gently, and lifting the cloak, shook it out and threw it over what had been Deleroy.

Then he took my sword and while I watched him idly, cleansed it with rushes from the floor.

Next I heard a sound from the neighbourhood of the fire, and bethinking me of Blanche turned to speak to her, though what I was going to say, God knows for I do not.

A terrible sight met my eyes and burned itself into my very soul so that it could never be forgot. Blanche was leaning back in the oak chair over which flowed her long, fair locks, and the front of her robe was red. I remembered how she had spilt the wine at the feast and thought I saw its stain, till presently, still staring, I noted that it grew and knew it to be caused by another wine, that of her blood. Also I noted that from the midst of it seen in the lamplight, just beneath the snake-encircled ruby heart, appeared the little handle of a dagger.

I sprang to her, but she lifted her hand and waved me back.

"Touch me not," she whispered, "I am not fit, also the thrust is mortal. If you draw the knife I shall die at once and first I would speak. I would have you know that I love you and hoped to be a good wife to you. What I said was true. That dead man tricked me with a false marriage when I was scarcely more than child, and afterwards would not mend it with an honest. Perchance he himself was wed, or he had other reasons, I do not know. My father guessed much but not all. I tried to warn you when you offered yourself, but you were deaf and blind and would not see or listen. Then I gave way, liking you well and thinking that I should find rest, as indeed I do; thinking also that I should be wealthy and able to shut that villain's mouth with gold. I never knew he was coming here or even that he had sailed home from France, but he broke in upon me, having learned that you were away, and was about to leave when you returned. He came for money for which he believed that I had wed, and thinking to win me back from one doomed by his lies to a traitor's death. You know the rest and for me there was but one thing to do. Be glad that you are no longer burdened with me and go find happiness in the arms of a more fortunate or a better woman. Fly, and swiftly, for Deleroy had many friends and the King himself loved him as a brother—as well he may. Fly, I say and forgive—forgive! Hubert, farewell!"

Thus she spoke, ever more slowly and lower, till with the last word her life left her lips.

Thus ended the story of my marriage with Blanche Aleys.

BOOK II

CHAPTER I

The New World

They were for ever silent now, who, but a breath before had been so full of life and the stir of mortal passion; Deleroy dead beneath the cloak upon the floor, Blanche dead in the oaken chair. We who remained alive were silent also. I glanced at Kari's face; it was as that of a stone statue on a tomb, only in it his large eyes shone, noting all things and, as I imagined in my distraught fancy, filled with triumph and fore-knowledge. Considering it in that strange calm of the spirit which sometimes supervenes on great and terrible events that for a while crush its mortality from the soul and set it free to marvel at the temporal pettiness of all we consider immediate and mighty, I wondered what was the aspect of my own.

At the moment, I, who on this day had passed the portals of so many emotions; that of the lover's longing for his bride won at last, only to be lost again, that of acute and necessary business, that of the ancient joy of battle and vengeance wreaked upon an evil man; that of the unshuttering of my eyes to the flame of a hellish truth, that of the self-murder and turning to cold clay before those same eyes of her whom I had hoped to clasp in honest love—I, I say, felt as though I too were dead. Indeed all within was dead, only the shell of flesh remained alive, and in my heart I echoed the words of my old uncle and of a wiser than he who went before him—"Vanity of vanities! All is vanity!"

It was Kari who spoke the first, Kari as ever calm and even-voiced, saying in his broken English of which but the substance is recorded:

"Things have happened, good things as I hold, though you, Master, may think otherwise for a little while. Yet in this rough land of savages and small justice these things may bring trouble. That lord brought a writing," and he nodded towards the document on the table, "and talked of death for *you*, Master—not for himself. And the lady, while she still lived, she say—'Fly, fly or die!' And now?" and he glanced at the two bodies.

I looked at him vacantly for the numbness following the first shock was passing away and all the eating agony of my loss began to fix its fangs upon my heart.

"Whither can I fly?" I asked. "And why should I fly? I am an innocent man and for the rest, the sooner I am dead the better."

"My Master must fly," answered Kari, in swift, broken words, "because he still live and is free. Also sorrow behind, joy before. Kari, who hate women and read heart, Kari who drink this same bitter water long ago, guess these things coming and think and think. No need that Master trouble, Kari settle all and tell Master that if he do what he say, everything come right."

"What am I to do?" I asked with a groan.

"Ship *Blanche* on great river ready for sea. Master and Kari sail in her before daybreak. Here leave everything; much land, much wealth—what matter? Life more than these things which can get again. Come. No, one minute, wait."

Then he went to the body of Deleroy and with wonderful swiftness took off it the chain coat he wore beneath his tunic, which he put on his own body. Also he took his sword and buckled it about him, while the parchment writ he threw upon the fire. Then he extinguished the hanging lamp and gave me one of the candles, taking the other himself.

At the door I held up my candle and by the light of it looked my last on the ashen face of Blanche, which face I knew must go with me through all my life's days.

Kari locked the stout oaken door of the solar from the outside and took me into my chamber, where was the armour of the knight whom I had killed on Hastings hill, which armour I had caused to be altered to fit myself. Swiftly he buckled it on to me, throwing over all a long, dark robe such as merchants wear. From the cupboard too he brought the big black bow and a sheath of arrows, also a purseful of gold pieces from where they were kept, and with them the leathern bag which he had worn when I found him on the quay.

We went into the room where the feast had been held and there drank some wine, though eat I could not. The cup from which I drank was, as it chanced, the same in which I had pledged Blanche at the bride-feast. Now I pledged her spirit whereon I prayed God's mercy.

We left the house and in the stable saddled two horses, strong, quiet beasts. Then by way of the back yard we rode out into the night, none seeing us, for by now all were asleep, and in that weather the streets were empty, even of such as walked them in darkness.

We reached the quay I know not how long afterwards whose mind was full of thoughts that blotted out all else. How strange had been my life—that was one of them. Within a few years I had risen to great wealth and won the woman I desired. And now where was the wealth and where was the woman, and what was I? One flying his native land by night with blood upon his hands, the blood of a King's favourite that, if he were taken, would bring him to the noose. Oh! how great was the contrast between the morn and the midnight of that day for me! "Vanity of vanities. All is vanity!"

I think that my mind must have wandered, for when my soul was swallowed in this deepest pit of hell, it seemed to me that he whom I had worshipped as a heavenly patron, St. Hubert, appeared striding by my horse with a shining countenance and said to me:

"Have good courage, Godson, and remember your mother's words—a wanderer shall you be, but where'er you go the good bow and the good sword shall keep you safe and I wander with you. Nor does all love die with one woman's passing breath."

This phantasy, as it were, lanced the abscess of my pain and for a while I was easier. Also something of hope came back to me. I no longer desired to die but rather to live and in life, not in the tomb, to find forgetfulness.

We reached the quay and placed the horses in a shed that served as stables there, ridding them of their bits and saddles that they might eat of the hay in the racks. The thought to do this came to me, which showed that my mind was working again since still I could attend to the wants of other creatures. Then we went to the quayside where was made fast that boat in which I had come ashore some hours gone. There was a moon which now and again showed between the drifting clouds, and by the light of it I saw that the *Blanche* lay safe at her anchors not a bowshot away. The gale had fallen much with the rising of the moon, as it often does and so it came about that although the boat was over large for two men to handle rightly, Kari and I, by watching our chance, were able to row it to the ship, on to which we climbed by the ladder.

Here we found a sailor on watch who was amazed to see us, and with his help, made the boat fast by the tow rope to the stern of the ship.

This done I caused the captain to be awakened and told him briefly that as the gale had abated and tide and wind served, I desired to sail at once. He stared at me, thinking me mad, whom he knew to have been married but that day.

Surely, he said, I should wait for the light and to gather up those of the ship's company who were still ashore. I answered that I would wait for nothing, and when he asked why, was inspired to tell him that it was because I went about the King's business, having letters from his Grace to deliver to his Envoys in the South Seas that brooked of no delay, since on them hung peace or war.

"Beware," I said to him, "how you, or any of you dare to disobey the King's orders, for you know that the fate of such is a short shrift and a long rope."

Then that captain grew frightened and summoned the sailors, who by now had slept off their drink, and to them he told my commands. They murmured, pointing to the sky, but when they saw me standing there, wearing a knight's armour and looking very stern with my hand upon my sword, when also through Kari I promised them double pay for the voyage, they too grew frightened, and having set some small sails, got up the anchors.

So it came about that within little more than an hour of our boarding of that ship, she was running out towards the sea fast as tide and wind could drive her. I think that it was not too soon, for as the quay vanished in the gloom I saw men with lanterns moving on it, and thought to myself that perhaps an alarm had been given and they were come to take me.

This captain was one who knew the river well and with the help of another sailor he steered us down its reaches safely. By dawn we had passed Tilbury and at full light were off Gravesend racing for the open sea. Now it was that behind us we perceived from the rushing clouds that the gale, which had lulled during the night, was coming up more strongly than ever and still easterly. The sailors grew afraid again and together with the captain vowed that it was madness to face the sea in such weather, and that we must anchor, or make the shore if we could.

I refused to listen to them, whereat they seemed to give way.

At that moment Kari, who had gone forward, called to me. I went to him and he pointed out to me men galloping along the bank and waving kerchiefs, as though to signal to us to stop.

"I think, Master," said Kari, "that some have entered the sun-room at your house."

I nodded and watched the men who galloped and waved. For some minutes I watched them, till suddenly I saw that the ship was altering her course so that her bow pointed first one way and then another, as though she were no longer being steered. We ran aft to learn the cause, and found this.

That crew of dastards, every man of them and the captain with them, had drawn up the boat in which Kari and I came aboard, that was still tied to the ship's stern, and slid down the rope into her, purposing to win ashore before it was too late. Kari smiled as though he were not astonished, but in my rage I shouted at them, calling them curs and traitors. I think that the captain heard my words for I saw him turn his head and look away as though in shame, but not the others. They were engaged in hunting for the oars, only to find them gone, for it would seem that they had been washed or had fallen overboard.

Then they tried to set some kind of a sail by aid of a boathook, but while they were doing this, the boat, which had drifted side on to the great waves raised by the gale upon the face of the broad river, overturned. I saw some of the men clinging to the boat and one or two scrambling on to her keel, but what chanced to them and the others I do not know, who had rushed to the steering gear to set the ship upon her course again, lest her fate should be that of the boat, or we should go ashore and be captured by those who galloped on the bank, or be drowned. This was the last I ever saw or heard of the crew of the *Blanche*.

The ship's bow came round and, driven by the ever increasing gale, she rushed on her course towards the sea, bearing us with her, two weak and lonely men.

"Kari," I said, "what shall we do? Try to run ashore, or sail on?"

He thought a while, then answered, pointing to those who galloped, now but tiny figures on the distant bank:

"Master, yonder is death, sure death; and yonder," here he pointed to the sea, "is death—perhaps. Master, you have a God, and I, Kari, have another God, mayhap same God with different name. I say—Trust our Gods and sail on, for Gods better than men. If we die in water, what matter? Water softer than rope, but I think not die."

I nodded, for the reasoning seemed good. Rather would I be drowned than fall into the hands of those who were galloping on the shore, to be dragged back to London and a felon's doom.

So I pressed upon the tiller to bring the *Blanche*

more into mid-channel, and headed for the sea. Wider and wider grew the estuary and farther and farther away the shores as the *Blanche* scudded on beneath her small sails with the weight of the gale behind her, till at last there was the open sea.

Within a few feet of the tiller was a deck-house, in which the crew ate, built of solid oak and clamped with iron. Here was food in plenty ; ale, too, and with these we filled ourselves. Also, leaving Kari to hold the tiller, I took off my armour and in place of it clothed myself in the rough sea garments that lay about with tall greased boots, and then sent him to do likewise.

Soon we lost sight of land and were climbing the great ocean billows, whose foamy crests rolled and spurted wherever the eye fell. We could set no course but must go where the gale drove us, away, away we knew not whither. As I have said the *Blanche* was new and strong and the best ship that ever I had sailed in upon a heavy sea. Moreover her hatches were closed down, for this the sailors had done after we weighed, so she rode the waters like a duck, taking no harm. Oh ! well it was for me that from my childhood I had had to do with ships and the sailing of them, and flying from the following waves thus was able to steer and keep the *Blanche's* poop right in the wind, which seemed to blow first from one quarter and then from that.

Now over my memory of these events there comes a great confusion and sense of amazement. All became fragmentary and disjointed, separated also by what seemed to be considerable periods of time—days or weeks perhaps. There was a sense of endless roaring seas before which the ship fled on and on, driven by a continuous screaming gale, that I noted dimly, seemed to blow first from the north-west and then steadily from the east.

I see myself, very distinctly, lashing the tiller to iron rings that were screwed in the deck beams, and know that I did this because I was too weak to hold it any longer and desired to set it so that the *Blanche* should continue to drive straight before the gale. I see myself lying in the deck-house of which I have spoken, while Kari fed me with food and water and sometimes thrust into my mouth little pellets of I knew not what, which he took from the leathern bag he wore about him. I remembered that bag. It had been on his person when I rescued him at the quay, for I had seen it first as he washed himself afterwards, half full of something, and wondered what it contained. Later, I had seen it in his hand again when we left my house after the death of Blanche. I noted that whenever he gave me one of these pellets I seemed to grow strong for a while, and then to fall into sleep, deep and prolonged.

After more days—or weeks, I began to behold marvels and to hear strange voices. I thought that I was talking with my mother and with my patron, St. Hubert; also that Blanche came to me and explained everything, showing how little she had been to blame for all that had happened to me and her. These things made me certain that I was dead and I was glad to be dead, since now I knew there would be no more pain or strivings; that the endeavours which make up life from hour to hour had ceased and that rest was won. Only then appeared my uncle, John Grimmer, who kept quoting his favourite text at me—"Vanity of vanities. All is vanity," he said, adding: "Did I not tell you that it was thus years ago? Now you have learned it for yourself. Only, Nephew Hubert, don't think that you have finished with vanities yet, as I have, for I say that there are plenty more to come for you."

Thus he seemed to talk on about this and other matters, such as what would happen to his wealth and whether the hospital would be quick to seize the lands to which he had given it the reversion, till I grew quite tired of him and wished that he would go away.

Then at length there was a great crash that I think disturbed him, for he did go, saying that it was only another "vanity," after which I seemed to fall asleep for weeks and weeks.

I woke up again for a warmth and brightness on my face caused me to open my eyes. I lifted my hand to shield them from the brightness and noted with a kind of wonder that it was so thin that the light shone through it as it does through parchment, and that the bones were visible beneath the skin. I let it fall from weakness, and it dropped on to hair which I knew must be that of a beard, which set me wondering, for it had been my fashion to go clean-shaven. How then did I come by a beard? I looked about me and saw that I was lying on the deck of a ship, yes, of the *Blanche* itself, for I knew the shape of her stern, also certain knots in one of the uprights of the deck-house that formed a rude resemblance to a human face. Nothing of this deck-house was left now, however, except the corner posts between which I lay, and to the tops of these was lashed a piece of canvas as though to keep off the sun and the weather.

With difficulty I lifted my head a little and looked about me. The bulwarks of the ship had gone but some of the uprights to which the planks had been nailed remained, and between them I perceived tall-stemmed trees with tufts of great leaves at the top of them, which trees seemed to be within a few yards of me. Bright-winged birds flew about them and in their crowns I saw apes such as the sailors used to bring home from Barbary. It would seem, then, that I must be in a river (in fact it was a little bay or creek, on either side of which these trees appeared).

Noting these and the creeping plants with beautiful flowers, such as I had never seen that climbed up them, and the sweet scents that floated on the air, and the clear light, now I grew sure that I was dead and had reached Paradise. Only then how came it that I still lay on the ship, for never had I heard that such things also went to Paradise? Nay, I must dream; it was nothing but a dream that I wished were true, remembering as I did the terrors of that gale-tossed sea. Or, if I did not dream, then I was in some new world.

While I mused thus I heard a sound of soft footsteps and presently saw a figure bending over me. It was Kari, very thin and hollow-eyed, much indeed as he had been when I found him on the quay in London, but still Kari without doubt. He looked at me in his grave fashion, then said softly:

"Master awake?"

"Yes, Kari," I said, "but tell me, where am I?"

He did not answer at once but went away and returned presently with a bowl from which he bade me drink, holding it to my lips. I did so, swallowing what seemed to be broth though I thought it strangely flavoured, after which I felt much stronger, for whatever was in that broth ran through my veins like wine. At last he spoke in his queer English.

"Master," he said, "when we still in Thames river, you ask me whether we should run ashore into the hands of the hunters who try to catch us, or sail on. I answer, 'You have God and I have God and better fall into hands of gods than into hands of men.' So we sail on into the big storm. For long long we sail, and though once it turn, always the great wind blew behind us. You grow weak and your mind leave you, but I keep you alive with medicine that I have and for many days I stay awake and steer. Then at last my mind leave me too and I know no more. Three days ago I wake up and find the ship in this place. Then I eat more medicine and get strength, also food from people on the shore who think us gods. That all the story, except that you live, not die. Your God and my God bring us here safe."

"Yes, Kari, but where are we?"

"Master, I think in that country from which I come; not in my own land which still far away, but still in that country. You remember," he added with a flash of his dark eyes, "I always say that you and I go there together one day."

"But what is the country, Kari?"

"Master, not know its name. It big and have many names, but you first white man who ever come here, that why people think you God. Now you go sleep again; to-morrow we talk."

I shut my eyes, being so very tired, and as I learned afterwards, slept for twelve hours or more, to awake on the morning of the following day, feeling wonderfully stronger and able to eat with appetite. Also Kari brought me water and washed me, and clean clothes which he had found in the ship that I put on.

Thus it went on for a long while and day by day I recovered strength till at length I was almost as I had been when I married Blanche Aleys in the church of St. Margaret at Westminster. Only now sorrow had changed me within and without my face had grown more serious, while to it hung a short yellow beard which, when I looked at my reflection, seemed to become me well enough. That beard puzzled me much, since such are not grown in a day, although it is true that as yet it was not over long. Weeks must have passed since it began to sprout upon my chin and as we had been but three days in this place when I woke up, those weeks without doubt were spent upon the sea.

Whither, then, had we come? Driving all the while before a great gale, that for most of our voyage had blown from the east, as, if Kari were right, we had done, this country must be very far away from England. That it was so, indeed there could be no doubt, since here everything was different. For example, having been a mariner from my childhood, I had been taught and observed something of the stars, and noted that the constellations had changed their places in the heavens, also that some with which I was familiar were missing, while other new ones had appeared. Further, the heat was great and constant, even at night being more than that of our hottest summer day, and the air was full of stinging insects, which at first troubled me much, though afterwards I grew hardened to them. In short, everything was changed and I was indeed in a new world that was not told of in Europe, but what world? What world? At least the sea joined it to the old, for beneath me was still the *Blanche*, which timber by timber I had seen built up upon the shores of Thames from oaks cut in my own woods.

As soon as I was strong enough, I went over the ship, or what was left of her. It was a marvel that she had floated for so long, since her hull was shattered. Indeed, I do not think she could have done so, save for the fine wool that was packed into the lower part of her, which wool seemed to have swollen when it grew wet and to have kept the water out. For the rest she was but a hulk, since both her masts were gone, and much of the deck with them. Still she had kept afloat and driving into this creek, had beached herself upon the mud as though it were the harbour that she sought.

How had we lived through such a journey? The answer seemed to be, after we were too weak to find or take food, by means of the drug that Kari cherished in his skin bag, and water of which there was plenty left at hand in barrels, since the *Blanche* had been provisioned for a long voyage to Italy and farther. At least we had lived for weeks and weeks, being still young and very strong, and not having been called upon to suffer great cold, since it would appear that although the gale continued, after the first few days of our flight before it, the weather had turned warm.

During this time of my recovery, every morning Kari would go ashore, which he did by means of planks set upon the mud, since we were within a few feet of the bank of the creek into which a streamlet ran. Later he would return, bringing with him fish and wildfowl, and corn of a sort that I did not know, for its grains were a dozen times the size of wheat, flat-sided and if ripe, of a yellow colour, which he said he had purchased from those who dwelt upon the land. On this good food I feasted, washing it down with ale and wine from the ship's stores; indeed never before did I eat so much, not even when I was a boy.

At length, one morning Kari made me put on my armour, the same which I had taken from the French knight, and fled in from London, that he had burnished till it shone like silver, and seat myself in a chair upon what remained of the poop of the ship. When I asked him why, he answered in order that he might show me to the inhabitants of that land. In this chair he bade me sit and wait, holding the shield upon my arm and the bare sword in my right hand.

As I had come to know that Kari never did anything without a reason and remembered that I was in a strange country where, lacking him, I should not have lived nor could continue to do so, I fell into his humour. Moreover, I promised that I would remain still and neither speak, nor smile, nor rise from my chair unless he bade me. So there I sat glittering in the hot sunshine which burned me through the armour.

Then Kari went ashore and was absent for some time. At length amongst the trees and undergrowth I heard the sound of people talking in a strange tongue. Presently they appeared on the bank of the creek, a great number of them; very curious people, brown-skinned with long, lank black hair and large eyes, but not over tall in stature; men, women and children together.

Among them were some who wore white robes whom I took to be their gentlefolk, but the most of them had only cloths or girdles about their middles. Leading the throng was Kari, who, as it appeared from the bushes, waved his hand and pointed me out seated in the shining armour on the ship, the visor up to show my face and the long sword in my hand. They stared, then with a low, sighing exclamation, one and all fell upon their faces and rubbed their brows upon the ground.

As they lay there Kari addressed them, waving his arms and pointing towards me from time to time. Afterwards I learned that he was telling them I was a god, for which lie may his soul be forgiven.

The end of it was that he bade them rise and led certain of them who wore the white robes, across the planks to the ship. Here, while they hung back, he advanced towards me, bowing and kissing the air till he drew near, when he went upon his knees and laid his hands upon my steel-clad feet. More, from the bosom of his robe he drew out flowers which he placed upon my knees as though in offering.

"Now, Master," he whispered to me, "rise and wave your sword and shout aloud, to show that you are alive and not an image."

So up I sprang, circling Wave-Flame about my head and roaring like any bull of Bashan, for my voice was always loud and carried far. When they saw the bright sword whirling through the air and heard these bellowings, uttering cries of fear, those poor folk fled. Indeed most of them fell from the plank into the mud, where one stuck fast and was like to drown, had not Kari rescued him which his brethren were in too great haste to do.

After they had gone Kari came and said that everything went well and that henceforward I was not a man but the Spirit of the Sea come to earth, such a spirit as had never been dreamed of even by the wizards.

Thus then did I, Hubert of Hastings, become a god among those simple people, who had never before so much as heard of a white man, or seen armour or a sword of steel.

CHAPTER II

The Rocky Isle

For another week or more I remained upon the *Blanche* waiting till my full strength returned, also because Kari said I must do so. When I asked him why, he replied for the reason that he wished news of my coming to spread far and wide throughout the land from one tribe to another, which it would do with great swiftness, flying, as he put it, like a bird. Meanwhile, every day I sat upon the poop in the armour for an hour or more, and both these people and others from afar came to look at me, bringing me presents in such quantity that we knew not what to do with them. Indeed, they built an altar and sacrificed wild creatures to me, and birds, burning them with fire. Both those that I had seen and the other folk from a long way off made this offering.

At last one night, when, having eaten, Kari and I were seated together in the moonshine before we slept, I turned on him suddenly, hoping thus to surprise the truth out of his secret heart, and said:

"What is your plan, Kari? For, know, I weary of this life."

"I was waiting for the Master to ask that question," he replied with his gentle smile. (Again I give not the very words he spoke in his bad English, but the substance of them.) "Now will the Master be pleased to listen? As I have told the Master, I believe that the gods, his God and my God, have brought me back to that part of the world which is unknown to the Master, where I was born. I believed this from the first hour that my eyes opened on it after our swoon, for I knew the trees and the flowers and the smell of the earth, and saw that the stars in the heavens stood where I used to see them. When I went ashore and mingled with the natives, I discovered that this belief was right, since I could understand something of their talk and they could understand something of mine. Moreover, among them was a man who came from far away, who said that he had seen me in past years, wandering like one mad, only that this man whom he had seen wore the image of a certain god about his neck, whose name was too high for him to mention. Then I opened my robe and showed him that which I wear about my neck, and he fell down and worshipped it, crying out that I was the very man."

"If so, it is marvellous," I said. "But what shall we do?"

"The Master can do one of two things. He can stop here, where these simple people will make him their king and give him wives and all that he desires, and so live out his life, since of return to the land whence he came there is no hope."

"And if there were I would not go," I interrupted.

"Or," went on Kari, "he can try to travel to my country. But that is very far away. Something of the journey which I made when I was mad comes back and tells me that it is very, very far away. First, yonder mountains must be crossed till another sea is reached, which is no great journey, though rough. Then the coast of that sea must be followed southward, for I know not how far, but, as I think, for months or years of journeying, till at length the country of my people is reached. Moreover, that ourneying is hard and terrible, since the road runs through forests and deserts where dwell savage tribes and huge snakes and wild beasts, like those painted on the flag of your country, and where famine and sicknesses are common. Therefore my counsel to the Master is that he should leave it unattempted."

Now I thought a while, and asked what he meant to do if I took this counsel of his. To which he replied:

"I shall wait here a while till I see the Master made a king amongst these people and established in his rule. Then I shall start on that journey alone, hoping that what I could do when I was mad I shall be able to do again when I am not mad."

"I thought it," I said. "But tell me, Kari, if we were to make this journey and perchance live to reach your people, how would they welcome us?"

"I do not know, Master; but I think that of the master they would make a god, as will all the other people of this country. Perhaps, too, they will sacrifice this god that his strength and beauty may enter into them. As for me, some of them will try to kill me and others will cling to me. Who will conquer I do not know, and to me it matters little. I go to take my own and to be avenged, and if in seeking vengeance I die—well, I die in honour."

"I understand," I said. "And now, Kari, let us start as soon as possible before I become as mad from staring at those trees and flowers and those big-eyed natives, that you say would make me a king, as you tell me you were when you left your country. Whether we shall ever find that country I cannot say. But at least we shall have done our best and, if we fail, shall perish seeking, as in this way or in that it is the lot of all brave men to do."

"The Master has spoken," said Kari, even more quietly than usual though as he spoke I saw his dark eyes flash and a trembling as of joy run down his body. "Knowing all, he has made his choice, and whatever happens, being what he is, he will not blame me. Yet because the Master has thus chosen, I say this—that if we reach my country, and if, perchance, I become a king there, even more than before I shall be the Master's servant."

"That is easy to promise now, Kari, but it will be time to talk of it when we do reach your land," I said laughing, and asked him when we were to start.

He replied not yet awhile, as he must make plans, and that in the meantime I must walk upon the shore so that my legs might grow strong again. So there every day I walked in the cool of the morning and in the evening, not going out of sight of the wreck. I went armed and carrying my big bow, but saw no one, since the natives had been warned that I should walk and must not be looked upon while I did so. Therefore, even when I passed through one of their villages of huts built of mud and thatched with leaves, it seemed to be deserted.

Still, in the end the bow did not come amiss, for one evening, hearing a little noise in a big tree under which I was about to pass that reminded me of the purring of a cat, I looked up and saw a great beast of the tiger sort lying on the bough of the tree and watching me. Then I drew the bow and sent an arrow through that beast, piercing it from side to side, and down it came roaring and writhing, and biting at the arrow till it died.

After this I returned to the ship and told Kari what had happened. He said it was fortunate I had killed the beast, which was of a very fierce kind and if I had not seen it, would have leapt on me as I passed under the tree. Also he sent natives to skin it who when they saw that it was pierced through and through by the arrow, were amazed and thought me an even greater god than before, their own bows being but feeble and their arrows tipped with bone.

Three days after the killing of this beast we started on our journey into a land unknown. For a long while before Kari and I had been engaged in collecting all the knives we could find in the ship, also arrows, nails, axes, tools of carpentering, clothes and I know not what besides, which goods we tied up in bundles wrapped in sailcloth, each bundle weighing from thirty to forty pounds, to serve as presents to natives or to trade away with them. When I asked who would carry them, Kari answered that I should see. This I did at dawn on the following morning when there arrived upon the shore a great number of men, quite a hundred indeed, who brought with them two litters made of light wood jointed like reeds, only harder, in which Kari said he and I were to be carried. Among these men he parcelled out the loads which they were to bear upon their heads, and then said that it was time for us to start in the litters.

So we started, but first I went down into a cabin and kneeling on my knees, thanked God for having brought me safe so far, and prayed Him and St. Hubert to protect me on my further wanderings, and if I died, to receive my soul. This done I left the ship and while the natives bowed themselves about me, entered my litter which was comfortable enough, having grass mats to lie on and other mats for curtains, very finely woven, so that they would turn even the heaviest rain.

Then away we went, eight men bearing the pole to which each litter was slung, on their shoulders, while others carried the bundles upon their heads.

Our road ran through forest uphill and on the crest of the first hill I descended from the litter and looked back.

There in the creek below lay the wreck of the *Blanche*, now but a small black blot showing against the water, and beyond it the great sea over which we had travelled. Yonder broken hulk was the last link which bound me to my distant home thousands of miles across the ocean, that home which my heart told me I should never see again, for how could I win back from a land that no white foot had ever trod?

On the deck of this ship Blanche herself had stood and smiled and talked, for once we visited it together shortly before our marriage, and I remembered how I had kissed her in its cabin. Now Blanche was dead by her own hand and I, the great London merchant, was an outcast among savages in a country of which I did not even know the name, where everything was new and different. And there the ship with her rich cargo, after bearing us so bravely through weeks of tempest, must lie until she rotted in the sun and rain and never again would my eyes behold her. Oh! then it was that a sense of all my misery and loneliness gripped my heart as it had not done before since I rode away after killing Deleroy with the sword Wave-Flame and I wondered why I had been born, and almost hoped that soon I might die and go to seek the reason.

Back into the litter I crept and there hid my face and wept like a child. Truly I, the prosperous merchant of London town who might have lived to become its mayor and magistrate and win nobility, was now an outcast adventurer of the humblest. Well, so God had decreed and there was no more to say.

That night we camped upon a hilltop past which rushed a river in the vale below and were troubled with heat and insects that hummed and bit, for to these as yet I was not accustomed, and ate of the food that we had brought with us, dried flesh and corn.

Next morning with the light we started on again, up and down mountains and through more forests, following the course of the river and the shores of a lake. So it went on until on the third evening from high land we saw the sea beneath us, a different sea from that which we had left, for it seemed that we had been crossing an isthmus, not so wide but that if any had the skill, a canal might be cut across it joining those two great seas.

Now it was that our real travels began, for here, after staring at the stars and brooding apart for a long while, Kari turned southwards. With this I had nothing to do who did not greatly care which way he turned. Nor did he speak to me of the matter, except to say that his god and such memory as remained to him through his time of madness, told him that the land of his people lay towards the south, though very far away.

So southwards we went, following paths through the forests with the ocean on our right hand. After a week of this wearisome marching we came to another tribe of natives of whose talk those with us could understand enough to tell them our story. Indeed the rumour that a white god had appeared in the land out of the sea had already reached them, and therefore they were prepared to worship me. Here our people left us, saying that they dared not go further from their own country.

The scene of their departure was strange, since every one of them came and rubbed his forehead in the dust before me and then went away, walking backwards and bowing. Still their going did not make a great difference to us, since the new tribe was much as the old one, though if anything, rather less clothed and more dirty. Also it accepted me as a god without question and gave us all the food we needed. Moreover, when we left their land men were provided to carry the litters and the loads.

Thus then, passing from tribe to tribe, we travelled on southward, ever southwards, finding always that the rumour of the coming of "the god" had gone before us. So gentle were all these people, that not once did we meet with any who tried to harm us or to steal our goods, or who refused us the best of what they had. Our adventures, it is true, were many. Thus, twice we came to tribes that were at war with other tribes, though on my appearance they laid down their arms, at any rate for a time, and bore our litters forward.

Again, sometimes we met tribes who were cannibals and then we suffered much from want of meat, since we dared not touch their food unless it were grain. In the town of the first of these cannibal people, being moved with fury, I killed a man whom I found about to murder a child and eat her, sweeping off his head with my sword. For this deed I expected that they would murder us, but they did not. They only shrugged their shoulders and saying that a god can do as he pleases, took away the slain man and ate him.

Sometimes our road ran through terrible forests where the great trees shut out the light of day, and a path must be hacked through the undergrowth. Sometimes it was haunted by tigers or tree lions such as I have spoken of, against which we must watch continuously, especially at night, keeping the brutes off by means of fires. Sometimes we were forced to wade great rivers, or worse still, to walk over them on swaying bridges made of cables of twisted reeds that until I grew accustomed to them, caused my head to swim, though never did I permit myself to show fear before the natives. Again, once we came to swampy lands that were full of snakes which terrified me much, especially after I had seen some natives whom they bit, die within a few minutes.

Other snakes there were also, as thick as a man's body, and four or five paces in length, which lived in trees and killed their food by coiling round it and pressing it to death. These snakes, it was said, would take men in this fashion, though I never saw one of them do so. At any rate they were terrible to look on, and reminded me of their forefather through whose mouth Satan talked with Mother Eve in the Garden of Eden, and thus brought us all to woe.

Once too, on the bank of a great river, I saw such a snake that at the sight of it my knees knocked together. By St. Hubert, the beast was sixty feet or more in length; its head was of the bigness of a barrel, and its skin was of all the colours of the rainbow. Moreover it seemed to hold me with its eyes, for till it slipped away into the river, I could not move a foot.

Month after month we travelled thus, covering a matter of perhaps five miles a day, since sometimes the country was open and we crossed it with speed. Yet although our dangers were so many, strangely enough during all this time, even in that heat neither of us fell sick, as I think because of the herb which Kari carried in his bag, that I found was named *Coca*, whereof we obtained more as we went and ate from time to time. Nor did we ever really suffer from starvation, since when we were hungry we took more of this herb which supported us until we could find food. These mercies I set down to the good offices of St. Hubert watching from Heaven over me, his poor namesake and godson, though perhaps the skill and courage of Kari which provided against everything, had something to do with them.

At length in the ninth month of our travelling, as Kari reckoned it by means of knots which he tied on pieces of native string, for I had long lost count of time, we came to the borders of a great desert that the natives said stretched southwards for a hundred leagues and more and was without water. Moreover, to the east of this desert rose a chain of mountains bordered by precipices up which no man could climb. Here, therefore, it seemed as though our journey must end, since Kari had no knowledge of how he crossed or went round this desert in his madness of bygone years, if indeed he ever travelled that road at all, a matter of which I was not certain.

For a week or more we remained among the tribe that lived in a beautiful watered valley upon the borders of this desert, wondering what we should do. For my part I was by now so tired of travelling upon an endless quest, that I should have been glad to stay among that tribe, a very gentle and friendly people, who like all the rest believed me to be a god, and make my home there till I died. But this was not Kari's mind which was set fiercely upon winning back to his own country that he believed to lie towards the south.

Day by day we sat there regaining our strength upon the good food of that valley, and staring first at the desert to the south, then at the precipices on our left hand, and lastly at the ocean upon our right. Now this people, I should say, drew their wealth from the sea as well as from the land, since they were great fishermen, and went out upon it in rude boats or rafts made of a wooden frame to which were lashed blown-up skins and bundles of dried reeds. Upon these boats, frail as they seemed, such as further south were called *balsas,* they made considerable journeys to distant islands where they caught vast quantities of fish, some of which they used to manure their land. Moreover, besides the oars, they rigged a square cotton sail upon the *balsas* which enabled them to run before the wind without labour, steering the craft by means of a paddle at the stern.

While we were there I observed that on the springing up of a wind from the north, although it was of no great strength, the *balsas* all came to shore and were drawn up out of reach of the waves. When I inquired why through Kari, the answer given was because the fishing season was over, since that wind from the north would blow for a long time without changing and those who went out in it upon the sea might be driven southwards to return no more. They stated indeed that often this had happened to venturesome men who had vanished away and been lost.

"If you wish to travel south, there is a way of doing so," I said to Kari.

At the time he made no answer, but on the following day asked me suddenly if I dared attempt such a journey.

"Why not?" I answered. "It is as easy to die in the water as on land and I weary of journeying through endless swamps and forests or of crossing torrents and climbing mountain ridges."

The end of it was that for a knife and a few nails Kari purchased the largest *balsa* that these people had, provisioning it with as much dried fish, corn and water in earthenware jars as it would carry together with ourselves, and such of our remaining goods as we wished to take with us. Then he announced that I, the god who had come out of the sea, desired to return into the sea with himself, my servant.

So on a certain fine morning when the wind was blowing steadily but not too strongly from the north, we embarked upon that *balsa* while the simple savages made obeisance with wonder in their eyes, hoisted the square canvas, and sailed away upon what I suppose was one of the maddest voyages ever made by man.

Although it was so clumsy the *balsa* moved through the water at a good rate, covering quite two leagues the hour, I should say, before that strong and steady wind. Soon the village that we had left vanished; then the mountains behind it grew dim and in time vanished also, and there remained nothing but the great wilderness upon our left and the vast sea around. Steering clear of the land so as to avoid sunken rocks, we sailed on all that day and all the night that followed, and when the light came again perceived that we were running past a coastline that was backed by high mountains on some of which lay snow. By the second evening these mountains had become tremendous, and between them I saw valleys down which ran streams of water.

Thus we went on for three days and nights, the wind from the north blowing all the while and the *balsa* taking no hurt, by the end of which time I reckoned that we had travelled as far along the coast as we had done in six months when we journeyed over land, at which I rejoiced. Kari rejoiced also, because he said that the shape and greatness of the mountains we were passing reminded him of those of his own country, to which he believed that we were drawing near.

On the fourth morning, however, our troubles began, since the friendly wind from the north grew steadily stronger, till at length it rose to a gale. Soon our little rag of canvas was torn away, but still we rushed on before the following seas at a very great speed.

Now I thought of trying to make the land, but found that we could not do so with the oars, because of the current that set out towards the ocean against which it was impossible to urge our clumsy craft. Therefore we must content ourselves with trying to keep her head straight with the steering oar, but even then we were often whirled round and round.

About two hours after noon the sky clouded over, and there burst upon us a great thunder-storm with torrents of rain ; also the wind grew stronger and stronger.

Now we could no longer steer or do anything except lie flat upon the bottom of the *balsa*, gripping the cords with which it was tied together, to save ourselves from being washed overboard, since often the foaming crests of the waves broke upon us. Indeed, it was marvellous that this frail craft should hang together at all, but owing to the lightness of the reeds and the blown-up skins that were tied in them, still she floated and, whirling round and round, sped upon her southward path. Yet I knew that this could not endure for very long, and committed my soul to God as well as I was able in my half-drowned state, wishing that my miseries were ended.

The darkness came down, but still the thunder roared and the lightning blazed, and by the flare of it I caught sight of snow-capped mountains far away upon the coast, also of Kari clinging to the reeds of the *balsa* at my side, and from time to time kissing the golden image of Pachacamac which hung about his neck. Presently he set his lips against my ear and shouted:

"Be bold! Our gods are still with us in storm."

"Yes," I answered, "and soon we shall be with our gods—in peace."

After this I heard no more of him, and fell to thinking with such wits as were left to me of how many perils we had passed since we saw the shores of Thames, and that it seemed sad that all should have been for nothing, since it would have been better to die at the beginning than now at the end, after so much misery. Then the glare of the lightning shone upon the handle of the sword Wave-Flame, which was still strapped about me, and I remembered the rune written upon it which my mother had rendered to me upon the morning of the fight against the Frenchmen. How did it run?

He who lifts Wave-Flame on high
In love shall live and in battle die;
Storm-tossed o'er wide seas shall roam
And in strange lands shall make his home.
Conquering, conquered shall he be,
And far away shall sleep with me.

It fitted well, though of the love I had known little and that most unhappy, and the battle in which I must die was one with water. Also, I had conquered nothing who myself was conquered by Fate. In short, the thing could be read two ways, like all prophecies, and only one line of it was true beyond a doubt—namely, that Wave-Flame and I should sleep together.

A while later the lightning shone awesomely, like to the swords of a whole army of destroying angels, so that the sky became alive with fire. In its light for an instant I saw ahead of us great breakers, and beyond them what looked like a dark mass of land. Now we were in them, for the first of those hungry, curling waves got a hold of the *balsa* and tossed it up dizzily, then flung it down into a deep valley of water. Another came and another, till my senses reeled and went. I cried to St. Hubert, but he was a land saint and could not help me; so I cried to Another greater than he.

My last vision was of myself riding a huge breaker as though it were a horse. Then there came a crash and darkness.

Lo! it seemed to me as though one were calling me back from the depths of sleep. With trouble I opened my eyes, only to shut them again because of the glare of the light. Then after a while I sat up, which gave me pain, for I felt as if I had been beaten all over, and looked once more. Above me shone the sun in a sky of deepest blue; before me was the sea almost calm, while around were rocks and sand, among which crawled great reptiles that I knew for turtles, as I had seen many of them in our wanderings. Moreover, kneeling at my side, with the sword that he had taken from the body of Deleroy still strapped about him, was Kari, who bled from some wound and was almost white with encrusted salt, but otherwise seemed unharmed. I stared at him, unable to open my mouth from amazement, so it was he who spoke the first, saying, in a voice that had a note of triumph in it:

"Did I not tell you that the gods were with us? Where is your faith, O White Man? Look! They have brought me back to the land of which I am Prince."

Now there was that in Kari's tone which in my weak state angered me. Why did he scold me about faith? Why did he address me as "White Man" instead of "Master"? Was it because he had reached a country where he was great and I was nothing? I supposed so, and answered:

"And are these your subjects, O noble Kari?" and I pointed to the crawling turtles. "And is this the rich and wondrous land where gold and silver are as mud?" and I pointed to the barren rocks and sand around.

He smiled at my jest, and answered more humbly:

"Nay, Master, yonder is my land."

Then I looked, following his glance, and saw many leagues away across the water two snowclad peaks rising above a bank of clouds.

"I know those mountains," he went on; "without doubt they are one of the gateways of my land."

"Then we might as well be in London for all the hope we have of passing that gate, Kari. But tell me what has chanced."

"This, I think. A very great wave caught us and threw us right over those rocks on to the shore. Look—there is the *balsa*," and he pointed to a broken heap of reeds and pierced skins.

With his help I rose and went to it. Now none could know that it had been a boat. Still, the *balsa* it was and nothing else, and tied in its tangled mass still remained those things which we had brought with us, such as my black bow and armour, though all the jars were broken.

"It has borne us well, but will never bear us again," I said.

"That is so, Master. But if we were in my own

country yonder I would set its fragments in a case of gold and place them in the Temple of the Sun as a memorial."

Then we went to a pool of rainwater that lay in a hollow rock near by, and drank our fill, for we were very thirsty. Also among the ruins of the *balsa* we found some of the dried fish that was left to us, and having washed it, filled ourselves. After this we limped to the crest of the land behind and perceived that we were on a little island, perhaps two hundred English acres in extent, whereon nothing grew except some coarse grass. This island, however, was the haunt of great numbers of seafowl which nested there; also of the turtles that I have mentioned, and of certain beasts like seals or otters.

"At least we shall not starve," I said, "though in the dry season we may die of thirst."

Now there on that island we remained for four long months. For food we ate the turtles, which we cooked over fires that Kari made by cunningly twirling a pointed piece of driftwood in the hollow of another piece that he filled with the dust of dried grass. Had he lacked that knowledge we must have starved or lived on raw flesh. As it was, we had plenty with this meat and that of birds and their eggs, also of fish that we caught in the pools when the tide was down. From the shells of the turtles, by the help of stones we built us a kind of hut to keep off the sun and the rain, which in that hot place was sufficient shelter; also, when the stench was out of them, we used other shells in which to catch rainwater that we stored as best we could against seasons of drought. Lastly, with my big bow which was saved with the armour, I shot sea-otters, and from their pelts we made us garments after rubbing the skins with turtle fat and handling them to make them soft.

Thus, then, we lived from moon to moon upon that desert place, till I thought I should go mad with loneliness and despair, for no help came near us. There were the mountains of the mainland far away, but between them and us stretched leagues of sea that we could not swim, nor had we anything of which to make a boat.

"Here we must remain until we die!" at last I cried in my wretchedness.

"Nay," answered Kari, "our gods are still with us and will save us in their season."

This, indeed, they did in a strange fashion.

CHAPTER III

THE DAUGHTER OF THE MOON

FOR the fourth time since we were cast away on this island the huge full moon shone in a sky of wondrous blue. Kari and I watched it rise between the two snow-clad peaks far away that he had called a gateway to his land, which was so near to us and yet it would seem more distant than Heaven itself. Heaven we might hope to reach upon the wings of spirit when we died, but to that country how could we come?

We watched that great moon climb higher and higher up a ladder of little bar-like clouds, till wearying we let our eyes fall upon the glittering pathway which its light made upon the bosom of the placid sea. Suddenly Kari started and stared.

"What is it?" I asked idly.

"I thought I saw something yonder far away where Quilla's footsteps make the waters bright," he said, speaking in his own language in which now we often talked together.

"Quilla's?" I exclaimed. "Oh! I forgot: that is the lady moon's name in your tongue, is it not? Well, come, Quilla, and I will wed and worship you, as 'tis said the ancients did, and never turn to look upon another, be she woman, or goddess, or both. Only come and take me from this accursed isle and in payment I'll die for you, if need be, when first I've taught you how to love as star or woman never loved before."

"Hush!" said Kari in a grave voice, when he had listened to this mad stuff that burst through my lips from the spring of a mind distraught by misery and despair.

"Why should I hush?" I asked. "Is it not pleasant to think of the moon wearing a lovely woman's shape and descending to give a lonely mortal love and comfort?"

"Because, Master, to me and my people the Moon is a goddess who hears prayer and answers it. Suppose, then, that she heard you and answered you and came to you and claimed your love, what then?"

"Why then, friend Kari," I raved on, "then I should welcome her, for that love goes a-begging, ready as ripe fruit to be plucked by the first hand if it be fair enough, ready to melt beneath the first lips if they be warm enough. 'Tis said that it is the man who loves and the woman who accepts the love. But that is not true. It is the man, Kari, who waits to be loved and pays back just as much as is given to him, and no more, like an honest merchant; for if he does otherwise, then he suffers for it, as I have learned. Therefore, come, Quilla, and love as a Celestial can and I swear that step by step I'll keep pace with you in flesh and spirit through Heaven, or through Hell, since love I must have, or death."

"I pray you, talk not so," said Kari again, in a frightened voice, "since those words of yours come from the heart and will be heard. The goddess is a woman too, and what woman will turn from such a bait?"

"Let her take it then. Why not?"

"Because, O friend, because *Quilla* is wed to *Yuti*; the Moon is the Sun's wife, and if the Sun grows jealous what will happen to the man who has robbed the greatest of the world's gods?"

"I do not know and I do not care. If Quilla would but come and love me, I'd take my chance of Yuti whom as a Christian I defy."

Kari shuddered at this blasphemy, then having once more scanned that silver pathway on the waters, but without avail for the great fish or drifting tree or whatever he had seen, was gone, prayed after his fashion at night, to Pachacamac, Spirit of the Universe, or to the Sun his servant, god of the world, I know not which, and rolling himself in his rug of skins, crept into our little hut to sleep.

But as yet I did not sleep, for though Kari hated both, this talk of love and women had stirred my blood and made me wakeful. So I took a rough comb that I had fashioned from the shell of a turtle, and dragged it through my long fair beard, which, growing fast, now hung down far upon my breast, and through the curling hair that lay upon my shoulders, for I had become as other wild men are, and sang to myself there by the little fire which we kept burning day and night and tried to think of happy things that never should I know again.

At length the fit passed and I grew weary and laid myself down by the fire, for the night being so fine and warm I would not go into the hut, and there sleep found me.

I dreamed in my sleep. I dreamed that a very beautiful woman who wore upon her naked breast the emblem of the moon fashioned in crystal, stood over me, looking down upon me with large dark eyes. And as she looked she sighed. Thrice she sighed, each time more deeply than the last. Then she knelt down by me—or so it seemed in my dream, and laid a tress of her long dark hair against my yellow locks, as though she would match them together. She did more indeed—in my dream—for lifting that tress of fragrant hair, she let it fall like thistledown across my face and mouth, and then kissed the hair, for I felt her breath reach me through its strands.

The dream ended thus, though I wished very much that it would go on, and I felt as though it had gone away as such visions do. A while later, as I suppose, I awoke quite suddenly, and opened my eyes. There, near to me glittering in the full light of the brilliant moon, stood the woman of my dream, only now her naked breast was covered with a splendid cloak broidered with silver, and on her dark locks was a feathered headdress, in front of which rose the crescent of the moon, likewise fashioned in silver. Also in her hand she held a little silver spear.

I stared at her, for move I could not. Then remembering my crazy talk with Kari, uttered one word, only one. It was—*Quilla.*

She bowed her head and answered in a voice soft as the murmur of the wind through rushes, speaking in the rich language called Quichua that Kari had taught me. In this tongue, as I have told, we talked together for practice, during our journeys and on the island, so that now I knew it well.

"So indeed am I named after my mother, the Moon," she said. "But how did you know it, O Wanderer, whose skin is white as the foam of the sea and whose hair is yellow as the fine gold in the temples?"

"I think you must have told me when you knelt over me just now," I said.

I saw the red blood run to her brow, but she only shook her head, and answered,

"Nay, my mother, the Moon, must have told

you: or perchance you learned it in the spirit. At least, Quilla am I named and you called me aright."

Now I stood up and stared at her, overcome by the strangeness of the business, and she stared at me. A marvellously beautiful woman she was in her dazzling robe and headdress, and lighter coloured than any native I had seen, almost white indeed in the moonlight save for the copper tinge that marked her race; tall too, yet not over tall; slim and straight as an arrow, but high-breasted and round-limbed and with a wild grace in her movements like to that of a hawk upon the wing. Also to my fancy in her face there was something more than common youthful beauty, something spiritual, such as great artists show upon the carven countenances of saints.

Indeed she might well have been one whose human blood was mixed with some other alien strain—as she had called herself, a daughter of the Moon.

A question rose to my lips and burst from them; it was

"Tell me, O Quilla, are you wife or maid?"

"Maid am I," she answered, "yet one who is promised as a wife," and she sighed, then went on quickly as though this matter were something of which she did not wish to talk, "And tell me, O Wanderer, are you god or man?"

Now I grew cunning and answered,

"I am a Son of the Sea as you are a Daughter of the Moon."

She turned her head and glanced at the radiance which lay upon the face of the deep, then said as though to herself,

"The moon shines upon the sea and the sea mirrors back the moon, yet they are far apart and never may draw near."

"Not so, O Quilla. Out of the sea does the moon

rise and, her course run, into the sea's white arms she sinks to sleep at last."

Again the red blood ran to her brow and her great eyes fell, those eyes of which never before had I seen the like.

"It seems that they speak our tongue in the sea, and prettily," she murmured, adding, "But is it not from and into Heaven that the Moon rises and departs ?"

At that moment to my grief our talk came to an end, for out of the hut crept Kari. He rose to his feet and stood there as ever calm and dignified, looking first at Quilla and then at me.

"What did I tell you, Master ?" he said in English. "Did I not say that prayers such as yours are answered ? Lo ! here is that Child of the Moon for whom you sought, clothed in beauty and bringing her gifts of love and woe."

"Yes," I exclaimed, "and I am glad that she is here. For the rest, were she but mine, I think I should not grudge her price whate'er it be."

Quilla looked at Kari frowning over the spear that when he appeared she had lifted, as though to defend herself, which in my case she had not thought needful.

"So the sea breeds men of my own race also," she said, addressing him. "Tell me, O Stranger, how did you and yonder white god come to this isle ?"

"Riding on the ocean billows, riding for thousands of leagues," he answered. "And you, O Lady, how did you come to this isle ?"

"Riding on the moonbeams," she replied, smiling, "I, the daughter of the Moon, who am named Moon and wear her symbol on my brow."

"Did I not tell you so ?" exclaimed Kari to me with a gloomy air.

Then Quilla went on,

"Strangers, I was out fishing with two of my maidens and we had drifted far from land. As the sun sank I caught sight of the smoke of your fire, and having been told that this isle was desert, my heart drew me to discover who had lit it. So, though my maidens were afraid, hither I sailed and paddled, and the rest you know. Hearken! I will declare myself. I am the only child of Huaraca, King of the People of the Chancas, born of his wife, a princess of the Inca blood who now has been gathered to her Father, the Sun. I am here on a visit to my mother's kinsman, Quismancu, the Chief of the Yuncas of the Coastlands, to whom my father, the King, has sent an embassy on matters of which I know nothing. Behind yonder rock is my *balsa* and with it are the two maidens. Say, is it your wish to bide here upon this isle, or to return into the sea, or to accompany me back to the town of Quismancu? If so, we must sail ere the weather breaks, lest we should be drowned?"

"Certainly it is my wish to accompany you, Lady, though a god of the sea cannot be drowned," I said quickly before Kari could speak. Indeed he did not speak at all, he only shrugged his shoulders and sighed, like one who accepts some evil gift from Fate, because he must.

"So be it!" exclaimed Quilla. "Now I go to make ready the *balsa* and to warn the maidens lest they should be frightened. When you are prepared you will find us yonder behind the rock."

Then she bowed in a stately fashion and departed, walking with the proud, light step of a deer.

From our little hut I took out my armour and with Kari's help, put it on, because he declared that thus it would be more easily carried, though I think he had other reasons in his mind.

"Yes," I answered, "unless the *balsa* oversets, when I shall find mail hard to swim in."

"The *balsa* will not overset, sailing beneath the moon with that Moon-lady for a pilot," he replied heavily. "Had the sun been up, it might have been different. Moreover the path into a net is always wide and easy."

"What net?" I asked.

"One that is woven of woman's hair, I think. Already, if I mistake not, such a net has been about your throat, Master, and next time it will stay there. Hearken now to me. The gods thrust us into high matters. The Yuncas of whose chief this lady is a guest, are a great people whom my people have conquered in war, but who wait the opportunity to rebel, if they have not already done so. The Chancas, of whose king she is the daughter, are a still greater people who for years have threatened war upon my people."

"Well, what of it, Kari? With such questions this lady will have nothing to do."

"I think she has much to do with them. I think that she knows more than she seems to know, and that she is an envoy from the Chancas to the Yuncas. To whom is she affianced, I wonder? Some Great One, doubtless. Well, we shall learn in time; and meanwhile, I pray you, Master, remember that she says she *is* affianced, and that in this land men are very jealous even of a white god who rises from the sea."

"Of course I shall remember," I answered sharply. "Have I not had enough of women who are affianced?"

"By your prayer to the moon this night, which the moon answered so well and quickly, one might think not. Also this daughter of hers is fair, and perchance when she gave her hand she kept her heart. Listen again, Master. Of me and of whom I am, say nothing, save that you found me on this island where I dwelt a hermit when you rose from the sea. As for my name, why it is Zapana. Remember that if you breathe my rank and history, however much sweet lips may try to cozen them out of you, you bring me to my death, who now do not wish to die, having a vengeance to accomplish and a throne to win. Therefore treat me as a dog, as one of no account, and be silent even in your sleep."

"I will remember, Kari."

"That is not enough—swear it."

"Good. I swear it—by the moon."

"Nay, not by the moon, for the moon is woman and changes. Swear it by this," and from beneath his skin robe he drew out the golden image of Pachacamac. "Swear it by the Spirit of the Universe, of whom Sun and Moon and Stars are but the servants, the Spirit whom all men worship in this shape or in that."

So to please him I laid my hand upon the golden symbol and swore. Then, very hurriedly, we made up a tale of how, clad in my armour, I had risen from the sea and found him on the island, and how knowing me for a white god who once in ages past had visited that land and who, as prophecy foretold, should return to it in days to come, he had worshipped me and become my slave.

This done we went down to the rock, Kari walking after me and bearing all our small possessions and with them Deleroy's sword. Passing round the rock we saw the *balsa* drawn up to the sand, and by it the lady Quilla, who now had put off her fine robes and again was attired as a fishing-girl as I had seen her in my dream, and with her two tall girls in the same scanty garments. When these saw me in the glittering armour, which in our long idle hours we had polished till it shone like silver, with the shield upon my arm and the casque upon my head and the great sword girded about my middle and the black bow in my hand, they screamed with fear and fell upon their faces, while even Quilla started back and glanced towards the boat.

"Fear not," I said. "The gods are kind to those who do them service, though to those who would harm them they are terrible."

Kari also went to them and whispered in their ears what tale I know not. In the end they rose trembling, and having motioned to me to be seated in it, with the help of Kari pushed the *balsa*, which I noted with joy was large and well made, down into the sea. Then one by one they climbed in, Quilla taking the steering-oar, while Kari and the two maidens hoisted the little sail and paddled till we were clear of the island, where the gentle wind caught the *balsa*. Then they shipped the paddles, and although full laden, we sailed quietly towards the mainland.

Now I was at the bow of the *balsa* and Quilla was at its stern, and between us were the others, so that during all that long night's journey I had no speech with her and must content myself with gazing over my shoulder at her beauty as best I could, which was not well, because of Kari, who ever seemed to come between my eyes and hers.

Thus the long hours went by till at length when we were near the land the moon sank, and we sailed on through the twilight. Then came the dawn, and there in front of us we saw the lovely strand green with palms and corn crops, fertile with waters, and set as in a frame within a ring of snow-clad mountains, two of them the great peaks that we had seen from our isle.

On the shore was a city of white, flat-roofed houses, and rising above it, perchance the half of a mile from the sea, a hill four or five hundred feet in height and terraced. On the top of the hill stood a mighty building, painted red, that from the look of it I took to be one of the churches of these people, in the centre of which gleamed great doors that, as I found afterwards, were covered with plates of gold.

"Behold the temple of Pachacamac, Master," whispered Kari, bowing his head and kissing the air in token of reverence.

By this time watchmen, who had been set there to search the sea for the boat of Quilla, had noted our approach. They shouted and pointed to me who sat in the prow clad in my armour upon which the sun glittered, then began to run to and fro as though in fear or excitement, so that ere we reached the shore a great crowd had gathered. Meanwhile, Quilla had put on her silver-broidered mantle and her head-dress of feathers, crowned with the crescent of the moon. As we touched the beach she came forward, and for the first time during that night spoke to me, saying:

"Remain here in the *balsa*, Lord, while I talk with these people, and when I summon you be pleased to come. Fear not—none will harm you."

Then she sprang from the prow of the *balsa* to the shore, followed by her two maidens, who dragged it further up the beach, and went forward to talk with certain white-robed men in the crowd. For a long while she talked, turning now and again to point at me. At length these men, accompanied by a number of others, ran forward. At first I thought they meant mischief and grasped my sword-hilt, then, remembering what Quilla had said, remained seated and silent.

Indeed, there was no cause for fear, for when the white-robed chiefs or priests and their following were close to me, suddenly they prostrated themselves and beat their heads upon the sand, from which I learned that they too believed me to be a god. Thereon I bowed to them and, drawing my sword—at the sight of which I saw them stare and shiver, for to these people steel was unknown—held it straight up in front of me in my right hand, the shield with the cognizance of the three arrows being on my left arm.

Now all the men rose, and some of them of the humbler sort, creeping to the *balsa,* suddenly seized it and lifted it on to their shoulders, which, being but a light thing of reeds and blown-out skins, they could do easily enough. Then, preceded by the chiefs, they advanced up the beach into the town, I still remaining seated in the boat with Kari crouching behind me. So strange was the business that almost I laughed aloud, wondering what those grave merchants of the Cheap whom I had known in London would think if they could see me thus.

"Kari," I said, without turning my head, "what are they going to do with us? Set us in yonder temple to be worshipped with nothing to eat?"

"I think not, Master," answered Kari, "since there the lady Quilla could not come to speak with you if she would. I think that they will take you to the house of the king of this country where, I understand, she is dwelling."

This, indeed, proved to be the case, for we were borne solemnly up the main street of the town, that now was packed with thousands of people, some of whom threw flowers before the feet of the bearers, bowing and staring till I thought that their eyes would fall out, to a large, flat-roofed house set in a walled court-yard. Passing through the gates the bearers placed the *balsa* on the ground and fell back. Then from out of the door of the house appeared Quilla, accompanied by a tall, stately-looking man who wore a fine robe, and a woman of middle age also gorgeously apparelled.

"O Lord," said Quilla, bowing, "behold my kinsman the *Curaca*" (which is the name for a lesser sort of king) "of the Yuncas, named Quismancu, and his wife, Mira."

"Hail, Lord Risen from the Sea!" cried Quismancu. "Hail, White god clothed in silver! Hail, *Hurachi!*"

Why he called me "Hurachi" at the time I could not guess, but afterwards I learned that it was because of the arrows painted on my shield, "Hurachi" being their name for arrows. At any rate, thenceforth by this name of Hurachi I was known throughout the land, though when addressed for the most part I was called "Lord-from-the-Sea" or "God-of-the-Sea."

Then Quilla and the lady Mira came forward and, placing their hands beneath my elbows, assisted me to climb out of that *balsa*, which I think was the strangest way that ever a shipwrecked wanderer came to land.

They led me into a large room with a flat roof that was being hastily prepared for me by the hanging of beautiful broideries on the walls, and sat me on a carven stool, where presently Quilla and other ladies brought me food and a kind of intoxicating drink which they called *chicha,* that after so many months of water drinking I found cheering and pleasant to the taste. This food, I noted, was served to me on platters of gold and silver, and the cups also were of gold strangely fashioned, by which I knew that I had come to a very rich land. Afterwards I learned, however, that in it there was no money, all the gold and silver that it produced being used for ornament or to decorate the temples and the palaces of the *Incas*, as they called their kings, and other great lords.

CHAPTER IV

THE ORACLE OF RIMAC

IN this town of Quismancu I remained for seven days, going abroad but little, for when I did so the people pressed about me and stared me out of countenance. There was a garden at the back of the house surrounded by a wall built of mud bricks. Here for the most part I sat and here the great ones of the place came to visit me, bringing me offerings of robes and golden vessels and I know not what besides. To all of them I told the same story—or, rather, Kari told it for me—namely, that I had risen out of the sea and found him a hermit, named Zapana, on the desert island. What is more, they believed it and, indeed, it was true, for had I not risen out of the sea?

From time to time Quilla came to see me also in this garden, bearing gifts of flowers, and with her I talked alone. She would sit upon a low stool, considering me with her beautiful eyes, as though she would search out my soul. One day she said to me:

"Tell me, Lord, are you a god or a man?"

"What is a god?" I asked.

"A god is that which is adored and loved."

"And is a man never adored and loved, Quilla? For instance, I understand that you are to be married, and doubtless you adore and love him who will be your husband."

She shivered a little and answered:

"It is not so. I hate him."

"Then why are you going to marry him? Are you forced to do so, Quilla?"

"No, Lord. I marry him for my people's sake. He desires me for my inheritance and my beauty, and by my beauty I may lead him down that road on which my people wish that he should go."

"An old story, Quilla, but will you be happy thus?"

"No, Lord, I shall be very unhappy. But what does it matter? I am only a woman, and such is the lot of women."

"Women, like gods and men, are also sometimes loved and adored, Quilla."

She flushed at the words and answered:

"Ah! if that were so life might be different. But even if it were so and I found the man who could love and adore even for a year, for me it is now too late. I am sworn away by an oath that may not be broken, for to break it might bring death upon my people."

"To whom are you sworn?"

"To the Child of the Sun, no less a man; to the god who will be Inca of all this land."

"And what is this god like?"

"They say that he is huge and swarthy, with a large mouth, and I know that he has the heart of a brute. He is cruel and false also, and he counts his women by the score. Yet his father, the Inca, loves him more than any of his children, and ere long he will be king after him."

"And would you, who are sweet and lovely as the moon after which you are named, give yourself body and soul to such a one?"

Again she flushed.

"Do my own ears hear the White-God-from-the-

Sea call me sweet and lovely as the moon? If so, I thank him, and pray him to remember that the perfect and lovely are always chosen to be the sacrifice of gods."

"But, Quilla, the sacrifice may be all in vain. How long will you hold the fancy of this loose-living prince?"

"Long enough to serve my purpose, Lord—or, at least," she added with flashing eyes, "long enough to kill him if he will not go my country's road. Oh! ask me no more, for your words stir something in my breast, a new spirit of which I never dreamed. Had I heard them but three moons gone, it might have been otherwise. Why did you not appear sooner from the sea, my lord Hurachi, be you god or man?"

Then, with something like a sob, she rose, made obeisance, and fled away.

That evening, when we were alone in my chamber where none could hear us, I told Kari that Quilla was promised in marriage to a prince who would be Inca of all the land.

"Is it so?" said Kari. "Well, learn, Master, that this prince is my brother, he whom I hate, he who has done me bitter wrong, he who stole away my wife and poisoned me. Urco is his name. Does this lady Quilla love him?"

"I think not. I think that like you she hates him, yet will marry him for reasons of policy."

"Doubtless she hates him now, whatever she did a week ago," said Kari in a dry voice. "But what fruit will this tree bear? Master, are you minded to come with me to-morrow to visit the temple of Pachacamac in the inner sanctuary of which sits the god Rimac who speaks oracles?"

"For what purpose, Kari?" I answered moodily.

"That we may hear oracles, Master. I think that if you choose to go the lady Quilla would come with us, since perhaps she would like also to hear oracles."

"I will go if it can be done in secret, say at night, for I weary of being stared at by these people."

This I said because I desired to learn of the religion of this nation and to see new things.

"Perhaps it can be so ordered, Master. I will ask of the matter."

It seemed that Kari did ask, perhaps of the high priest of Pachacamac, for between all the worshippers of this god there was a brotherhood; perhaps of the lord Quismancu, or perhaps of Quilla herself—I do not know. At least, on this same day Quismancu inquired whether it would please me to visit the temple that night, and so the matter was settled.

Accordingly, after the darkness had fallen, two litters were brought into which we entered, Quilla and a waiting woman seating themselves in one of them and Kari and I in the other, for Quismancu and his wife did not come—why I cannot say. Then, preceded by another litter in which was a priest of the god, and surrounded by a guard of soldiers, through a rain-storm we were borne up the hill—it was but a little way—to the temple.

Here, before the golden doors on which the lightning glimmered fitfully, we descended and were led by white-robed men bearing lanterns, through various courts to the inner sanctuary of the god, on the threshold of which I crossed myself, not loving the company of heathen idols. So far as I could see by the lamplight it was a great and glorious place, and everywhere that the eye fell was gold—plates of gold on the walls, offerings of gold upon the floor, stars of gold upon the roof. The strange thing about this holy place, however, was that it seemed to be quite empty except for the aforesaid gold. There was neither altar nor image—nothing but a lamp-lit void

Here all prostrated themselves, save I alone, and prayed in silence. When they rose again, in a whisper I asked of Kari where was the god. To which he answered: "Nowhere, yet everywhere." This I thought a true saying, and indeed so solemn was the place that I felt as though I were surrounded by that which is divine.

After a while the priests, who were gorgeously apparelled, led us across the sanctuary to a door that opened upon some stairs. Down these stairs we went into a long passage that seemed to run beneath the earth, for the air in it was heavy. When we had walked a hundred paces or more in this narrow place, we came to other steps and another door, passing through which we found ourselves in a second temple, smaller than that which we had visited, but like to it rich with gold. In the centre of this temple sat the image of a man rudely fashioned of gold.

"Behold Rimac the Speaker!" whispered Kari.

"How can gold speak?" I asked.

Kari made no answer.

Presently the priests began to mutter prayers and incantations that I thought unholy, after which they laid offerings of what looked like raw flesh set in cups of gold before the idol, that I thought unholier still. Lastly they drew back and asked of what we would learn.

I made no answer who did not like the business. Nor did Kari say anything, but Quilla spoke out boldly, saying that we would learn of the future and what would befall us.

Now there was a long silence, and I confess that fear got hold of me, for it seemed to me as though spirits were moving in the air and through the darkness behind us—yes, as though I could hear their whisperings and the rustle of their wings. Suddenly, at the end of this silence, the golden image in front of us began to glow as though it were molten, and the emerald eyes that were set in its head to sparkle terribly, which frightened me so much that had it not been for shame's sake I would have run away, but because of this stood still and prayed to St. Hubert to protect me from the devil and his works. Presently I prayed still harder, for the image began to speak—yes, in a horrid, whistling voice it spoke, although no one was near to it. These were the words it said:

"Who is this clad in silver whose skin is white and whose hair is yellow? Such an one I have not seen for a thousand years, and such as he it is that shall possess themselves of the Land of Tavantinsuyu, shall steal its wealth, shall slay its people, and shall cast down its gods. But not yet, not yet! Therefore this is the command of Pachacamac, uttered by the voice of Rimac the Speaker, that none do harm to or cross the will of this mighty seaborn lord, since he shall be as a strong wall to many and his sword shall be red with the blood of the wicked."

The whistling voice ceased while the priests and all there stared at me, for they seemed to think its words fateful. Then suddenly it began again:

"And who is this that came out of the sea with the Shining One, having wandered further than any of his ancient blood? I know. I know, yet I may not say, since the Spirit of spirits whose image he wears upon his heart bids me be silent. Be bold! Be bold! Prosper and grow great, Child of Pachacamac, for thy wanderings are not yet done. Still there is a mountain to be climbed, and on the crest of it hangs a fringe of Heaven's gold."

Again the voice ceased, while this time all stared

at Kari, who shook his head humbly as though bewildered by what he could not understand. Once more the image spoke:

"Who is this daughter of the Sun, in whose veins play moonbeans and who is fairer than the evening star? One, I think, whom men shall desire and because of whom shall flow the blood of the great. One whose thought is swift as the lightning and subtle as the snake, one in whom passion burns like fire in the womb of the mountain, but who is filled with spirit that dances above the fire and who longs for things that are afar. Daughter of the Sun in whose blood run the moonbeams, thou shalt slip from the hated arms and the Sun shall be thy shelter, and in the beloved arms thou shalt sleep at last. Yet from the vengeance of the god betrayed fly fast and far!"

Again the voice ceased, and I thought that all was over. But it was not so, for after a little space the golden figure of the oracle glowed more fiercely than before and the emerald eyes shone more terribly, and in a kind of scream it spoke, saying:

"The snows of Tavantinsuyu shall be red with blood, the waters of her rivers shall be full of blood. Yes, ye three shall wade through blood, and in a rain of blood shall pluck the fruit of your desires. Still for a while the gods of Tavantinsuyu shall endure and its kings shall reign and its children shall be free. But in the end death for the gods and death for the kings and death for the people. Still, not yet—not yet! None who live shall see it, nor their children, nor their children's children. Rimac the Voice has spoken; treasure ye his words and interpret them as ye will."

The whistling voice died away like the thin cry of some starving child in a desert, and there was a great silence. Then in a moment the figure of gold ceased to glow and the eyes of emerald to burn, leaving the thing but a dead lump of metal. The priests prostrated themselves, and rising, led us from the place without a word, but in the light of the lamps I saw that their faces were full of terror—so full that I doubted whether it could be feigned.

As we had come, so we went, and at last found ourselves outside the glittering temple doors where the litters awaited us.

"What did it mean?" I whispered to Quilla, who was by my side.

"For you and the other I know not," she answered hurriedly; "but for me I think that it means death. Yet not until—not until——" And she ceased.

At that moment the moon appeared from behind the rain-clouds and shone upon her upturned face, and in her eyes there was a glory.

Now, as I learned afterwards, these words of its most famous oracle went all through the land and caused great talk and wonder mixed with fear, for none of such import had been spoken by it for generations. More, they shaped my own fortunes, for, as I came to know, Quismancu and his people had determined that I should not be allowed to go from among them. Not every day did a white god rise from the sea, and they desired that having come to them, there he should bide to be their defence and boast, and with him that hermit named Zapana, to whom, as they believed, he had appeared upon the desert isle. But after Rimac had spoken all this was changed, and when I said it was my will to depart and accompany Quilla upon her journey home to her father, Huaraca, King of the Chancas, as by swift messenger this King invited me to do, Quismancu answered that if I so desired I must be obeyed as the god Rimac had commanded, but that nevertheless he was sure that we should meet again.

Now, thinking these things over I wondered much whether that oracle came out of the golden Rimac or perchance from the heart of Quilla, or of Kari, or of both of them, who desired that I should leave the Yuncas and travel to the Chancas and further. I did not know, nor was I ever to learn, since about matters to do with their gods these people are as secret as the grave. I asked Kari and I asked Quilla, but both of them stared at me with innocent eyes, and replied who were they to inspire the golden tongue of Rimac? Nor, indeed, did I ever learn whether Rimac the Speaker was a spirit or but a lump of metal through which some priest talked. All I know is that from one end of Tavantinsuyu to the other he was believed to be a spirit who spoke the very will of God to those who could understand his words, though this as a Christian man I could not credit.

So it came about that some days later, with Quilla and Kari and certain old men who, I took it, were priests or ambassadors, or both, I departed on our journey. As we went the people wept around my litter for sorrow, real or feigned, for we travelled in litters guarded by some two hundred soldiers armed with axes of copper and bows, and cast flowers before the feet of the bearers. But I did not weep, for though I had been very kindly treated there and, indeed, worshipped, glad was I to see the last of that city and its people who wearied me.

Moreover, I felt that there I was in the midst of plots, though of what these were I knew nothing, save that Quilla, who to the outward eye was but a lovely, innocent maiden, had a hand in them. Plots there were indeed, for, as I came to understand in time, they were nothing less than the preparing of a great war which the Chancas and the Yuncas were to wage against their over-lord, the Inca, the king of the mighty nation of the Quichuas, who had his home at a city called Cuzco far inland. Indeed, there and then this alliance was arranged, and by Quilla—Quilla, who proposed to sacrifice herself and by the gift of her person to his heir, to throw dust in the eyes of the Inca, whose dominion her father planned to take and with it the imperial crown of Tavantinsuyu.

Leaving the coastland, we were borne forward through the passes of great mountains, upon a wonderful road so finely made that never had I seen its like in England. At times we crossed rivers, but over these were thrown bridges of stone. Or mayhap we came to swamps, yet there the road still ran, built upon deep foundations in the mud. Never did it turn aside; always it went on, conquering every hindrance, for this was one of the Inca's roads that pierced Tavantinsuyu from end to end. We came to many towns, for this land was thickly populated, and for the most part slept in one of them each night. But always my fame had gone before me, and the *Curacas*, or chiefs of the towns, waited upon me with offerings as though I were indeed divine.

For the first five days of that journey I saw little of Quilla, but at length one night we were forced to camp at a kind of rest-house upon the top of a high mountain pass, where it was very cold, for the deep snow lay all about. At this place, as here were no *Curacas* to trouble me, I went out alone when Kari was elsewhere, and climbed a certain peak which was not far from the rest-house, that thence I might see the sunset and think in quiet.

Very glorious was the scene from that high point. All round me stood the cold crests of snow-clad mountains towering to the very skies, while between them lay deep valleys where rivers ran like veins of silver. So immense was the landscape that it seemed to have no end, and so grand that it crushed the spirit, while above arched the perfect sky in whose rich blue the gorgeous lights of evening began to gather as the great sun sank behind the snowy peaks.

Far up in the heavens floated one wide-winged bird, the eagle of the mountains, which is larger than any other fowl that I have ever seen, and the red light playing on it turned it to a thing of fire. I watched that bird and wished that I too had pinions which could bear me far away to the sea and over it.

And yet did I wish to go who had no home left on all the earth and no kind heart that would welcome me? A while ago I should have answered, "Yes, anywhere out of this loneliness," but now I was not so sure. Here at least Kari was my friend if a jealous one, though of late, as I could see, he was thinking of other things than friendship—dark plottings and high ambitions of which as yet he said little to me.

Then there was that strange and beautiful woman, Quilla, to whom my heart went out and not only because she was beautiful, and who, as I thought at times, looked kindly on me. But if so, what did it avail, seeing that she was promised in marriage to some high-placed native man who would be a king? Surely I had known enough of women who were promised in marriage to other men, and should do well to let her be.

Thinking thus, desolation took hold of me and I sat myself down on a rock and covered my face with my hands that I might not see the tears, which I knew were gathering in my eyes, as they fell from them.

Yes, there in the midst of that awful solitude, I, Hubert of Hastings, whose soul it filled, sat down like a lost child and wept.

Presently I felt a touch upon my shoulder and let fall my hands, thinking that Kari had found me out, to hear a soft voice, the voice of Quilla, say,

"So it seems that the gods can weep. Why do you weep, O God-from-the-Waves who here are named Hurachi?"

"I weep," I answered, "because I am a stranger in a strange land; I weep because I have not wings whereon I can fly away like that great bird above us."

She looked at me a while, then said, most gently,

"And whither would you fly, O God-from-the-Sea? Back into the sea?"

"Cease to call me a god," I answered, "who, as you know well, am but a man though of another race to yours."

"I thought it but I did not know. But whither would you fly, O Lord Hurachi?"

"To the land where I was born, Lady Quilla; the land that I shall never see again."

"Ah! doubtless there you have wives and children for whom your heart is hungry."

"Nay, now I have neither wife nor child."

"Then once you had a wife. Tell me of that wife. Was she fair?"

"Why should I tell you a sad story? She is dead."

"Dead or living, you still love her, and where there is love there is no death."

"Nay, I only love what I thought she was."

"Was she false, then?"

"Yes, false and yet true. So true that she died because she was false."

"How can a woman be both false and true?"

"Women can be all things. Ask the question of your own heart. Can you not perchance be both false and true?"

She thought a while and, leaving this matter, said,

"So, having once loved, you can never love again."

"Why not? Perchance I can love too much. But what would be the use when more love would but mean more loss and pain?"

"Whom could you love, my lord Hurachi, seeing that the women of your own folk are far away?"

"I think one who is very near, if she would pay back love for love."

Quilla made no answer, and I thought that she was angry and would go away. But she did not; indeed, she sat herself down upon the stone at my side and covered her face with her hands as I had done and began to weep as I had done. Now in my turn I asked her,

"Why do you weep?"

"Because I too must know loneliness, and with it shame, Lord Hurachi."

At these words my heart beat and passion flamed up in me. Stretching out my hand I drew hers away and in the dying light gazed at the face beneath. Lo! on its loveliness there was a look which could not be misread.

"Do you, then, also love?" I whispered.

"Aye, more, I think, than ever woman loved before. From the moment when first I saw you sleeping in the moonbeams on the desert isle, I knew my fate had found me and that I loved. I fought against it because I must, but that love has grown and grown, till now I am all love, and, having given everything, have no more left to give."

When I heard this, making no answer, I swept her

into my arms and kissed her, and there she lay upon my breast and kissed me back.

"Let me go and hear me," she murmured presently, "for you are strong and I am weak."

I obeyed, and she sank back upon the stone.

"My lord," she said, "our case is very sad, or at least my case is sad, since though you being a man may love often, I can love but once, and, my lord, it may not be."

"Why not?" I asked hoarsely. "Your people think me a god; cannot a god take whom he wills to wife?"

"Not when she is vowed to another god, he who will be Inca; not when on her, mayhap, hangs the fate of nations."

"We might fly, Quilla."

"Whither could the God-from-the-Sea fly and whither could fly the daughter of the Moon, who is vowed to the son of the Sun in marriage, save to death?"

"There are worse things than death, Quilla."

"Aye but my life is in pawn. I must live that my people may not die. Myself I offered it to this cause and now, being royal, I cannot take it back again for my own joy. It is better to be shamed with honour than to be loved in the lap of shame."

"What then?" I asked hopelessly.

"Only this, that above us are the gods, and—heard you not the oracle of Rimac that declared to me that I should slip from the hated arms, that the Sun should be my shelter, and in the beloved arms I should sleep at last, though from the vengeance of the god betrayed I must fly fast and far? I think that this means death, but also it means life in death and—O arms beloved, you shall fold me yet. I know not how, but have faith—for you shall fold me yet.

Meanwhile, tempt me not from the path of honour, since this I know, that it alone can lead me to my home. Yet who is the god betrayed from whom I must fly? Who, who?"

Thus she spoke and was silent, and I too was silent. Yes, there we sat, both silent in the darkness, searching the heavens for a guiding star. And as we sat, presently I heard the voice of Kari saying,

"Have I found you, Lord, and you also, Lady Quilla? Return, I pray you, for all search and are frightened."

"Why?" I answered. "The lady Quilla and I study this wondrous scene."

"Yes, Lord, though to those who are not god-born it would be difficult in this darkness. Suffer now that I show you the path."

CHAPTER V

KARI GOES

As it chanced during the remaining days of that journey, Quilla and I were not again alone together (that is to say, except once for a few minutes), for we were never out of eyeshot of someone in our company. Thus Kari clung to me very closely indeed, and when I asked him why, told me bluntly that it was for my safety's sake. A god to remain a god, he said, should live alone in a temple. When he began to mix with others of the earth and to do those things they did, to eat and to drink, to laugh and to frown, even to slip in the mud or to stumble over the stones in the common path, those others would come to think that there was small difference between god and man. Especially would they think so if he were observed to love the company of women or to melt beneath their soft glances.

Now I grew sore at the sting of these arrows which of late he had loved to shoot at me, and without pretending to misunderstand him, said outright:

"The truth is, Kari, that you are jealous of the Lady Quilla as once you were jealous of another."

He considered the matter in his grave fashion, and answered:

"Yes, Master, that is the truth, or part of it. You saved my life and sheltered me when I was alone in a strange land, and for this and for yourself I came to love you very greatly, and love, if it be true, is always jealous and always hates a rival."

" There are different sorts of loves," I said ; " that of man for man is one, that of man for woman is another."

" Yes, Master, and that of woman for man is a third ; moreover, there is this about it—it is the acid which turns all other loves sour. Where are a man's friends when a woman has him by the heart ? —although perchance they love him better than ever will the woman who at bottom loves herself best of all. Still, let that be, for so Nature works, and who can fight against Nature ? What Quilla takes, Kari loses and Kari must be content to lose."

" Have you done ? " I asked angrily, who wearied of his homilies.

" No, Master. The matter of jealousy is small and private ; so is the matter of love. But, Master, you have not told me outright whether you love the Lady Quilla, and, what is more important, whether she loves you."

" Then I will tell you now. I do and she does."

" You love the Lady Quilla and she says that she loves you, which may or may not be true, or if true to-day may be false to-morrow. For your sake I hope that it is not true."

" Why ? " I said in a rage.

" Because, Master, in this land there are many sorts of poison, as I have learned to my cost. Also there are knives, if not of steel, and many who might wish to discover whether a god who courts women like a man can be harmed by poisons or pierced by knives. Oh ! " he added, in another tone, ceasing from his bitter jests, " believe me that I would shield, not mock you. This Lady Quilla is a queen in a great game of pieces such as you taught me to play far away in England, and without her perchance that game cannot be won, or so those who play it think.

Now you would steal that queen and thereby, as they also think, bring death and destruction on a country. It is not safe, Master. There are plenty of fair women in this land; take your pick of them, but leave that one queen alone."

"Kari," I answered, "if there be such a game, are you not perchance one of the players on this side or on that?"

"It may be so, Master, and if you have not guessed it, perhaps one day I will tell you upon which side I play. It may even be that for my own sake I should be glad to see you lift this queen from off the board, and that what I tell you is for love of you and not of myself, also of the Lady Quilla, who, if you fall, falls with you down through the black night into the arms of the Moon, her mother. But I have said enough, and indeed it is foolish to waste breath in such talk, since Fate will have its way with both of you, and the end of the game in which we play is already written in Pachacamac's book for every one of us. Did not Rimac speak of it the other night? So play on, play on, and let Destiny fulfil itself. If I dared to give counsel it was only because he who watches the battle with a general's eye sees more of it than he who fights."

Then he bowed in his stately fashion and left me, and it was long ere he spoke to me again of this matter of Quilla and our love for one another.

When he was gone my anger against him passed, since I saw that he was warning me of more than he dared to say, not for himself, but because he loved me. Moreover, I was afraid, for I felt that I was moving in the web of a great plot that I did not understand, of which Quilla and those cold-eyed lordlings of her company and the chief whose guest I had been, and Kari himself, and many others as yet unknown to me, spun the invisible threads. One day these might choke me. Well, if they did, what then? Only I feared for Quilla—greatly I feared for Quilla.

On the day following my talk with Kari at length we reached the great city of the Chancas, which, after them, was called Chanca—at least I always knew it by that name. From the dawn we had been passing through rich valleys where dwelt thousands of these Chancas who, I could see, were a mighty people that bore themselves proudly and like soldiers. In multitudes they gathered themselves together upon either side of our road, chiefly to catch a sight of me, the white god who had risen from the ocean, but also to greet their princess, the Lady Quilla.

Indeed, now I learned for the first time how high a princess she was, since when her litter passed these folk prostrated themselves, kissing the air and the dust. Moreover, as soon as she came among them Quilla's bearing changed, for her carriage grew more haughty and her words fewer. Now she seldom spoke save to issue a command, not even to myself, although I noted that she studied me with her eyes when she thought that I was not observing her.

During our midday halt I looked up and saw that an army was approaching us, five thousand men or more, and asked Kari its meaning.

"These," he answered, "are some of the troops of Huaracha, King of the Chancas, whom he sends out to greet his daughter and only child, also his guest, the White God."

"Some of the troops! Has he more, then?"

"Aye, Master, ten times as many, as I think. This is a great people; almost as great as that of the Incas who live at Cuzco. Come now into the tent and put on your armour, that you may be ready to meet them."

I did so, and, stepping forth clad in the shining steel, took my stand where Kari showed me, upon a rise of ground. On my right at a little distance stood Quilla, more splendidly arrayed than I had ever seen her, and behind her her maidens and the captains and counsellors of her following.

The army drew nearer, marshalled in regiments and halted on the plain some two hundred yards away, Presently from it advanced generals and old men, clad in white, whom I took to be priests and elders. They approached to the number of twenty or more and bowed deeply, first to Quilla, who bent her head in acknowledgment, and then to myself. After this they went to speak with Quilla and her following, but what they said I did not know. All the while, however, their eyes were fixed on me. Then Quilla brought them to me, and one by one they bowed before me, saying something in a language which I did not understand well, for it was somewhat different from that which Kari had taught me.

After this we entered the litters, and, escorted by that great army, were borne forward down valleys and over ridges till about sunset we came to a large cup-like plain in the centre of which stood the city called Chanca. Of this city I did not see much except that it was very great, as the darkness was falling when we entered, and afterwards I could not go out because of the crowds that pressed about me. I was borne down a wide street to a house that stood in a large garden which was walled about. Here in this fine house I found food prepared for me, and drink, all of it served in dishes and cups of gold and silver; also there were women who waited upon me, as did Kari who now was called Zapana and seemed to be my slave.

When I had eaten I went out alone into the garden,

for on this plain the air was very warm and pleasant. It was a beautiful garden, and I wandered about among its avenues and flowering bushes, glad to be solitary and to have time to think. Amongst other things I wondered where Quilla might be, for of her I had seen nothing from the time that we entered the town. I hated to be parted from her, because in this vast strange land into which I had wandered she was the only one for whom I had come to care and without whom I felt I should die of loneliness.

There was Kari, it is true, who I knew loved me in his fashion, but between him and me there was a great gulf fixed, not only of race and faith, but of something new which I did not wholly understand. In London he had been my servant and his ends were my ends; on our wanderings he had been my companion in great adventures. But now I knew that other interests and desires had taken a hold of him, and that he trod a road of which I could not see the goal; and no longer thought much of me save when what I did or desired to do came between him and that goal.

Therefore Quilla alone was left to me, and Quilla was about to be taken away. Oh! I wearied of this strange land with its snowclad mountains and rich valleys, its hordes of dark-skinned people with large eyes, smiling faces, and secret hearts; its great cities, temples, and palaces filled with useless gold and silver; its brilliant sunshine and rushing rivers; its gods, kings, and policies. They were alien to me, every one of them, and if Quilla were taken away and I were left quite alone, then I thought that it would be well to die.

Something moved behind a palm trunk of the avenue in which I walked, and not knowing whether it were beast or man, I laid my hand upon my sword which I still wore, although I had taken off the armour.

Before I could draw it my wrist was grasped and a soft voice whispered in my ear:

"Fear nothing; it is I—Quilla."

Quilla it was, wrapped in a long hooded cloak such as the peasant women wear in the cold country, for she threw back the hood and a beam of starlight fell upon her face.

"Hearken!" she said. "It is dangerous to both of us, but I have come to bid you farewell."

"Farewell! I feared it would be thus, but why so soon, Quilla?"

"For this reason, Love and Lord. I have seen my father the King, and made my report to him of the matter with which I was sent to deal among the Yuncas. It pleased him, and since his mood was gracious, I opened my heart to him and told him that no longer did I wish to be given in marriage to Urco, who will soon put on the Inca fringe, for, as you know, it is to him that I am promised!"

"What did he answer, Quilla?"

"He answered: 'This means, Daughter, that you have met some other man to whom you do wish to be given in marriage. I will not ask his name, since if I knew it it would be my duty to kill him, however high and noble he might be.'"

"Then he guesses, Quilla?"

"I think he guesses; I think that already some have whispered in his ear, but he does not wish to listen who desires to remain deaf and blind."

"Did he say no more, Quilla?"

"He said much more; he said this—now I tell you secrets, Lord, and place my honour in your keeping, for having given you all the rest, why should I not give you that also? He said: 'Daughter, you who have been my ambassador, you, my only child, who know all my counsel, know also that there is about to be the greatest war that the land of Tavantinsuyu has ever known, war between the two mighty nations of the Quichuas of Cuzco whereof the old Upanqui is king and god, and the Chancas whereof I am king and you, if you live, in a day to come will be the queen. No longer can these two lions dwell in the same forest; one of them must devour the other; nor shall I fight alone, since on our side are all the Yuncas of the coast who, as you report to me, are ripe for rebellion. But, as you also report, and as I have learned from others, they are not yet ready. Moons must go by before their armies are joined to mine and I throw off the mask. Is it not so?'

"I answered that it was so, and my father went on:

"'Then during that time, Daughter, a dust must be raised that will hide the shining of my spears, and, Daughter, you are that dust. To-morrow the old Inca Upanqui visits me here with a small army. I read your thought. It is—Why do you not kill him and his army? Daughter, for this reason. He is very aged and about to lay down his sceptre, who grows feeble of mind and body. If I killed him what would it serve me, seeing that he has left his son, Urco, who will be Inca, ruling at Cuzco, and that of his soldiers not one in fifty will be with him here? Moreover, he is my guest, and the gods frown on those who slay their guests, nor will men ever trust them more.'

"Now I answered: 'You spoke of me as a cloud of dust, Father; how, then, can this poor dust serve your ends and those of the Chanca people?'

"'Thus, Daughter,' he answered. 'With your own consent you are promised in marriage to Urco. Upanqui the Inca has heard rumours that the Chancas prepare for war. Therefore, he who travels on his last journey through certain of his dominions, comes to lead you away to be Urco's bride, saying to himself, "If those rumours are true, King Huaracha will withhold his only child and heiress, since never will he make war upon Cuzco if she rules there as its queen." Therefore, if I refuse you to him, he will withdraw and begin the war, rolling down his thousands upon us before we are ready, and bringing the Chancas to destruction and enslavement. Therefore also not only my fate, but the fate of all your country lies in your hand.'

"'Father,' I said, 'tell me, who was ever dear to you that lack sons, is there no escape? Must I eat this bitter bread? Before you answer, learn that you have guessed aright, and that I who, when I made that promise, cared for no man, have come to feel the burning of love's fire.'

"Now he looked at me a while, then said: 'Child of the Moon, there is but one escape, and it must be sought—in the moon. The dead cannot be given in marriage. If your strait is so sore, though it would cut me to the heart, perchance it is better that you should die and go whither doubtless he whom you love will soon follow you. Depart now and take counsel with Heaven in your sleep. To-morrow, before Upanqui comes, we will talk again.'

"So I knelt and kissed the hand of the King my father, and left him, wondering at his nobleness who could show such a road to his only child, though its treading would mean woe to him and mayhap the ruin of his hopes. Still that road is an old one among the women of my people, and why should I not walk it, as thousands have done before me?"

"How came you here?" I asked hoarsely.

"Lord, I guessed that you would be walking in this garden which joins on to that of the palace, and

—none were about, and—the door in the wall was open. Indeed, it was almost as though I were left alone and unwatched of set purpose. So I came and sought—and found, having a question to put to you."

"What question, Quilla ?"

"This, shall I live or shall I die ? Speak the word and I obey. Yet ere you speak, remember that if I live we meet for the last time, since very soon I go hence to become the wife of Urco and play the part that is prepared for me ?"

Now when I, Hubert, heard these words I felt as though my heart would burst within my breast and knew not what to say. So to gain time I asked her :

"Which do you desire—to live or to die ?"

She laughed a little as she answered :

"That is a strange question, Lord. Have I not told you that if I live I must do so befouled as one of Urco's women as, if I die, I die clean and take my love with me to where Urco cannot come, but where, mayhap, another may follow at the appointed time."

"Which time would be very soon, I think, Quilla, seeing that he who had spoiled all this pretty plot would scarcely be left long upon the earth, even if he wished to stay there. Yet I say : Do not die—live on."

"To become Urco's woman ! That is strange counsel from a lover's lips, Lord ; such as would scarcely have been given by any of our nobles."

"Aye, Quilla, and it is given because I am not of your people and do not think as they think, who reject their customs. You are not yet Urco's wife, and may be rid of him by other paths than that of death, but from the grave there is no escape."

"And in the grave there is no more fear, Lord. Thither Urco cannot come ; there are neither wars nor plottings ; there honour does not beckon and love hold back. I say that I will die and make an end, as for like causes many of my blood have done, though not here and now. When I am about to be delivered to Urco, then I will die, and perchance not alone. Perchance he will accompany me," she added slowly.

"And if this happens, what shall I do ? "

"Live on, Lord, and find other women to love you, as a god should. There are many in this land fairer and wiser than I, and, save myself, you may take whom you will."

"Listen, Quilla. I have a story to tell you."

Then, as briefly as I could, I set out the tale of Blanche and of her end, while she hung upon my every word.

"Oh ! I grieve for you," she said, when I had finished.

"You grieve for me, and yet, what she did for my sake, you would do also, so that, as it were, both my hands must be dyed with blood. This first terror I have borne, but if a second falls upon me then I know that I shall go mad and perish in this way or in that, and you, Quilla, will be my murderess."

"No, no, not that ! " she murmured.

"Then swear to me by your god and by your spirit that you will do yourself no harm, whatever chances, and that if die you must, it shall be with me for company."

"Is your love so great that you would dare this for my sake, Lord ? "

"I think so, though not till all else had failed. I think that if you were taken from me, Quilla, I could not live on here in loneliness and exile—however great the sin But do you swear ? "

"Aye, Love and Lord, I swear, for your sake. Moreover, I add to the oath. If perhaps we should escape these perils and come together, I will be such a wife to you as never man has had. I will wrap you round with love and lift you up to be a king, that you may live in glory forgetting your home across the sea, and all the sorrows that befell you there. Children you shall have also of whom you need not be ashamed, though my dark blood runs in them, and armies at command and palaces filled with gold, and all royal joys. And if perchance the gods declare against us, and we pass from the world together, then I think, oh! then I think that I shall give you finer gifts than these, though what they are I know not yet, since to the power of love there is no end——here on earth or yonder in the skies."

I stared at her face in the starlight, and oh! it had grown splendid. No longer was it that of a woman, since through it, like light through pearl, shone a soul divine. It might have been a goddess who stood beside me, for those eyes were holy and her embrace that wrapped me close was not that of the flesh alone.

"I must be gone," she whispered, "but now I go without fear. Perchance we may not speak again for long, but trust me always. Play your part and I will play mine. Follow me wherever I am taken and keep near to me, if you may, as ever my spirit shall be near to you. Then what matters anything, even if we are slain? Farewell, beloved, kiss me and farewell."

Another moment and she had glided away and was lost in the shadows.

She was gone, and I stood amazed and overcome. Oh! what a love it was that this alien woman had given to me and how could I be worthy of it? Now I forgot my griefs; now I no longer mourned because I was an outcast who nevermore might look upon the land where I was born, nor see the face of one of my own race or blood. All my loss was paid back to me again and yet again, in the coin of the glory of this woman whom I had won. Dangers rose about us, but I feared them no more, because I knew that her love's conquering feet would stamp them flat and lead me safe to a joyful treasure-house of splendour of spirit and of body where we should dwell side by side, triumphant and unafraid.

Whilst I thought thus, lost in a rapture such as I had not felt since Blanche kissed me at the mouth of the Hastings cave after I had killed the three Frenchmen with as many arrows from my black bow, I heard a sound and looked up to see a man standing before me.

"Who is it?" I asked, grasping my sword, for his face was hidden in the shadows.

"I," answered a voice which I knew to be that of Kari.

"Then how did you come here? I saw no one pass the open ground."

"Master, you are not the only one who loves to walk in gardens in the quiet of the night. I was here before yourself, behind yonder tree," and he pointed to a palm, not three paces distant.

"Then Kari, you must have seen——"

"Yes, Master, I saw and heard, not everything, because there came a point at which I shut my eyes and stopped my ears, but still much."

"I am minded to kill you, Kari," I said between my teeth, "who play the spy upon me."

"I guessed it would be so, Master," he replied in his gentlest voice, "and for that reason as you will notice, I am standing out of reach of your sword. You wonder why I am here. I will tell you. It is not from any desire to watch your love-makings which weary me, who have seen such before, but rather that I might find secrets, of which love is always the loser, and those secrets I have learned. How could I have come by them otherwise, Master ? "

" Surely you deserve to die," I exclaimed furiously.

" I think not, Master. But listen and judge for yourself. I have told you something of my story, now you shall hear more, after which we will talk of what I do or do not deserve. I am the eldest son of the Inca Upanqui, and Urco, of whom you have been talking is my younger brother. But Upanqui, our father, loved Urco's mother while mine he did not love, and swore to her before she died that against right and law, Urco, her son, should be Inca after him. Therefore he hated me because I stood in Urco's path ; therefore too many troubles befell me, and I was given over into Urco's hand, so that he took my wife and tried to poison me, and the rest you know. Now it was needful to me to learn how things went, and for this reason I listened to the talk between you and a certain lady It told me that Upanqui, my father, comes here to-morrow, which indeed I knew already, and much else that I had not heard. This being so I must vanish away, since doubtless Upanqui or his councillors would know me again, and as they are all of them friends of Urco, perhaps I should taste more poison and of a stronger sort."

" Whither will you vanish, Kari ? "

" I know not, Master, or if I know, I will not say who have but just been taught afresh how secrets can pass from ear to ear. I must lie hid, that is enough. Yet do not think that therefore I shall desert you who, while I live, will watch over you, a stranger in my country, as you watched over me when I was a stranger in your England."

" I thank you," I answered, " and certainly you watch well—too well sometimes, as I have found to-night."

"You think it pleases me to spy upon you and a certain lady," went on Kari with an unruffled voice, "but it is not so. What I do is for good reasons, amongst others that I may protect you both, and if I can, bring about what you desire. That lady has a great heart, as I learned but now, and after all you did well to love her, as she does well to love you. Therefore, although the dangers are so many, if I am able, I will help you in your love and bring you together, yes, and save her from the arms of Urco. Nay, ask me not how, for I do not know, and the case seems desperate."

"But if you go, what shall I do alone?" I asked alarmed.

"Bide here, I think, Lord, giving it out that your servant Zapana has deserted you. Indeed it seems that this you must do, since the King of this country will scarcely suffer you to be the companion of his daughter upon her marriage journey to Cuzco, even if Upanqui so desires. Nor would it be wise, for if he did, misfortune might befall you on the road. There are some women, Lord, who cannot keep their love out of their eyes, and henceforward there will be plenty to watch the eyes and hearken to the most secret sighings of one of the greatest of them. Now farewell until I come to you again or send others on my behalf. Trust me, I pray you, since to whomever else I may seem false, to you I am true; yes, to you and to another because she has become a part of you."

Then before I could answer Kari took my hand and touched it with his lips. Another moment and I had lost sight of him in the shadows.

CHAPTER VI

THE CHOICE

THAT night I slept but ill who was overwhelmed with all that had befallen me of good and evil. I had gained a wondrous love, but she who gave it was, it seemed, about to be lost to me, aye, and to be thrown to another whom she hated, to forward the dark policies of a great and warlike people. I had spoken to her with high words of hope, but of it in my heart there was little. She would follow what she held to be her duty to the end, and that end, if she kept her promise and did not die as she desired to do—was—the arms of Urco. From these I could see no escape for her, and the thought maddened me. Moreover, Kari was gone leaving me utterly alone among these strangers, and whether he would return again I did not know. Oh! almost I wished that I were dead.

The morning broke at last and I arose and called for Zapana. Then came others who said that my servant, Zapana, could not be found, whereat I affected surprise and anger. Still these others waited on me well enough, and I rose and ate in pomp and luxury. Scarcely had I finished my meal than there appeared heralds who summoned me to the presence of the King Huaracha.

I went borne in a litter although an arrow from my black bow would have flown from door to door. At the portal of the palace which was like others I had seen, only finer, I was met by soldiers and gaily dressed servants and led across a courtyard within, which I could see was prepared for some ceremony, to a small chamber on the further side. Here, when my eyes grew accustomed to the half-darkness, I perceived a man of some sixty years of age, and behind him two soldiers. At once I noted that everything about this man was plain and simple; the chamber, which was little more than four white-washed walls with a floor of stone, the stool he sat on, even his apparel. Here were no gold or silver or broidered cloths, or gems, or other rich and costly things such as these people love, but rather those that are suited to a soldier. A soldier he looked indeed, being burly and broad and scarred upon his homely face, in which gleamed eyes that were steady and piercing.

As I entered the King Huaracha, for it was he, rose from his stool and bowed to me, and I bowed back to him. Then he motioned to one of the soldiers to give me another stool, upon which I sat myself, and speaking in a strong, low voice, using that tongue which Kari had taught me, said:

"Greeting, White-God-from-the-Sea, or golden-bearded man named the Lord Hurachi, I know not which, of whom I have heard so much and whom I am glad to behold in my poor city. Say, can you understand my talk?"

Thus he spoke searching me with his eyes, though all the while I perceived that they rested rather on my armour and the great sword, Wave-Flame, than on my face.

I gave him back his greeting and answered that I understood the tongue he used though not so very well, whereon he began to speak about the armour and the sword, which puzzled him who had never seen steel.

"Make me some like them," he said, "and I will give you ten times their weight in gold, which after all is of no use since with it one cannot kill enemies."

"In my country with it one can corrupt them," I answered, "or buy them to be friends."

"So you have a country," he interrupted shrewdly. "I thought that the gods had none."

"Even the gods live somewhere," I replied.

He laughed and turning to the two soldiers, who also were staring at my mail and sword, bade them go. When the heavy door had shut behind them and we were quite alone, he said:

"My Lord Hurachi, I have heard from my daughter how she found you in the sea, a story indeed. I have also heard, or guessed, it matters not which, that her heart has turned towards you, as is not strange, seeing the manner of man you are, if indeed you be not more than man, and that women are ever prone to love those whom they think they have saved. Is this true, my Lord Hurachi?"

"Ask of the Lady Quilla, O King."

"Mayhap I have asked and at least it seems that you make no denial. Now hearken, my Lord Hurachi. You are my honoured guest and save one thing, all I have is yours, but you must talk no more alone with the Lady Quilla in gardens at night."

Now, making no attempt to deny or explain which I saw would be useless, since he knew all, I asked boldly:

"Why not?"

"I thought that perchance my daughter had told you, Lord Hurachi, but if you desire to hear it from my own lips also, for this reason. The Lady Quilla is promised in marriage and if she lives that promise must be fulfilled, since on it hangs the fate of nations. Therefore, it is, although I grieve to part such a pair, that you and she must meet no more in gardens or elsewhere. Know that if you do, you will bring about her death and your own, if gods can die."

Now I thought a while and answered.

"These are heavy words, King Huaracha, seeing that I will not hide from you that I love your daughter well and that she, who is great-hearted, loves me well and desires me for her husband."

"I know it and I grieve for both of you," he said courteously."

"King Huaracha," I went on, "I see that you are a soldier and the lord of armies, and it has come into my mind that perchance you dream of war."

"The gods see far, White Lord."

"Now god or man, I also am a soldier, King, and I know arts of battle which perhaps are hidden from you and your people; also I cannot be harmed by weapons because of magic armour that I wear, and none can stand before me in fight because of this magic sword I carry, and I can direct battles with a general's mind. In a great war, King, I might be useful to you were I the husband of your daughter and therefore your son and friend, and perchance by my skill make the difference to you and your nation between victory and defeat."

"Doubtless this is so, O Son-of-the-Sea."

"In the same fashion, King, were I upon the side of your enemies, to them I might bring victory and to you defeat. Whom do you desire that I should serve, you or them?"

"I desire that you should serve me," he replied with eagerness. "Do so and all the wealth of this land shall be yours, with the rule of my armies under me. You shall have palaces and fields and gold and silver, and the fairest of its daughters for wives, and be worshipped as a god, and for aught I know, be king after me, not only of my country but mayhap of another that is even greater."

"It is a good offer, King, but not enough. Give

me your daughter Quilla, and you may keep all the rest."

"White Lord, I cannot, since to do so I must break my word."

"Then, King, I cannot serve you, and unless you kill me first—if you are able—I will be, not your friend, but your enemy."

"Can a god be killed, and if so can a guest be killed? Lord, you know that he cannot. Yet he can remain a guest. To my country you have come, Lord, and in my country you shall stay, unless you have wings beneath that silver coat. Quilla goes hence but here you bide, my Lord Hurachi."

"Perchance I shall find the wings," I answered.

"Aye, Lord, for it is said that the dead fly, and if I may not kill you, others may. Therefore my counsel to you is to stay here, taking such things as my poor country can give you and not to try to follow the moon (by this he meant Quilla) to the golden city of Cuzco, which henceforth must be her home."

Now having no more to say, since war had been declared between us, as it were, I rose to bid this king farewell. He also rose, then, as though struck by a sudden thought, said that he desired to speak with my servant, Zapana, he whom the Lady Quilla had found with me in the island of the sea. I replied that he could not since Zapana had vanished, I knew not where.

At this intelligence he appeared to be disturbed and was beginning to question me somewhat sternly as to who Zapana might be and how I had first come into his company, when the door of the room opened and through it Quilla entered even more gorgeously robed and looking lovelier than ever I had seen her. She bowed, first to the king and then to me, saying:

"Lord and Father, I come to tell you that the

Inca Upanqui draws near with his princes and captains."

"Is it so, Daughter?" he answered. "Then make your farewell here and now to this White Son of the Sea, since it is my will that you depart with Upanqui who comes to escort you to Cuzco, the City of the Sun, there to be given as wife to the Prince Urco, son of the Sun, who soon will sit on the Inca's throne."

"I make my farewell to the Lord Hurachi as you command," she answered, curtseying, and in a very quiet voice, "but know, my father, that I love this White Lord as he loves me, and that therefore although I may be given to the Prince Urco, as a gold cup is given, never shall he drink from the cup and never will I be his wife."

"You have courage, Daughter, and I like courage," said Huaracha. "For the rest, settle the matter as you will and if you can slip from the coils of this snake of an Urco unpoisoned, do so, since my bargain is fulfilled and my honour satisfied. Only hither you shall not return to the Lord Hurachi, nor shall the Lord Hurachi go to you at Cuzco."

"That shall be as the gods decree, my father, and meanwhile I play my part as *you* decree. Lord Hurachi, fare you well till in life or death we meet again."

Then she bowed to me, and went, and presently without more words we followed after her.

In front of the palace there was a great square of open ground surrounded by houses, except towards the east, and on this square was marshalled an army of men all splendidly arrayed and carrying copper-headed spears. In front of these was pitched a great pavilion made of cloths of various colours. Here King Huaracha, simply dressed in a robe of white cotton but wearing a little crown of gold and carrying a large spear, took his seat upon a throne, while to his right on a smaller throne, sat Quilla, and on his left stood yet another throne ornamented with gold, that was empty. Between the throne of Huaracha and that which was empty, stood a chair covered with silver on which I was bidden to take my seat, so placed that all could see me, while behind and around were lords and generals.

Scarcely were we arranged when from the dip beyond the open space appeared heralds who carried spears and were fantastically dressed. These shouted that the Inca Upanqui, the Child of the Sun, the god who ruled the earth, drew near.

"Let him approach!" said Huaracha briefly, and they departed.

A while later there arose a sound of barbarous music and of chanting and from the dip below emerged a glittering litter borne upon the shoulders of richly clothed men, all of whom I was told afterwards, were princes by blood, and surrounded by beautiful women who carried jewelled fans, and by councillors. It was the litter of the Inca Upanqui, and after it marched a guard of picked warriors, perhaps there were a hundred of them, not more.

The litter was set down in front of the throne; gilded curtains were drawn and out of it came a man whose attire dazzled the eyes. It seemed to consist of gold and precious stones sewn on to a mantle of crimson wool. He wore a head-dress also of as many colours as Joseph's coat, surmounted by two feathers, which he alone might bear, from which head-dress a scarlet fringe that was made of tasselled wool hung down upon his forehead. This was the Inca's crown, even to touch which was death, and its name was *Lautu*. He was a very old man for his white locks and beard hung down upon his splendid garments and he supported himself upon his royal staff that was headed by a great emerald. His fine-cut face also, though still kingly, was weak with age and his eyes were blear. At the sight of him all rose and Huaracha descended from his throne, saying in a loud voice:

"Welcome to the land of the Chancas, O Upanqui, Inca of the Quichuas."

The old monarch eyed him for a moment, then answered in a thin voice:

"Greeting to Huaracha, *Curaca* of the Chancas."

Huaracha bowed and said:

"I thank you, but here among my own people my title is not *Curaca* but King, O Inca."

Upanqui drew himself up to his full height and replied:

"The Incas know no kings throughout the land of Tavantinsuyu save themselves, O Huaracha."

"Be it so, O Inca; yet the Chancas, who are unconquered, know a king, and I am he. I pray you be seated, O Inca."

Upanqui stood still for a moment frowning and as I thought, was about to make some short answer, when suddenly his glance fell upon me and changed the current of his mind.

"Is that the White-god-from-the-Sea?" he asked, with an almost childish curiosity. "I heard that he was here and to tell the truth that is why I came, just to look at him, not to bandy words with you, O Huaracha, who they say can only be talked to with a spear point. What a red beard he has and how his coat shines. Let him come and worship me.'

"He will come, but I do not think that he will worship. They say he is a god himself, O Inca."

"Do they? Well now I remember there are strange prophecies about a white god who should rise out of the sea, as did the forefather of the Incas. They say, too, that this god shall do much mischief to the land when he comes. So perhaps he had better not draw too near to me, for I like not the look of that great sword of his. By the Sun my father, he is tall and big and strong" (I had risen from my chair) " and his beard is like a fire; it will set the hearts of all the women burning, though perhaps if he is a god he does not care for women. I must consult my magicians about it, and the head-priest of the Temple of the Sun. Tell the White god to make ready to return with me to Cuzco."

"The Lord Hurachi is my guest, O Inca, and here he bides with me," said Huaracha.

"Nonsense, nonsense! When the Inca invites anyone to his court, he must come. But enough of him for the present. I came here to talk of other matters. What were they? Let me sit down and think."

So he was conducted to his throne upon which he sat trying to collect his mind, which I saw was weak with age. The end of it was that he called to his aid a stern-faced, shifty-eyed, middle-aged minister, whom after I came to know as the High-priest Larico, the private Councillor of himself and of his son, Urco, and one of the most powerful men in the kingdom. This noble, I noted, was one who had the rank of an Ear-man, that is, he wore in his ear, which like that of Kari, was stretched out to receive it, a gold disc of the size of an apple, whereon was embossed the image of the sun.

At a sign and a word from his dotard master this Larico began to speak for him as though he were the Inca himself, saying;

"Hearken, O Huaracha. I have undertaken this toilsome journey, the last I shall make as Inca, for be it known to you that I purpose to divest myself of the royal Fringe in favour of the Prince Urco, begotten of me in the body and of the Sun in the spirit, and to retire to end my days in peace at my palace of Yucay, waiting there patiently until it pleases my father, the Sun, to take me to his bosom."

Here Larico paused to allow this great news to sink into the minds of his hearers, and I thought to myself that when I died I would choose to be gathered to any bosom rather than to that of the Sun, which put me in mind of hell. Then he went on:

"Rumours have reached me, the Inca, that you, Huaracha, Chief of the Chancas, are making ready to wage war upon my Empire. It was to test these rumours, although I did not believe them, that a while ago I sent an embassy to ask your only child, the lady Quilla in marriage to the Prince Urco, promising, since he has no sister whom he may wed and since on the mother's side she, your daughter, has the holy Inca blood in her veins, that she should become his *Coya*, or Queen, and the mother of him who shall succeed to the throne."

"The embassy came, and received my answer, O Inca," said Huaracha.

"Yes, and the answer was that the Lady Quilla should be given in marriage to the Prince Urco, but as she was absent on a visit, this could not happen until she returned. But since then, O Huaracha, more rumours have reached me that you still prepare for war and seek to make alliances among my subjects, tempting them to rebel against me. Therefore I am here myself to lead away the Lady Quilla and to deliver her to the Prince Urco."

"Why did not the Prince Urco come in person, O Inca?"

"For this reason, Huaracha, from whom I desire

to hide nothing. If the Prince had come, you might have set a trap for him and killed him, who is the hope of the Empire."

"So I might for you, his father, O Inca."

"Aye, I know it, but what would that avail you while the Prince sits safe at Cuzco ready to assume the Fringe? Also I am old and care not when or how I die, whose work is done. Moreover few would desire to anger the gods by the murder of an aged guest, and therefore I visit you sitting here in the midst of your armies with but a handful of followers, trusting to your honour and to my father the Sun, to protect me. Now answer me—will you give the hand of your daughter to my son and thereby make alliance with me, or will you wage war upon my empire and be destroyed, you and your people together?"

Here Upanqui, who hitherto had been listening in silence to the words of Larico, spoken on his behalf, broke in saying:

"Yes, yes, that is right, only make him understand that the Inca will be his over-lord, since the Inca can have no rivals in all the land."

"My answer is," said Huaracha, "that I will give my daughter in marriage as I have promised, but that the Chancas are a free people and accept no over-lord."

"Foolishness, foolishness!" said Upanqui. "As well might the tree say that it would not bend before the wind. However, you can settle that matter afterwards with Urco, and indeed with your daughter, who will be his queen and is your heiress, for I understand you have no other lawful child. Why talk of war and other troubles when thus your kingdom falls to us by marriage? Now let me see this Lady Quilla who is to become my daughter."

Huaracha, who had listened to all this babble

with a stern set face, turned to Quilla and made a sign. She descended from her chair and advancing, stood before the Inca, a vision of splendour and of beauty, and bowed to him. He stared at her a while, as did all his company, then said :

" So you are the Lady Quilla. A fair woman, a very fair woman and a proud, one who ought to be able to lead Urco aright if anyone can. Well named too after the moon, for the moonlight seems to shine in your eyes, Lady Quilla. Indeed and indeed were I but a score of years younger I should tell Urco to seek another queen and keep you for myself."

Then Quilla spoke for the first time, saying :

" Be it as you will, O Inca. I am promised in marriage to the Child of the Sun and which child is nothing to me."

" Well said, Lady Quilla, and why should I wonder ? Though I grow old they tell me that I am still handsome, a great deal better looking than Urco in fact, who is a rough man and of a coarser type. You ask my wives when you come to Cuzco ; one of them told me the other day that there was no one so handsome in the whole city, and earned a beautiful present for her pretty speech. What is it you say, Larico ? Why are you always interfering with me ? Well, perhaps you are right, and, Lady Quilla, if you are ready, it is time to start. No, no, I thank you, Curaca, but I will not stop for any feasting who desire to be back at my camp before dark, since who knows what may happen to one in the dark in a strange country ? "

Then at last Huaracha grew angry.

" Be it as you will, O Inca," he said, " but know that you offer me a threefold insult. First you refuse the feast that has been made ready for you whereat you were to meet all the notables of my kingdom.

Secondly you give me, who am a king, the title of a petty chief who owns your rule. Thirdly you throw doubts upon my honour, hinting that I may cause you to be murdered in the dark. Now I am minded to say to you, 'Begone from my poor country, Lord Inca, in safety, but leave my daughter behind you.'"

Now at these words I, Hubert, saw the fires of hope burn up in the large eyes of Quilla, as they did in my own heart, for might they not mean that she would escape from Urco after all? But, alas, they were extinguished like a brand that is dipped in water.

"Tush, tush!" said the old dotard, "what a fire-eater are you, friend Huaracha. Know that I never care to eat, except at night; also that the chill of the air after my father the Sun has set, makes my bones ache, and as for titles—take any one you like, except that of Inca."

"Mayhap that is the one I shall take before all is done," broke in the furious Huaracha, who would not be quieted by the councillors whispering in his ears.

It was at this moment that the minister and high-priest, Larico, who had been noting all that passed with an impassive face, said coldly:

"Be not wroth, O King Huaracha, and lay not too much weight upon the idle words of the glorious Inca, since even the gods will doze at times when they are weighed down by the burden of years and the cares of Empire. No affront was meant to you and least of all does the Inca or any one of us, dream that you would tarnish your honour by offering violence to your guests by day or by night. Yet know this, that if, after all that has been sworn, you withhold your daughter, the Lady Quilla, from the house of

Urco who is her lord to be, it will breed instant war, since as soon as word of it comes to Cuzco, which will be within twenty hours, for messengers wait all along the road, the great armies of the Inca that are gathered there will begin to move. Judge then if you have the strength to withstand them, and choose whether you will live on in glory and honour, or bring yourself to death and your people to slavery. Now, King Huaracha, speaking on behalf of Urco, who within some few moons will be Inca, I ask you—will you suffer the Lady Quilla to journey with us to Cuzco and thereby proclaim peace between our peoples or will you keep her here against your oath and hers, and thereby declare war?"

Huaracha sat silent, lost in thought and the old Inca Upanqui began to babble again, saying:

"Very well put, I could not have said it better myself; indeed, I did say it, for this coxcomb of a Larico, who thinks himself so clever just because I made him high-priest of the Sun under me and he is of my blood, is after all nothing but the tongue in my mouth. You don't really want to die, Huaracha, do you, after seeing most of your people killed and your country wasted? For you know that is what must happen. If you do not send your daughter as you promised, within a few hours a hundred thousand men will be marching on you and another hundred thousand gathering behind them. Anyhow please make up your mind one way or another, as I wish to leave this place."

Huaracha thought on a while. Then he descended from his throne and beckoned to Quilla. She came and he led her towards the back part of the pavilion behind and a little to the left of the chair on which I sat where none could hear their talk save me, of whom he seemed to take no note, perhaps because he had forgotten me, or perhaps because he desired that I should know all.

"Daughter," he said in a low voice, "what word? Before you answer remember that if I refuse to send you, now for the first time I break my oath."

"Of such oaths I think little," answered Quilla. "Yet of another thing I think much. Tell me, my father, if the Inca declares war and attacks us, can we withstand his armies?"

"No, Daughter, not until the Yuncas join us for we lack sufficient men. Moreover, we are not ready, nor shall be for another two moons or more."

"Then it stands thus, Father. If I do not go the war will begin, and if I do go it seems that it will be staved off until you are ready, or perhaps for always, because I shall be the peace-offering and it will be thought that I, your heiress, take your kingdom as my marriage portion to be joined to that of the Incas at your death. Is it thus?"

"It is, Quilla. Only then you will work to bring it about that the Land of the Incas shall be joined to the Land of the Chancas, and not that of the Chancas to that of the Incas, so that in a day to come as Queen of the Chancas you shall reign over both of them and your children after you."

Now I, Hubert, watching Quilla out of the corners of my eyes, saw her turn pale and tremble.

"Speak not to me of children," she said, "for I think that there will be none, and talk not of future glories, since for these I care nothing. It is for our people that I care. You swear to me that if I do not go your armies will be defeated and that those who escape the spear will be enslaved?"

"Aye, I swear it by the Moon your mother, also that I will die with my soldiers."

"Yet if I go I leave behind me that which I love,"

here she glanced towards me, "and give myself to shame, which is worse than death. Is that your desire, my Father?"

"That is not my desire. Remember, Daughter, that you were party to this plan, aye, that it sprang from your far-seeing mind. Still, now that your heart has changed I would not hold you to your bargain, who desire most of all things to see you happy at my side. Choose therefore, and I obey. On your head be it."

"What shall I say, O Lord, whom I saved from the Sea?" asked Quilla in a piercing whisper, but without turning her head towards me.

Now an agony took hold of me for I knew that what I bade her, that she would say and that perchance upon my answer hung the fate of all this great Chanca people. If she went they would be saved, if she remained perchance she would be my wife if only for a while. For the Chancas I cared nothing and for the Quichuas I cared nothing, but Quilla was all that remained to me in the world and if she went, it was to another man. I would bid her bide. And yet—and yet, if her case were mine and the fate of England hung upon my breath, what then?

"Be swift," she whispered again.

Then I spoke, or something spoke through me, saying:

"Do what honour bids you, O Daughter of the Moon, for what is love without honour? Perchance both shall still be yours at last."

"I thank you, Lord, whose heart speaks as my heart," she whispered for the third time, then lifting her head and looking Huaracha in the eyes, said:

"Father, I go, but that I will wed this Urco I do not promise."

CHAPTER VII

The Return of Kari

So Quilla, seated in a golden litter and accompanied by maidens as became her rank, soon was borne away in the train of the Inca Upanqui, leaving me desolate. Before she went, under pretence of bidding me farewell, none denying her, she gained private speech with me for a little while.

" Lord and Lover," she said, " I go to what fate I know not, leaving you to what fate I know not, and as your lips have said, it is right that I should go. Now I have something to ask of you—that you will not follow me as I know it is in your heart to do. But last night I prayed of you to dog my steps and wherever I might go to keep close to me, that the knowledge of your presence might be my comfort. Now my mind is different. If I must be married to this Urco, I would not have you see me in my shame. And if I escape marriage you cannot help me, since I may only do so by death or by taking refuge where you cannot come. Also I have another reason."

" What reason, Quilla ? " I asked.

" This ; I ask that you will stop with my father and give him your help in the war that must come. I would see this Urco crushed, but without that help I am sure that the Chancas and the Yuncas are too weak to overthrow the Inca might. Remember that if I escape marriage thus only can you hope to win me, namely by the defeat and death of Urco. Say then that you will stay here and help to lead the Chanca armies, and say it swiftly, since that dotard, Upanqui, frets to be gone. Hark! his messengers call and search; my women can hold them back no more."

"I will stay," I answered hoarsely.

"I thank you, and now farewell, till in life or death we meet again. Thoughts come to my mind which I have no time to utter."

"To mine also, Quilla, and here is one of them. You know the man who was with me on the island. Well, he is more than he seems."

"So I guessed, but where is he now?"

"In hiding, Quilla. If you should chance to find him, bear in mind that he is an enemy of Urco and one not friendless; also that he loves me after his fashion. Trust him, I pray you. Urco is not the only one of the Inca blood, Quilla."

She glanced at me quickly and nodded her head. Then without more words, for officers were pressing towards us, she drew a ring off her finger, a thick and ancient golden ring on which were cut what looked like flowers, or images of the sun, and gave it to me.

"Wear this for my sake. It is very old and has a story of true love that I have no time to tell," she said.

I took it and in exchange passed to her that ancient ring which my mother had given to me, the ring that had come down to her with the sword Wave-Flame, saying:

"This too is old and has a story; wear it in memory of me."

Then we parted and presently she was gone.

I stood watching her litter till it vanished in the evening haze. Then I turned to go to find myself face to face with Huaracha.

"Lord-from-the-Sea," he said, "you have played a man's—or a god's—part to-day. Had you bidden my daughter bide here, she would have done so for love of you and the Chanca people must have been destroyed, for as that old Inca or his spokesman told us, the breaking of my oath would have been taken as a declaration of instant war. Now we have breathing time and in the end things may go otherwise."

"Yes," I answered, "but what of Quilla and what of me?"

"I know not your creed or what with you is honour, White Lord, but among us whom perhaps you think of small account, it is thought and held that there are times when a man or a woman, especially if they be highly placed, must do sacrifice for the good of the many who cling to them for guidance and for safety. This you and my daughter have done and therefore I honour both of you."

"To what end is the sacrifice made?" I asked bitterly. "That one people may struggle for dominion over another people, no more."

"You are mistaken, Lord. Not for victory or to increase my dominions do I desire to war upon the Inca, but because unless I strike I shall presently be struck, though for a little while this marriage might hold back the blow. Alone in the midst of the vast territories over which the Incas rule, the Chancas stem their tide of conquest and remain free amongst many nations of slaves. Therefore for ages these Incas, like those who ruled before them at Cuzco, have sworn to destroy us, and Urco has sworn it above all."

"Urco might die or be deposed, Huaracha."

"If so another would put on the Fringe and be vowed to the ancient policy that does not change from generation to generation. Therefore I must fight or perish with my people. Hearken, Lord-from-the-Sea! Stay here with me and become as my brother and a general of my armies, for where will they not follow when you lead, who are held to be a god? Then if we conquer, in reward, from a brother you shall become a son, and to you after me I swear shall pass the Chanca crown. Moreover, to you, if she can be saved, I will give in marriage, her whom you love. Think before you refuse. I know not whence you come, but this I know that you can return thither no more, unless, indeed, you are a spirit. Here your lot is cast till death. Therefore make it glorious. Perchance you might fly to the Inca and there become a marvel and a show, furnished with gold and palaces and lands, but always you would be a servant, while I offer to you a crown and the rule of a people great and free."

"I care nothing for crowns," I answered sighing. "Still, such was Quilla's prayer, perchance the last that ever she will make to me. Therefore I accept and will serve you and your cause, that seems noble, faithfully to the end, O Huaracha."

Then I stretched out my hand to him and so our compact was sealed.

On the very next day my work began. Huaracha made me known to his captains, commanding them to obey me in all things, which, looking on me as half divine, they did readily enough.

Now, of soldiering I knew little who was a seaman bred, yet as I had learned, a man of the English race in however strange a country he finds himself can make a path there to his ends.

Moreover, in London I had heard much talk of armies and their ordering and often watched troops at their exercise; also I knew how to handle bow and sword, and was accustomed to the management of men. So putting all these memories together, I set myself to the task of turning a mob of half-savage fellows with arms into an ordered host. I created regiments and officered them with the best captains that I could find, collecting in each regiment so far as possible, the people of a certain town or district. These companies I drilled and exercised, teaching them to use such weapons as they had to the best purpose.

Also I caused them to shape stronger bows on the model of my own with which I had shot the three Frenchmen far away at Hastings that, as it was said, once had been the battle-bow of Thorgrimmer the Norseman my ancestor, as the sword Wave-Flame was his battle-sword. When these Chancas saw how far and with what a good aim I could shoot with this bow, they strove day and night to learn to equal me, though it is true they never did. Also I bettered their body-armour of quilting by setting sheets of leather (since in that country there is no iron), taken from the hides of wild animals and of their long-haired native sheep, between the layers of cotton. Other things I did also, too many and long to record.

The end of it was that within three months Huaracha had an army of some fifty thousand men who, if not well trained, still kept discipline, and could move in regiments; who knew also how to shoot with their bows and to use their copper-headed spears and axes of that metal, or of hard stone, to the best purpose.

Then at length came the Yuncas to join us, thirty or forty thousand of them, wild fellows and brave enough, but undisciplined. With these I could do little since time was lacking, save send some of the officers whom I had trained, to teach their chiefs and captains what they were able.

Thus I was employed from dawn till dark and often after it, in talk with Huaracha and his generals, or in drawing plans with ink that I found a means to make, upon parchment of sheepskin and noting down numbers and other things, a sight at which these people who knew nothing of writing, marvelled very much. Great were my labours, yet in them I found more happiness than I had known since that fatal day when I, the rich London merchant, Hubert of Hastings, had stood before the altar of St. Margaret's church with Blanche Aleys. Indeed, every cranny of my time and mind being thus filled with things finished or attempted, I forgot my great loneliness as an alien in a strange land, and once more became as I had been when I trafficked in the Cheap.

But toil as I would, I could not forget Quilla. During the day I might mask her memory in its urgent business, but when I lay down to rest she seemed to come to me as a ghost might do and to stand by my bed, looking at me with sad and longing eyes. So real was her presence that sometimes I began to believe that she must have died to the world and was in truth a ghost, or else that she had found the power to throw her soul afar, as it is said certain of these Indian folk, if so they should be called, can do. At least there she seemed to be while I remained awake and afterwards when I slept, and I know not whether her strange company joyed or pained me more. For alas! she could not talk to me, or tell me how it fared with her, and, to speak truth, now that she was the wife of another man, as I supposed, I desired to forget her if I could.

For of Quilla no word reached us. We heard that she had come safely to Cuzco and after that nothing more. Of her marriage there was no tidings; indeed she seemed to have vanished away. Certain of Huaracha's spies reported to him, however, that the great army which Urco had gathered to attack him had been partly disbanded, which seemed to show that the Inca no longer prepared for immediate war.

Only then what had happened to Quilla, whose person was the price of peace? Perhaps she was hidden away during the preparations for her nuptials; at least I could think of nothing else, unless indeed she had chosen to kill herself or died naturally.

Soon, however, all news ceased, for Huaracha shut his frontiers, hoping that thus Urco might not learn that he was gathering armies.

At length, when our forces were almost ready to march, Kari came, Kari whom I thought lost.

One night when I was seated at my work by lamplight, writing down numbers upon a parchment, a shadow fell across it, and looking up I saw Kari standing before me, travel-worn and weary, but Kari without doubt, unless I dreamed.

"Have you food, Lord?" he asked while I stared at him. "I need it and would eat before I speak."

I found meat and native beer and brought them to him, for it was late and my servants were asleep, waiting till he had filled himself, for by this time I had learned something of the patience of these people. At length he spoke, saying:

"Huaracha's watch is good, and to pass it I must journey far into the mountains and sleep three nights without food amid their snows."

"Whence come you?" I asked.

"From Cuzco, Lord."

"Then what of the Lady Quilla? Does she still live? Is she wed to Urco?"

"She lives, or lived fourteen days ago, and she is not wed. But where she is no man may ever come. You have looked your last on the Lady Quilla, Lord."

"If she lives and is unwed, why?" I asked, trembling.

"Because she is numbered among the Virgins of

the Sun our Father, and therefore inviolate to man. Were I the Inca, though I love you and know all, should you attempt to take her, yes, even you, I would kill you if I could, and with my own sword. In our land, Lord, there is one crime which has no forgiveness, and that is to lay hands upon a Virgin of the Sun. We believe, Lord, that if this is done, great curses will fall upon our country, while as for the man who works the crime, before he passes to eternal vengeance, he and all his house and the town whence he came, must perish utterly, and that false virgin who has betrayed our father, the Sun, must die slowly and by fire."

"Has this ever chanced?" I asked.

"History does not tell it, Lord, since none have been so wicked, but such is the law."

I thought to myself that it was a very evil law, and cruel; also that I would break it if I found opportunity, but made no answer, knowing when to be silent and that I might as well strive to move a mountain from its base, as to turn Kari from the blindness of his folly bred of a false faith. After all, could I blame him, seeing that we held the same of the sacredness of nuns and, it was said, killed them if they broke their vows?

"What news, Kari?" I asked.

"Much, Lord. Hearken. Disguised as a peasant who had come into this country to barter wool from a village near to Cuzco, I joined myself to the train of the Inca Upanqui, among whose lords I found a friend who had loved me in past years and kept my secret as he was bound to do, having passed into the brotherhood of knights with me while we were lads. Through him, in place of a man who was sick, I became one of the bearers of the Lady Quilla's litter and thus was always about her and at times had speech with her in secret, for she knew me again notwithstanding my disguise and uniform. So I became one of those who waited on her when she ate and noted all that passed.

"After the first day the Inca Upanqui, he who is my father and whose lawful heir I am, although he discarded me for Urco and believes me dead, made it a habit to take his food in the same tent or rest-house chamber as the Lady Quilla. Lord, being very clever, she set herself to charm him, so that soon he began to dote upon her, as old, worn-out men sometimes do upon young and beautiful women. She, too, pretended to grow fond of him and at last told him in so many words that she grieved it was not he that she was to marry whose wisdom she hung upon, in place of a prince who, she heard, was not wise. This, she said because she knew well that the Inca would never marry any more and indeed had lived alone for years. Still, being flattered, he told her it was hard that she should be forced to wed one to whom she had no mind, whereon she prayed him, even with tears, to save her from such a fate. At last he vowed that he would do so by setting her among the Virgins of the Sun on whom no man may look. She thanked him and said that she would consider the matter, since, for reasons that you may guess, Lord, she did not desire to become a Virgin of the Sun and to pass the rest of the days in prayer and the weaving of the Inca's garments.

"So it went on until when we were a day's march from Cuzco, Urco, my brother, came to meet his promised bride. Now, Urco is a huge man and hideous, one whom none would believe to have been born of the Inca blood. Coarse he is, and dissolute, given to drink also, though a great fighter and brave in battle, and quick-brained when he is sober. I was present when they met and I saw the Lady Quilla shiver and turn pale at the sight of him, while he on his part, devoured her beauty with his eyes. They spoke but few words together, yet before these were done, he told her it was his will that they should be wed at once on the day after she came to Cuzco, nor would he listen to the Inca Upanqui who said, being cunning and wishing to gain time, that due preparation must be made for so great a business.

"Thereupon Urco grew angry with his father, who both fears and loves him, and answered that, being almost Inca, this matter was one which he would settle for himself. So fierce was he that Upanqui became afraid and went away. When they were alone Urco strove to embrace Quilla, but she fled from him and hid with her maidens in a private place. After this, at the feast Urco took much drink according to his custom and was led away to sleep by his lords. Then Quilla waited upon the Inca and said:

"'O Inca, I have seen the Prince and I claim your promise to save me from him. O Inca, abandoning all thought of marriage, I will become the bride of our Father the Sun.'

"Upanqui, who was wroth with Urco because he had crossed his will, swore by the Sun itself that he would not fail her, come what might, since Urco should learn that he was not yet Inca."

"What happened then?" I asked, staring him in the eyes.

"After this, Lord, when we were halted before making the state entry into Cuzco, for a moment the Lady Quilla found opportunity for private speech with me. This is what she said:

"'Tell my father, King Huaracha, that I have fulfilled his oath, but that I cannot marry Urco. Therefore I seek refuge in the arms of the Sun, as the oracle Rimac foretold that I should do, having to choose between this fate and that of death. Tell my Lord-from-the-Sea what has befallen me and bid him farewell from me. Still say to him that he must keep a good heart, since I do not believe that all is ended between us.'

"Then we were parted and I saw her no more."

"And did you hear no more, Kari?"

"I heard much, Lord. I heard that when Urco learned that the Lady Quilla had vanished away into the House of Virgins, whither he might not come, and that he was robbed of the bride whom he desired, he grew mad with rage. Indeed, of this I saw something myself. Two days later, with thousands of others I was in the great square in front of the Temple of the Sun, where the Inca Upanqui sat in state upon a golden throne to receive the praise of his people upon his safe return after his long and hard journey, and as some reported, to lay down his Incaship in favour of Urco; also to tell the people that the danger of war with the Chancas had passed away. Scarcely had the ceremony begun when Urco appeared at the head of a number of lords and princes of the Inca blood, who are of his clan, and I noted that he was drunk and furious. He advanced to the foot of the throne, almost without obeisance, and shouted:

"'Where is the Lady Quilla, daughter of Huaracha, who is promised to me in marriage, Inca? Why have you hidden her away, Inca?'

"'Because the Sun, our Father, has claimed her as his bride and has taken her to dwell in his holy house, where never again may the eyes of man behold her, Prince!' answered Upanqui.

"'You mean that robbing me, you have taken her for yourself, Inca,' shouted Urco again.

"Then Upanqui stood up and swore by the Sun that this was not so and that what he had done was done by the decree of the god and at the prayer of the Lady Quilla, who having seen Urco, had declared that either she would be wed to the god or die by her own hand, which would bring the vengeance of the Sun upon the people.

"Then Urco went mad. He raved at the Inca and while all present shivered with fear, he cursed the Sun our Father, yes, even when a cloud came up in the clear sky and veiled the face of the god, heedless of the omen, he continued his curses and blasphemy. Moreover, he said that soon he would be Inca and that then, if he must tear the House of Virgins stone from stone, as Inca he would drag forth the Lady Quilla and make her his wife.

"Now at these words Upanqui stood up and rent his robes.

"'Must my ears be outraged with such blasphemies?' he cried. 'Know, son Urco, that this day I was minded to take off the Royal Fringe and to set it on your head, crowning you Inca in my place while I withdrew to pass the remainder of my days at Yucay in peace and prayer. My will is changed. This I shall not do. My life is not done and strength returns to my mind and body. Here I stay as Inca. Now I see that I am punished for my sin.'"

"'What sin?' shouted Urco.

"'The sin of setting you before my eldest lawful son, Kari, whose wife you stole; Kari, whom also it is said you poisoned and who at least has vanished and is doubtless dead.'

"Now, Lord, when I, Kari, heard this my heart melted in me and I was minded to declare myself to Upanqui my father. But while I weighed the matter for a moment, knowing that if I did so, such words as these might well be my last since Urco had many of his following present, who perhaps would fall upon and kill me, suddenly my father Upanqui fell forward in a swoon. His lords and physicians bore him away.

Urco followed and presently the multitude departed this way and that. Afterwards we were told that the Inca had recovered but must not be disturbed for many days."

"Did you hear more of Quilla, Kari?"

"Yes, Lord," he answered gravely. "It was commonly reported that, through some priestess in his pay, Urco had poisoned her, saying that as she had chosen the Sun as husband, to the Sun she should go."

"Poisoned her!" I muttered, wellnigh falling to the ground. "Poisoned her!"

"Aye, Lord," but be comforted for this was added —that she who gave the poison was taken in the act by her who is named the Mother of the Virgins, and handed over to the women who cast her into the den of serpents, where she perished, screaming that it was Urco who had forced her to the deed."

"That does not comfort me, man. What of Quilla? Did she die?"

"Lord, it is said not. It is said that the Mother of the Virgins dashed away the cup as it touched her lips. But this is said also, that some of the poison flew into her eyes and blinded her."

I groaned, for the thought of Quilla blinded was horrible.

"Again take comfort, Lord, since perchance she may recover from this blindness. Also I was told, that although she can see nothing, her beauty is not marred; that the venom indeed has made her eyes seem larger and more lovely even than they were before."

I made no answer, who feared that Kari was deceiving me or perhaps was himself deceived and that Quilla was dead. Presently he continued his story in the same quiet, even voice, saying:

"Lord, after this I sought out certain of my

friends who had loved me in my youth and my mother also while she lived, revealing myself to them. We made plans together, but before aught could be done in earnest, it was needful that I should see my father, Upanqui. While I was waiting till he had recovered from the stroke that fell upon him, some spy betrayed me to Urco, who searched for me to kill me and wellnigh found me. The end of it was that I was forced to fly, though before I did so, many swore themselves to my cause who would escape from the tyranny of Urco. Moreover, it was agreed that if I returned with soldiers at my back, they and their followers would come out to join me to the number of thousands, and help me to take my own again so that I may be Inca after Upanqui, my father. Therefore I have come back here to talk with you and Huaracha

" Such is my tale."

CHAPTER VIII

THE FIELD OF BLOOD

WHEN on the morrow Huaracha, King of the Chancas, heard all this story and that Urco had given poison to his daughter Quilla, who, if she still lived at all, did so, it was said, as a blind woman, a kind of madness took hold of him.

"Now let war come; I will not rest or stay," he cried, "till I see this hound, Urco, dead and hang up his skin stuffed with straw as an offering to his own god, the Sun."

"Yet it was you, King Huaracha, who sent the Lady Quilla to this Urco for your own purposes," said Kari in his quiet fashion.

"Who and what are you that reprove me?" asked Huaracha turning on him. "I only know you as the servant or slave of the White Lord from the Sea, though it is true I have heard stories concerning you," he added.

"I am Kari, the firstborn lawful son of Upanqui and by right heir to the Inca throne, no less, O Huaracha. Urco my brother robbed me of my wife, as through the folly of my father, upon whose heart Urco's mother worked, he had already robbed me of my inheritance. Then, to make sure, he strove to poison me as he has poisoned your daughter, with a poison that would make me mad and incapable of rule, yet leave me living—because he feared lest the curse of the Sun should fall upon him if he murdered me. I recovered from that bane and wandered to a far land. Now I have returned to take my own, if I am able. All that I say I can prove to you."

For a while Huaracha stared at him astonished, then said:

"And if you prove it, what do you ask of me, O Kari?"

"The help of your armies to enable me to overthrow Urco, who is very strong, being the Commander of the Quichua hosts."

"And if your tale be true and Urco is overthrown, what do you promise me in return?"

"The independence of the Chanca people, who otherwise must soon be destroyed, and certain other added territories which you covet, while I am Inca."

"And with this my daughter, if she still lives?" asked Huaracha looking at him.

"Nay," replied Kari firmly. "As to the Lady Quilla I promise nothing. She has vowed herself to my Father the Sun, and what I have already told the Lord Hurachi here, who loves her I tell you. Henceforward no man may look upon her, who is the Bride of the Sun, for if I suffered this, certainly the curse of the Sun would fall upon me and upon my people. He who lays a hand upon her I will strive to slay"—here he looked at me with meaning—"because I must or be accurst. Take all else, but let the Lady Quilla be. What the Sun has, he holds for ever."

"Perhaps the Moon, her mother, may have something to say in that matter," said Huaracha gloomily. "Still, let it lie for the while."

Then they fell to discussing the terms of their alliance and, when it came to battle, what help Kari could bring from among those who clung to him in Cuzco."

After this Huaracha took me to another chamber, where we debated the business.

"This Kari, if he be Kari himself, is a bigot," he said, "and if he has his way, neither you nor I will ever set eyes on Quilla again, because to him it is sacrilege. So, what say you?"

I answered that it would be best to make an alliance with Kari, whom I knew to be honest and no Pretender, since without his help I did not think that it would be possible to defeat the armies of the People of the Incas. For the rest we must trust to chance, making no promises as to Quilla.

"If we did they would avail little," said Huaracha, "seeing that without doubt she is dead and only vengeance remains to us. There is more poison in Cuzco, White Lord!"

Eight days later we were marching on Cuzco, a great host of us, numbering at least forty thousand Chancas and twenty-five thousand of the rebellious Yuncas, who had joined our standard.

On we marched by the great road over mountains and across plains, driving with us numberless herds of the native sheep for food, but meeting no man, since so soon as we were out of the territory of the Chancas all fled at our approach. At length one night we camped upon a hill named Carmenca and saw beneath us at a distance, the mighty city of Cuzco standing in a valley through which a river ran. There it was with its huge fortresses built of great blocks of stone, its temples, its palaces, its open squares and its countless streets bordered by low houses. Moreover, beyond and around it we saw other things, namely the camps of a vast army dotted with thousands of white tents.

"Urco is ready for us," said Kari to me grimly as he pointed to these tents.

We camped upon the hill Carmenca and that night there came to us an embassy which spoke in the names of Upanqui and Urco, as though they reigned jointly. This embassy of great lords who all wore discs of gold in their ears, asked us what was our purpose. Huaracha answered—to avenge the murder of the Lady Quilla, his daughter, that he heard had been poisoned by Urco.

"How know you that she is dead?" asked the spokesman.

"If she is not dead," replied Huaracha, "show her to us."

"That may not be," replied the spokesman, "since if she lives, it is in the House of the Virgins of the Sun, whence none come out and where none go in. Hearken, O Huaracha. Go back whence you came, or the countless army of the Incas will fall upon you and destroy you, you and your handful together."

"That is yet to be seen," answered Huaracha, and without more words the embassy withdrew.

That night also men crept into our camp secretly, who were of the party of Kari. Of Quilla they seemed to know nothing, for none spoke of those over whom the veil of the Sun had fallen. They told us, however, that the old Inca, Upanqui, was still in Cuzco and had recovered somewhat from his sickness. Also they said that now the feud between him and Urco was bitter, but that Urco had the upper hand and was still in command of the armies. These armies, they declared, were immense and would fight us on the morrow, adding however, that certain regiments of them who were of the party of Kari, would desert to us in the battle. Lastly they said that there was great fear in Cuzco, since none knew how that battle would end, which was understood by all to be one for the dominion of Tavantinsuyu.

They had nothing more to say except that they prayed the Sun for our success to save them from the tyranny of Urco. This prince, it appeared, suspected their conspiracy, for now the rumour that Kari lived was everywhere, and having obtained the names of some who were connected with it through his spies, he pursued them with murder and sudden death. They were poisoned at their food; they were stabbed as they walked through the streets at night; their wives, if young and fair, vanished away, as they believed into the houses of those who desired them; even their children were kidnapped, doubtless to become the servants of whom they knew not. They had complained of these things to the old Inca Upanqui, but without avail, since in such matters he was powerless before Urco who had command of the armies. Therefore they would even welcome the triumph of Huaracha, which meant that Kari would become Inca if with lessened territory.

Before they departed to play their parts, Kari brought them before me, who in their foolishness they worshipped, believing me to be in truth a god. Then he told them to have no fear, since I would command the armies of Huaracha in the battle.

Having surveyed the ground while the light lasted, for the most of that night, together with Huaracha and Kari, I toiled, making plans for the great fight that was to come. All being ready, I lay down to sleep awhile, wondering whether it were the last time I should do so upon the earth and, to tell the truth, not caring over much who, believing that Quilla was dead, had it not been for my sins which weighed upon me with none to whom I might confess them, should have been glad to leave the world and its troubles for whatever might lie beyond, even if it were but sleep.

There comes a time to most men when above everything they desire rest, and now that hour was with me, the exiled and the desolate. Here in this strange country and among these alien people I had found one soul which was akin to mine, that of a beautiful woman who loved me and whom I had come to love and desire. But what was the end of it? Owing to the necessities of statecraft and her own nobleness, she had been separated from me and although, as it would seem, she had as yet escaped defilement, was spirited away into the temple of some barbarous worship where I was almost sure death had found her. At the best she was blinded, and where she lay in her darkness no man might come because of the superstitions of these folk. Even if Kari became Inca, it would not help me or her, should she still live, since he was the fiercest bigot of them all and swore that he would kill me, his friend, rather than that I should touch her, the vowed to his false gods.

Or perhaps, through the priests, to save himself such sorrow, he would kill her. At the least, dead or not, she was lost to me, while I—utterly alone—must fight for a cause in which I had but one concern, to bring some savage prince to his end because of his crime against Quilla. And, if things went well and this chanced, what of the Future? Of what use to me were rewards that I did not want, and the worship of the vulgar which I hated? Rather would I have lived out my life as the humblest fisherman on Hastings beach, than be made a king over these glittering barbarians with their gold and gems which could buy nothing that I needed, not even a Book of Hours to feed my soul, or the sound of the English tongue to comfort my empty heart.

At length I fell asleep and as it seemed but a few minutes later, though really six hours had gone by, was awakened by Kari, who told me that the dawn was not far off and came to help me to buckle on my armour. Then I went forth and together with Huaracha arranged our army for battle. Our plan was to advance from our rising ground across a great plain beneath us which was called Xaqui, but afterwards became known by the name of Yahuar-pampa, or Field of Blood.

This plain lay between us and the city of Cuzco, and my thought was that we would march or fight our way across it and rush into the city which was unwalled, and there amidst its streets and houses await the attack of the Inca hosts that were encamped upon its further side, for thus protected by their walls we hoped that we should be more equal to them. Yet things happened otherwise, since with the first light, without which we did not dare to move over unknown ground, we perceived that during the darkness the Inca armies had moved round and through the town and were gathered by the ten thousand in dense battalions upon the further side of the plain.

Now we took counsel together and in the end decided not to attack as we had proposed, but to await their onslaught on the rocky ridge up which they must climb. So we commanded that our army, which was marshalled in three divisions, a breast and two wings with the Yuncas as a reserve behind, should eat and make ready. In the centre of our main division which numbered some fifteen thousand of the Chanca troops, and a little in front of it, was a low long hill upon the highest point of which I took my place, standing upon a rock with a group of captains and messengers behind me and a guard of about a thousand picked men massed upon the slopes and around the hill. From this high point I could see everything and in my glittering armour was visible to all, friends and foes together.

After a pause, during which the priests of the

Chancas and of the Yuncas behind us sacrificed sheep to the moon and the many other gods they worshipped, and those of the Quichuas, as I could see from my rock, made prayers and offerings to the rising sun, with a mighty shouting the Inca hosts began to advance across the plain towards us. Reckoning them with my eye I saw that they outnumbered us by two or three to one; indeed their hordes seemed to be countless and always more of them came on behind from the dim recesses of the city. Divided into three great armies they crept across the plain, a wild and gorgeous spectacle, the sunlight shining upon the forest of their spears and on their rich barbaric uniforms.

A furlong or more away they halted and took counsel, pointing to me with their spears as though they feared me. We stood quite still, though some of our generals urged that we should charge, but this I counselled Huaracha not to do, who desired that the Quichuas should break their strength upon us. At length some word was given; the splendid "rainbow Banner" of the Incas was unfurled and, still divided into three armies with a wide stretch of plain between each of them, they attacked, yelling like all the fiends of hell.

Now they had reached us and there began the most terrible battle that was told of in the history of that land. Wave after wave of them rolled up against us but our battalions, which I had not trained in vain, stood like rocks and slew and slew and slew till the dead could be counted by the thousand. Again and again they strove to storm the hill on which I stood, hoping to kill me, and each time we beat them back. Picking out their generals I loosed shaft after shaft from my long bow, and seldom did I miss, nor could their cotton-quilted armour turn those bitter arrows.

"*The shafts of the god! The shafts of the god!*" they cried, and shrank back from before me.

There appeared a man with a yellow fillet on his head and a robe that was studded with precious stones; a huge man with great limbs and flaming eyes; a loose-mouthed, hideous man who wielded a big axe of copper and carried a bow longer than any I had seen in that land. Hooking the axe to his belt, he set an arrow on the bow and let drive at me. It sped true and struck me full upon the breast, only to shatter on the good French mail, which copper could not pierce.

Again he shot and this time the arrow glanced from my helm. Then I drew on him and my shaft, that I had aimed at his head, cut the fringe about his brow and carried it far away. At this sight a groan went up from the lords about him, and one cried:

"An omen, O Urco, an evil omen!"

"Aye," he shouted, "for the White Wizard who shot the arrow."

Dropping the bow, he rushed up the hill at me roaring, axe aloft and followed by his company. He smote and I caught the blow upon my shield, and striking back with Wave-Flame, shore through the shaft of the axe that he had lifted to guard his head as though it had been made of reed, aye, and through the quilted cotton on his shoulder strengthened with strips of gold, and to the bone beneath.

Then a man slipped past me. It was Kari, striking at Urco with Deleroy's sword. They closed and rolled down the slope locked in each other's arms. What chanced after this, I do not know, for others rushed in and all grew confused, but presently Kari limped back somewhat shaken and bleeding, and I caught sight of Urco, little hurt, as it seemed, amidst his lords at the bottom of the slope.

At this moment I heard a great shouting and looking round, saw that the Quichuas had broken through our left and were slaughtering many, while the rest fled, also that our right was wavering. I sent messengers to Huaracha, bidding him call up the Yunca rearguard. They were slow in coming and I began to fear that all was lost, for little by little, the hordes of the men of Cuzco were surrounding us.

Then it was that Kari, or some with him, lifted a banner that had been wrapped upon a pole, a blue banner upon which was embroidered a golden sun. At the sight of it there was tumult in the Inca ranks, and presently a great body of men, five or six thousand of them that had seemed to be in reserve, ran forward shouting, "*Kari! Kari!*" and fell upon those who were pursuing our shattered left, breaking them up and dispersing them. Also at last the Yuncas came up and drove back the regiments that assailed our right, while from Urco's armies there rose a cry of "Treachery!"

Trumpets blew and the Inca host, gathering itself together and abandoning its dead and wounded, drew back sullenly on to the plain, and there halted in three bodies as before, though much lessened in number.

Huaracha appeared, saying:

"Strike, White Lord! It is our hour! The heart is out of them."

The signal was given and roaring like a hurricane, presently the Chancas charged. Down the slope they went, I at the head of them with Huaracha on one side and Kari on the other. The swift-footed Chancas outran me who was hindered by my mail. We charged in three masses as we had stood on the ridge, following those open lanes of ground up which the foe had not come, because these were less cumbered with dead and wounded. Presently I saw why those of Cuzco had left these lanes untrod, for of a sudden some warriors, who had outstripped me vanished. They had fallen into a pit covered over with earth laid upon canes, of which the bottom was set with sharp stakes. Others, who were running along the lanes of open ground to right and left, also fell into pits of which there were scores all carefully prepared against the day of battle. With trouble the Chancas were halted, but not before we had lost some hundreds of men. Then we advanced again across that ground over which the Inca host had retreated.

At length we reached their lines, passing through a storm of arrows and there began such a battle as I had never heard of or even dreamed. With axes, stone-headed clubs and spears, both armies fought furiously, and though the Incas still outnumbered us by two to one, because of my training our regiments drove them back. Lord after lord rushed at me with glaring eyes, but my mail turned their copper spears and knives of flint. Oh! Wave-Flame fed full that day and if Thorgrimmer my forefather could see us from his home in Vallhal, surely he must have sworn by Odin that never had he given it such a feast.

The Inca warriors grew afraid and shrank back.

"This Red-Beard from the sea is indeed a god. He cannot be slain!" I heard them cry.

Then Urco appeared, bloody and furious, shouting:

"Cowards! I will show you whether he cannot be slain."

He rushed onward to meet—not me, but Huaracha, who seeing that I was weary, had leapt in front of me. They fought and Huaracha went down and was dragged away by some of his servants.

Now Urco and I were face to face, he wielding a huge copper-headed club with which as my mail could not be pierced, he thought to batter out my life. I caught the blow upon my shield, but so great was the giant's strength that it brought me to my knees. Next second I was up and at him. Shouting, I smote with both hands, for my shield had fallen. The thick, turban-like headdress that Urco wore was severed, cut through as the axe had been, and Wave-Flame bit deep into the skull beneath.

Urco fell like a stunned ox and I sprang upon him to make an end. Then it was that a rope was flung about my shoulders, a noosed rope that was hauled tight. In vain I struggled. I was thrown down; I was seized by a score of hands and dragged away into the heart of Urco's host.

Waiting till a litter could be brought, they set me on my feet again, my arms still bound by the noose that these Indians call "laso," which they know so well how to throw, the red sword Wave-Flame still hanging by its thong from my right wrist. Whilst I stood thus, like a bull in a net, they gathered round, staring at me, not with hate as it seemed to me, but in fear and with reverence. When at length the litter came they aided me to enter it quite gently.

As I did so I looked back. The battle still raged but it seemed to me with less fury than before. It was as though both sides were weary of slaughter, their leaders being fallen. The litter was borne forward, till at length the noise of shouting and tumult grew low. Twisting myself round I peered through the back curtains and saw that the Inca host and that of the Chancas were separating sullenly, neither of them broken since they carried their wounded away with them. It was plain that the battle remained drawn for there was no rout and no triumph.

I saw too that I was entering the great city of Cuzco, where women and children stood at the doors of the houses gazing and, some of them, wringing their hands with tears upon their faces.

Passing down long streets and across a bridge, I came to a vast square round which stood mighty buildings, low, massive and constructed of huge stones. At the door of one of these the litter halted and I was helped to descend. Men beautifully clad in broidered linen led me through a gateway and across a garden where I noted a marvellous thing, namely: that all the plants therein were fashioned of solid gold with silver flowers, or sometimes of silver with golden flowers. Also there were trees on which were perched birds of gold and silver. When I saw this I thought that I must be mad, but it was not so, for having no other use for the precious metals, of which they had so much abundance, thus did these Incas adorn their palaces.

Leaving the golden garden I reached a courtyard surrounded by rooms, to one of which I was conducted. Passing its door, I found myself in a splendid chamber, hung with tapestries fantastically wrought and having cushioned seats, and tables of rich woods, incrusted with precious stones. Here servants or slaves appeared with a chamberlain who bowed deeply and welcomed me in the name of the Inca.

Then, as though I were something half divine, gently enough, they loosed the sword from my wrist, took the long bow from my back, with the few arrows that remained, also my dagger and hid them away. They unbound me, and freeing me from my armour, as I told them how, and the garments beneath, laved me with warm, scented water, rubbed my bruised limbs, and clothed me in wonderful soft garments, also scented and fastened about my middle with a golden belt. This done, food and spiced drinks of their native wine were brought to me in golden vessels. I ate and drank and, being very weary, laid myself down upon one of the couches to sleep. For now I no longer took any thought as to what might befall me, but received all as it came, good and ill together, entrusting my body and soul to the care of God and St. Hubert. Indeed, what else could I do who was disarmed and a prisoner?

When I awoke again, very stiff and bruised, but much refreshed, night had fallen, for hanging lamps were lit about the room. By their light I saw the chamberlain of whom I have spoken, standing before me. I asked him his errand. With many bows he said that if I were rested the Inca Upanqui desired my presence that he might speak with me.

I bade him lead on, and, with others who waited without, he conducted me through a maze of passages into a glorious chamber where everything seemed to be gold, for even the walls were panelled with it. Never had I dreamt of so much gold; indeed the sight of it wearied me till I could have welcomed that of humble brick or wood. At the end of this chamber that was also lit with lamps, were curtains. Presently these were drawn by two beautiful women in jewelled skirts and head-dresses, and behind them on a dais I saw a couch and on the couch the old Inca Upanqui looking feebler than when I had last beheld him in the Chanca city, and very simply clad in a white tunic. Only on his head he wore the red fringe from which I suppose he never parted day or night. He looked up and said:

"Greeting, White-Lord-from-the-Sea. So you have come to visit me after all, though you said that you would not."

"I have been brought to visit you, Inca," I answered.

"Yes, yes, they tell me they captured you in the

battle, though I expect that was by your own will as you had wearied of those Chancas. For what *laso* can hold a god ? "

" None," I answered boldly.

" Of course not, and that you are a kind of god there is no doubt because of the things you did in that battle. They say that the arrows and spears melted when they touched you and that you shot and cut down men by scores. Also that when the Prince Urco tried to kill you, although he is the strongest man in my kingdom, you knocked him over as though he had been a little child and hacked his head open, so that they do not know whether he will live or die. I think I hope he will die, for you see I have quarrelled with him."

I thought to myself that so did I, but I only asked :

" How did the battle end, Inca ? "

" As it began, Lord Hurachi. A great many men have been killed on both sides, thousands and thousands of them, and neither army has the victory. They have drawn back and sit growling at each other like two angry lions which are afraid to fight again. Indeed, I do not want them to fight and now that Urco cannot interfere, I shall put a stop to all this bloodshed, if I am able. Tell me, for you were with him, why does this Huaracha, who I hear is also wounded, want to make war on me with those troublesome Chancas of his ? "

" Because your son, the Prince Urco, has poisoned, or tried to poison his only child, Quilla."

" Yes, yes, I know and it was a wicked thing to do. You see, Lord, what happened was this. That lovely Quilla, who is fairer than her mother the Moon, was to have married Urco. But, Lord, as it chanced on our journey together, although I am old—well, she became enamoured of me, and prayed me to protect her from Urco. Such things happen to women, Lord, whose hearts, when they behold the divine, are apt to carry them away from the vulgar," and he laughed in a silly fashion like the vain old fool that he was.

"Naturally. How could she help it, Inca? Who after seeing you, would wish to turn to Urco?"

"No one, especially as Urco is a coarse and brutal fellow. Well, what was I to do? There are reasons why I do not wish to marry again at my age; indeed I am tired of the sight of women, who want time to pray and think of holy things; also if I had done what she wished, some might have thought that I had behaved badly to Urco. At the same time a woman's heart is sacred and I could not do violence to that of one so sweet and understanding and lovely. So I put her into the House of the Virgins of the Sun where she will be quite safe."

"It seems that she was not safe, Inca."

"No, because that violent man, Urco, being disappointed and very jealous, through some low creature of his, who waited on the Virgins, tried to poison her with a drug which would have made her all swollen and hideous and covered her face with blotches, also perhaps have sent her mad. Luckily one of the matrons, whom we call *Mama-conas*, knocked the cup away before she drank, but some of the horrible poison went into her eyes and blinded her."

"So she lives, Inca."

"Certainly she lives. I have learnt that for myself, because in this country it is not wise to trust what they tell you. You know as Inca I have privileges and although even I do not talk to them, I caused those Virgins of the Sun to be led in front of me, which in strictness, even I ought not to have done. It was a dreary business, Lord Hurachi, for though those Virgins may be so holy, many of them are very old and hideous and of course Quilla as a novice came last in the line conducted by two *Mamaconas* who are cousins of my own. The odd thing is that the poison seems to have made her much more beautiful than before, for her eyes have grown bigger and are glorious, shining like stars seen when there is frost. Well, there she is safe from Urco and every other man, however wicked and impious. But what does this Huaracha want ?"

"He wants his blinded daughter back, Inca."

"Impossible, impossible! Who ever heard of such a thing! Why Heaven and Earth would come together and the Sun, my father, and her husband, would burn us all up. Still, perhaps, we could come to an agreement for Huaracha must have had enough fighting and very likely he will die. Now I am tired of talking about the Lady Quilla and I want to ask you something."

"Speak on, Inca."

Suddenly the old dotard's manner changed; he became quick and shrewd, as doubtless he was in his prime, for this Upanqui had been a great king. At the beginning of our talk the two women of whom I have spoken and the chamberlain had withdrawn to the end of the chamber where they waited with their hands folded, like those who adore before an altar. Still he peered about him to make sure that none were within hearing, and in the end beckoned to me to ascend the dais and sit upon the couch beside him, saying:

"You see I trust you although you are a god from the sea who has been fighting against me. Now hearken. You had a servant with you, a very strange man, who is said also to have come out of the sea, though that I cannot believe since he is like one of our princes. Where is that man?"

"With the army of Huaracha, Inca."

"So I have heard. I heard also that in the battle he hoisted a banner with the sun blazoned on it, and that thereon certain regiments of mine deserted to Huaracha. Now, why did they do that?"

"I understand, Inca, that the kings of this land have many children. Perhaps he might be one of them."

"Ah! You are clever as a god should be. Well, I am a god also and the same thought has come to me, although as a fact I have only had two legitimate sons and the others are of no account. The eldest of these was an able and beautiful prince named Kari, but we quarrelled, and to tell the truth there was a woman in the matter, or rather two women, for Kari's mother fought with Urco's mother whom I loved, because she never scolded me, which the other did. So Urco was named to be Inca after me. Yet that was not enough for him who remained jealous of his brother Kari who outpassed him in all things, save strength of body. They wooed the same beautiful woman and Kari won her, whereon Urco seduced her from him, and afterwards he or someone killed her. At least she died, I forget how. Then the lords of the Inca blood began to turn towards Kari because he was royal and wise, which would have meant civil war when I had been gathered to the Sun. Therefore Urco poisoned him, or so it was rumoured; at any rate he vanished away, and often since than I have mourned him."

"The dead come to life again sometimes, Inca."

"Yes, yes, Lord-from-the-Sea, that happens; the gods who took them away bring them back—and, this servant of yours—they say he is so like to Kari that he might be the same man grown older. And—why did those regiments, all of them officered by men who used to love Kari, go over to Huaracha to-day, and why do rumours run through the land like the wind that springs up suddenly in fine weather? Tell me of this servant of yours and how you found him in the sea."

"Why should I tell you, Inca? Is it because you want to kill him who is so like to this lost Kari of yours?"

"No, no—gods can keep each other's counsel, can they not? It is because I would give—oh! half my godship to know that he is alive. Hark you, Urco wearies me, so much that sometimes I wonder whether he really is my son. Who can tell? There was a certain lord from the coastlands, a hairy giant who, they said, could eat half a sheep at a sitting and break the backs of men in his hands, of whom Urco's mother used to think much. But who can tell? No one except my father the Sun, and he guards his secrets—for the present. At least Urco wearies me with his coarse crimes and his drunkenness, though the army loves him because he is a butcher and liberal. We quarrelled the other day over the small matter of this Lady Quilla, and he threatened me till I grew wroth and said that I would not hand him my crown as I had purposed to do. Yes, I grew wroth and hated him for whose sake I had sinned because his mother bewitched me. Lord-from-the-Sea," here his voice dropped to a whisper, "I am afraid of Urco. Even a god such as I am can be murdered, Lord-from-the-Sea. That is why I will not go to Yucay, for there I might die and none know it, whereas here I still am Inca and a god whom it is sacrilege to touch."

"I understand, but how can I help you, Inca, who am but a prisoner in your palace?"

"No, no, you are only a prisoner in name. At the worst Urco will be sick for a long while, since the physicians say that sword of yours has bitten deep, and during that time all power is mine. Messengers are at your service; you are free to come and go as you will. Bring this servant of yours to my presence, for doubtless he trusts you. I would speak with him, O Lord-from-the-Sea."

"If I should do this, Inca, will the Lady Quilla be given back to her father?"

"Nay, it would be sacrilege. Ask what else you will, lands and rule and palaces and wives—not that. Myself I should not dare to lay a finger on her who rests in the arms of the Sun. What does it matter about this Quilla who is but one fair woman among thousands?"

I thought a while, then answered, "I think it matters much, Inca. Still, that this bloodshed may be stayed, I will do my best to bring him who was my servant to your presence if you can find me the means to come at him, and afterwards we will talk again."

"Yes, I am weary now. Afterwards we will talk again. Farewell, Lord-from-the-Sea."

CHAPTER IX

KARI COMES TO HIS OWN

WHEN I woke on the following morning in the splendid chamber of which I have spoken, it was to find that my armour and arms had been restored to me, and very glad was I to see Wave-Flame again. After I had eaten and, escorted by servants, walked in the gardens, for never could I be left alone, marvelling at the wondrous golden fruits and flowers, a messenger came to me, saying that the *Villaorna* desired speech with me. I wondered who this *Villaorna* might be, but when he entered I saw that he was Larico, that same stern-faced, cunning-eyed lord who had been the spokesman of the Inca when he visited the city of the Chancas. Also I learned that *Villaorna* was his title and meant "Chief priest."

We bowed to each other and all were sent from the chamber, leaving us quite alone.

"Lord-from-the-Sea," he said, "the Inca sends me, his Councillor and blood relative, who am head priest of the Sun, to desire that you will go on an embassy for him to the camp of the Chancas. First, however, it is needful that you should swear by the Sun that you will return thence to Cuzco. Will you do this?"

Now as there was nothing I desired more than to return to Cuzco where Quilla was, I answered that I would swear by my own god, by the Sun and by my sword, unless the Chancas detained me by force. Further I prayed him to set out his business.

He did so in these words :

" Lord, we have come to know, it matters not how, that the man who appeared with you in this land, is no other than Kari, the elder son of the Inca, whom we thought dead. Now it is in the Inca's mind, and in the minds of us, his councillors, to proclaim the Prince Kari as heir to the throne which soon he would be called upon to fill. But the matter is very dangerous, seeing that Urco still commands the army and many of the great lords who are of his mother's House, cling to him, hoping to receive advancement from him when he becomes Inca."

" But, Priest Larico, Urco, they say, is like to die and if so all this trouble will melt like a cloud."

" Your sword bit deep, Lord, but I have it from his physicians that as the brain is uncut he will not die, although he will be sick for a long while. Therefore we must act while he is sick, since it is not lawful to bring about his end, even if he could be come at. Time presses, Lord, for as you have seen, the Inca is old and feeble and his mind is weak. Indeed at times he has no mind, though at others his strength returns to him."

" Which means that I deal with you who are the Chief priest, and those behind you," I said looking him in the eyes.

" That is what it means, Lord. Now hearken while I tell you the truth. After the Inca I am the most powerful man in Tavantinsuyu, indeed for the most part the Inca speaks with my voice although I seem to speak with his. Yet I am in a snare. Heretofore I have supported Urco because there was no other who could become Inca, although he is a brutal and an evil man. Of late, however, since my return from the City of the Chancas I have quarrelled with Urco because he has lost that witch, the Lady Quilla, whom he desires madly and lays the blame on me, and it has come to my knowledge that when he succeeds to the throne, it is his purpose to kill me, which doubtless he will do if he can, or at the least to cast me from my place and power, which is as bad as death. Therefore, I desire to make my peace with Kari, if he will swear to continue me in my office, and this I can only do through you. Bring this peace about, Lord, and I will promise you anything you may wish, even perchance to the Incaship itself, should aught happen to Kari, or should he refuse my offers. I think that the Quichuas might welcome a white God from the Sea who has shown himself so great a general and so brave in battle, and who has knowledge and wisdom more than theirs, to rule over them," he added reflectively. "Only then, Lord, it would be needful to be rid of Kari as well as of Urco."

"To which I would never consent," I replied, "seeing that he is my friend with whom I have shared many dangers. Moreover I do not wish to be Inca."

"Is there then anything else that you wish very much, Lord? A thought came to me, yonder at the City of the Chancas. By the way, how lovely is that Lady Quilla and how royal a woman. It is most strange that she should have turned her mind towards an aged man like Upanqui."

We looked at each other.

"Very strange," I said. "It seems to me sad also that this beauteous Quilla should be immured in a nunnery for life. To tell you the truth, High-priest, since it is not good for man to live alone, rather than that such a thing should have happened, I would have married her myself, to which perchance she might have consented."

Again we looked at each other and I went on:

"I hinted as much to Kari after we heard she was

numbered amongst the Virgins, and asked him whether, should he become Inca, he would take her thence and give her to me."

"What did he answer, Lord?"

"He said that though he loved me like a brother, first he would kill me with his own hand, since such a deed would be sacrilege against the Sun. Last night also the Inca himself said much the same."

"Is it so, Lord? Well, we priests bring up our Incas to think thus. If we did not, where would our power be, seeing that we are the Voice of the Sun upon earth and issue his decrees?"

"But do you always think thus yourselves, O High-priest?"

"Not quite always. There are loopholes in every law of gods or men. For example, I believe I see one in the instance of this Lady Quilla. But before we waste more time in talking—tell me, White Lord, do you desire her, and if so, are you ready to pay me my price? It is that you shall assure to me the friendship of the Prince Kari, should he become Inca, and the continuance of my power and office."

"My answer is that I do desire this lady, O High-priest, and that if I can I will obtain from Kari the promise of what you seek. And now where is the loophole?"

"I seem to remember, Lord, that there is an ancient law which says—that none who are maimed may be the wives of the Sun. It is true that this law applies to them *before* they contract the holy marriage. Still, if the point came up before me as high-priest, I might perhaps find that it applied also to those who were maimed *after* marriage. The case is rare, for which precedents cannot be found if the search be thorough. Now through the wickedness of Urco, as it happens, this Lady Quilla has been blinded, and therefore is no longer perfect in her body. Do you understand ? "

" Quite. But what would Upanqui or Kari say ? The Incas you declare are always bigots and might interpret this law otherwise."

"I cannot tell, Lord, but let us cease from beating bushes. I will help you if I can, if you will help me if *you* can, though I daresay that in the end you, who are not a bigot, must take the law into your own hands, as perhaps the Lady Quilla, who is a moon-worshipper, would be willing to do also."

The finish of it was that this cunning priest and statesman and I made a bargain. If I could win Kari over to his interests, then he swore by the Sun, that he would gain me access to the Lady Quilla and help me to fly with her, if so we both wished, while I on my part swore to plead his cause with Kari. Moreover, as he showed me, there was little fear that either of us would break these oaths since henceforth each lay in the power of the other."

After this we passed on to public matters. I was charged to offer an honourable truce to Huaracha and the Chancas with permission to them to camp their armies in certain valleys near to Cuzco where they would be fed until Peace was declared, which Peace would give them all they needed, namely their freedom and safeguards from attack. For the rest I was to bring Kari and those who had deserted to him on the yesterday, into Cuzco where none would molest them.

Then he went, leaving me happier than I had been since I bade farewell to Quilla. For now at last I saw light, a faint uncertain light, it was true, only to be reached, if reached at all, through many difficulties and dangers, but still light. At last I had found some one in this land of black superstition who was not a bigot, and who, being the High-priest of the Sun, knew too much of his god to fear him or to believe that he would come down to earth and burn it up, should one of the hundreds of his brides seek another husband. Of course this Larico might betray me and Quilla, but I did not think he would, since he had nothing to gain thereby, and might have much to lose, for the reason that I was able, or he thought that I was able, to set Kari against him. At least I could only go forward and trust to fortune, though in fact hitherto she had never shown me favour where woman was concerned.

A while later I was being borne in one of the Inca's own litters, back to the camp of the Chancas, accompanied by an embassy of great lords.

We passed over that dreadful, bloodstained plain where, under a flag of truce, both sides were engaged in burying the thousands of their dead, and came to the ridge whence we had charged on the yester morn. Here sentries stopped us and I descended from my litter. When the Chancas saw me in my armour come back to them alive, they set up a great shouting and presently I and the lords with me were led to the pavilion of King Huaracha.

We found him lying sick upon a couch, for though he showed no wound he had been badly bruised upon the body by a blow from Urco's club and, as I feared, was hurt in the bowels. He greeted me with delight, since he thought that I might have been killed after I was captured, and asked how I came to appear in his camp in the company of our enemies. I told him at once what had chanced and that I was sworn to return to Cuzco when I had done my business. Then the Inca's ambassadors set out their proposals for a truce, and retired, while Huaracha discussed them with his generals and Kari, who also was overjoyed to see me safe.

The end of it was that they were accepted on the terms offered, namely that Huaracha and his army should withdraw to the valleys of which I have spoken, and there camp, receiving all the food they needed until a peace could be offered such as he would be willing to accept. Indeed, the Chancas were glad to agree to this plan for their losses in the battle had been very great and they were in no state to renew the attack upon Cuzco, which was still defended by such mighty hordes of brave warriors fighting for their homes, families and freedom.

So all was agreed on the promise that peace should be made within thirty days or sooner, and that if it were not the war should re-commence.

Then privately, I told Huaracha all that I had learned about Quilla and that I had still hopes of saving her, though what these were I did not tell him. When he had thought, he said that now the fate of Quilla must be left in the hands of the gods and mine, since not even for her could he neglect the opportunity of an honourable peace, seeing that another battle might mean destruction. Also he pointed out that he was hurt and I who had been general under him, was a prisoner and bound by my oath to return to prison, so that the Chancas had lost their leaders.

After this we parted, I promising to work for his cause and to come to see him again, if I might.

These matters finished I went aside with Kari to a place where none could hear us, and there laid before him the offers of Larico, the high-priest, showing him how the case stood. Of Quilla, however, I said nothing to him, though it pained me to keep back part of the truth, even from Kari. Yet, what was I to do, who knew that if I told him all and he became

Inca, or the Inca's acknowledged heir, he would work against me because of his superstitious madness, and perhaps cause Quilla to be killed by the priests, as one whose feet were set in the path of sacrilege? So on this matter I held my peace, nor did he ask me anything concerning Quilla who, I think, wished to hear nothing of that lady and what had befallen her.

When he had learned all, he said:

"This may be a trap, Lord. I do not trust yonder Larico, who has always been my enemy and Urco's friend."

"I think he is his own friend first," I answered, "who knows that if Urco recovers he will kill him, because he has taken the part of your father, Upanqui, in their quarrels, and suspects him."

"I am not sure," said Kari. "Yet something must be risked. Did I not tell you when we were sailing down the English river that we must put faith in our gods, yes, afterwards also, and more than once? And did not the gods save us? Well, now again I trust to my god," and drawing out the image of Pachacamac, which he wore round his neck, he kissed it, then turning, bowed and prayed to the sun.

"I will come with you," he said, when he had finished his devotions, "to live to be Inca, or to die, as the Sun decrees."

So he came and with him some of his friends, captains of those who had deserted to him in the battle. But the five thousand soldiers, or those who were left of them, did not come as yet because they feared lest they should be set upon and butchered by the regiments of Urco.

That night when we were back safe in Cuzco, Kari and the high-priest Larico talked together in secret. Of what passed between them he only told me that they had come to an agreement which satisfied them both. Larico said the same to me when next I saw him, adding:

"You have kept your word and served my turn, Lord-from-the-Sea, therefore I will keep mine and serve yours when the time comes. Yet be warned by me and say nothing of a certain lady to the Prince Kari, since when I spoke a word to him on the matter, hinting that her surrender to her father Huaracha would make peace with him more easy and lasting, he answered that first would he fight Huaracha, and the Yuncas as well, to the last man in Cuzco.

"To the Sun she has gone," he said, "and with the Sun she must stay, lest the curse of the Sun and of Pachacamac, the Spirit above the Sun, should fall on me and all of us."

Larico told me also that, fearing something, the great lords, who were of Urco's party, had borne him away in a litter to a strong city in the mountains about five leagues from Cuzco, escorted by thousands of picked men who would stay in and about that city.

On the next morning I was summoned to wait upon the Inca Upanqui, and went, wearing my armour. I found him in the same great chamber as before, only now he was more royally arrayed and with him were sundry of his high lords of the Inca blood, also certain priests, among them the *Villaorna* Larico.

The old king, who on that day seemed clear in his mind and well, greeted me in his kindly fashion and bade me set out all that had passed between me and Huaracha in the Chanca camp. This I did, only I hid from him how great had been the Chanca losses in the battle and how glad they were to declare a truce and rest.

Upanqui said that the matter should be attended to, speaking in a royal fashion as though it were one of little moment, which showed me how great an emperor he must be. Great he was indeed, seeing that all the broad land of England would have made but one province of his vast dominions, which in every part were filled with people who, unless they chanced to be in rebellion like the Yuncas lived but to do his will.

After this when I thought the audience was ended, a chamberlain advanced to the foot of the throne, and kneeling, said that a suppliant prayed speech with the Inca. Upanqui waved his sceptre, that long staff which I have described, in token that he should be admitted. Then presently up the chamber came Kari arrayed in the tunic and cloak of an Inca prince, wearing in his ear a disc carved with the image of the sun, and a chain of emeralds and gold about his neck. Nor did he come alone, for he was attended by a brilliant band of those lords and captains who had deserted to him on the day of the great battle. He advanced and knelt before the throne.

"Who is this that carries the emblems of the Holy Blood and is clothed like a Prince of the Sun?" asked Upanqui, affecting ignorance and unconcern, though I saw the colour mount to his pale cheeks and the sceptre shake in his withered hand.

"One who is indeed of the holy Inca Blood; one sprung from the purest lineage of the Sun," answered the stately Kari in his quiet voice.

"How then is he named?" asked the Inca again.

"He is named Kari, firstborn son of Upanqui, O Inca."

"Such a son I had once, but he is long dead, or so they told me," said Upanqui in a trembling voice.

"He is not dead, O Inca. He lives and he kneels before you. Urco poisoned him, but the Sun his father recovered him and the Spirit that is above all gods, supported him. The sea bore him to a far land, where he found a white god who befriended and cared for him," here he turned his head towards me. "With this god he returned to his own country and here he kneels before you, O Inca."

"It cannot be," said the Inca. "What sign do you bring who name yourself Kari? Show me the image of the Spirit above the gods that from his childhood for generations has been hung about the neck of the Inca's eldest son, born from the Queen."

Kari opened his robe and drew out that golden effigy of Pachacamac which he always wore.

Upanqui examined it, holding it close to his rheumy eyes.

"It seems to be the same," he said, "as I should know upon whose breast it lay until my first son was born. And yet who can be sure since such things may be copied?"

Then he handed back the image to Kari and after reflecting a while, said:

"Bring hither the Mother of the Royal Nurses."

Apparently this lady was in waiting, for in a minute she appeared before the throne, an old and withered woman with beady eyes.

"Mother," said the Inca, "you were with the *Coya* (that is the Queen) who has been gathered to the Sun, when her boy was born and afterwards nursed him for years. If you saw it, would you know his body again after he has come to middle age?"

"Aye, O Inca."

"How, Mother?"

"By three moles, O Inca, which we women used to call *Yuti*, *Quilla* and *Chasca*" (that is, the Sun, the Moon and the planet Venus), "which were the marks of good fortune stamped by the gods upon the Prince's back between the shoulders, set one above the other."

"Man who call yourself Kari, are you willing that this old crone should see your flesh?" asked Upanqui.

By way of answer Kari with a little smile stripped himself of his broidered tunic and other garments and stood before us naked to the middle. Then he turned his back to the Mother of the Nurses. She hobbled up and searched it with her bright eyes.

"Many scars," she muttered, "scars in front and scars behind. This warrior has known battles and blows. But what have we here? Look, O Inca, *Yuti*, *Quilla* and *Chasca*, set one above the other, though *Chasca* is almost hidden by a hurt. Oh! my fosterling, O my Prince whom I nursed at these withered breasts, are you come back from the dead to take your own again? O Kari of the Holy Blood; Kari the lost who is Kari the found!"

Then sobbing and muttering she threw her arms about him and kissed him. Nor did he shame to kiss her in return, there before them all.

"Restore his garments to the Royal Prince," said Upanqui, "and bring hither the Fringe that is worn by the Inca's heir."

It was produced without delay by the high-priest Larico, which told me at once that all this scene had been prepared. Upanqui took it from Larico, and beckoning Kari to him, with the priest's help bound it about his brow, thereby acknowledging him and restoring him as heir-apparent to the Empire. Then he kissed him on the brow and Kari knelt down and did his father homage.

After this they went away together accompanied only by Larico and two or three of the councillors of Inca blood and as I learned from Larico afterwards, told each other their tales and made plans to outwit, and if need were to destroy Urco and his faction.

On the following day Kari was established in a house of his own that was more of a fortress than a palace, for it was built of great stones with narrow gates, and surrounded by an open space. Upon this space, as a guard, were encamped all those who had deserted to him in the battle of the Field of Blood, who had returned to Cuzco from the camp of Huaracha now that Kari was accepted as the royal heir. Also other troops who were loyal to the Inca, were stationed near by, while those who clung to Urco departed secretly to that town where he lay sick. Moreover, proclamation was made that on the day of the new moon, which the magicians declared to be auspicious, Kari would be publicly presented to the people in the Temple of the Sun as the Inca's lawful heir, in place of Urco disinherited for crimes that he had committed against the Sun, the Empire and the Inca his father.

"Brother," said Kari to me, for so he called me now that he was an acknowledged Prince, when I went to greet him in his grandeur, "Brother, did I not tell you always that we must trust to our gods? See, I have not trusted in vain though it is true that dangers still lie ahead of me, and perhaps civil war."

"Yes," I answered, "your gods are in the way of giving you all you want, but it is not so with mine and me."

"What then do you desire, Brother, who can have even to the half of the kingdom?"

"Kari," I replied, "I cry not for the Earth, but for the Moon."

He understood and his face grew stern.

"Brother, the Moon alone is beyond you, for she inhabits the sky while you still dwell upon the earth," he answered with a frown, and then began to talk of the peace with Huaracha.

CHAPTER X

THE GREAT HORROR

THE day of the new moon came and with it the great horror that caused all the Empire of Tavantinsuyu to tremble, fearing lest Heaven should be avenged upon it.

Since Upanqui had found his elder son again he began to dote upon him, as in such a case the old and weak-minded often do, and would walk about the gardens and palaces with his arm around his neck, babbling to him of whatever was uppermost in his mind. Moreover his soul was oppressed because he had done Kari wrong in the past, and preferred Urco to him under the urging of that Prince's mother.

" The truth is, Son," I myself heard him say to Kari, " that we men who seem to rule the world, do not rule it at all, because always women rule us. This they do through our passions which the gods planted in us for their own ends, also because they are more single in their minds. The man thinks of many things, the woman only thinks of what she desires. Therefore the man whom Nature already has bemused, only brings a little piece of his mind to fight against her whole mind, and so is conquered ; he who was made for one thing only, to be the mate of the woman that she may mother more men in order to serve the wills of other women who yet seem to be those men's slaves."

" So I have learned, Father," answered the grave Kari, " and for this reason having suffered in the past, I am determined to have as little to do with women as is possible for one in my place. During my travels in other lands, as in this country, I have seen men great and noble brought to nothingness and ruin by their love for women; down into the dirt indeed, when their hands were full of the world's wealth and glory. Moreover I have noticed that they seldom learn wisdom, and that what they have done before, they are ready to do again, who believe anything that soft lips swear to them. Yes, even that they are loved for themselves alone, as I own to my sorrow, once I did myself. Urco could not have taken that fair wife of mine, Father, if she had not been willing to go when she saw that I had lost your favour and with it the hope of the Scarlet Fringe."

Here Kari looked at me, of whom I knew he was thinking all this time, and seeing that I could overhear his talk, began to speak of something else.

On the appointed day there was a great gathering of the nobles of the land, especially of those of the Inca blood, and of all that were "earmen," a class of the same rank as our peers in England, to hear the proclamation of Kari as the Inca's heir. It was made before this gorgeous company in the Great Temple of the Sun, which now I saw for the first time.

It was a huge and most wondrous place well named the "House of Gold." For here everything was gold. On the western wall hung an image of the sun twenty feet or more across, an enormous graven plate of gold set about with gems and having eyes and teeth of great emeralds. The roof too and the walls were all panelled with gold, even the cornices and column heads were of solid gold.

Opening out of this temple also were others dedicated to the moon and stars, that of the moon being clothed in silver, with her radiant face shaped in silver fixed to the western wall. So it was with the temple of the Stars, of the Lightning and of the Rainbow, which perhaps with its many colours that sprang from jewels, was the most dazzling of them all.

The sight of so much glory overwhelmed me, and it came into my mind that if only it were known of in Europe, men would die by the ten thousand on the chance that they might conquer this country and make its wealth theirs. Yet here, save for these purposes of ornament and to be used as offerings to the gods and Incas, it was of no account at all.

But in this temple of the Sun was a marvel greater than its gold. For on either side of the carved likeness of the sun, seated upon chairs of gold, sat the dead Incas and their queens. Yes, clothed in their royal robes and emblems, with the Fringe upon their brows, there they sat with their heads bent forward, so wonderfully preserved by the arts these people have, that except for the stamp of death upon their countenances, they might have been sleeping men and women. Thus in the dead face of the mother of Kari I could read her likeness to her son. Of these departed kings and queens there were many, since from the first Inca of whom history told all were gathered here in the holy House and under the guardianship of the effigy of their god, the Sun, from whom they believed themselves to be descended. The sight was so solemn that it awed me, as it did all that congregation, for I noted that here men walked with unsandalled feet and that in speaking none raised their voices high.

The old Inca, Upanqui, entered, gloriously apparelled and accompanied by lords and priests, while after him came Kari with his retinue of great men. The Inca bowed to the company whereon everyone in the great temple, save myself alone whose British pride kept me on my feet, standing like one left living on a battlefield among a multitude of slain, prostrated himself before his divine majesty. At a sign they rose again and the Inca seated himself upon his jewelled golden throne beneath the effigy of the sun, while Kari took his place upon a lesser throne to the Inca's right.

Looking at him there in his splendour on this day when he came into his own again, I bethought me of the wretched, starving Indian marked with blows and foul with filth whom I had rescued from the cruel mob upon the Thames-side wharf, and wondered at this enormous change of fortune and the chain of wonderful events by which it had been brought about.

My fortune also had changed, for then I was great in my own fashion, who now had become but a wanderer, welcomed indeed in this glittering new world of which yonder we knew nothing, because I was strange and different, also full of unheard of learning and skilled in war, but still nothing but an outcast wanderer, and so doomed to live and die. And as I thought, so thought Kari, for our glances met, and I read it in his eyes.

Yonder sat my servant who had become my lord, and though he was still my friend, soon I felt he would be lost in the State matters of that great Empire, leaving me more lonely than before. Also his mind was not as my mind, as his blood was not my blood, and he was the slave of a faith that to me was a hateful superstition doubtless begotten by the Devil, who under the name of *Cupay*, some worshipped in that land, though others declared that this *Cupay* was the God of the Dead.

Oh! that I could flee away with Quilla and at her side live out what was left to me of life, since of all these multitudes she alone understood and was akin to me, because the sacred fire of love had burned away our differences and opened her eyes. But Quilla was snatched from me by the law of their accursed faith, and whatever else Kari might give, he would never give me this lady of the Moon, since as he had said, to him this would be sacrilege.

The ceremonies began. First Larico, the high-priest of the Sun, clothed in his white sacerdotal robes, made sacrifice upon a little altar which stood in front of the Inca's throne.

It was a very simple sacrifice of fruit and corn and flowers, with what seemed to be strange-shaped pieces of gold. At least I saw nothing else, and am sure that nothing that had life was laid upon that altar after the fashion of the bloody offerings of the Jews, and indeed of those of some of the other peoples of that great land.

Prayers, however, were spoken, very fine prayers and pure so far as I could understand them, for their language was more ancient and somewhat different to that which was used in common speech ; also the priests moved about, bowing and bending the knees much as our own do in celebrating the mass, though whether these motions were in honour of the god or of the Inca, I am not sure.

When the sacrifice was over, and the little fire that burned upon the altar had sunk low, though I was told that for hundreds of years it had never been extinguished, suddenly the Inca began to speak. With many particulars that I had not heard before, he told the tale of Kari and of his estrangement from him in past years through the plottings of the mother of Urco who now was dead, like the mother of Kari. This woman, it would appear, had persuaded him, the Inca, that Kari was conspiring against him, and therefore Urco was ordered to take him prisoner, but returned only with Kari's wife, saying that Kari had killed himself.

Here Upanqui became overcome with emotion as

the aged are apt to do, and beat his breast, even shedding tears because most unjustly he had allowed these things to happen and the wicked to triumph over the good, for which sin he said he felt sure his father the Sun would bring some punishment on him, as indeed was to chance sooner than he thought. Then he continued his story, setting out all Urco's iniquities and sacrileges against the gods, also his murders of people of high and low degree and his stealing of their wives and daughters. Lastly he told of the coming of Kari who was supposed to be dead, and all that story which I have set out.

Having finished his tale, with much solemn ceremonial he deposed Urco from his heirship to the Empire which he gave back to Kari to whom it belonged by right of birth and calling upon his dead forefathers, one by one, to be witness to the act, with great formality once more he bound the Prince's Fringe about his brow. As he did this, he said these words,

" Soon, O Prince Kari, you must change this yellow circlet for that which I wear, and take with it all the burden of Empire, for know that as quickly as may be I purpose to withdraw to my palace at Yucay, there to make my peace with God before I am called hence to dwell in the Mansions of the Sun."

When he had finished Kari did homage to his father, and in that quiet, even voice of his, told his tale of the wrongs that he had suffered at the hands of Urco his brother and of how he had escaped, living but maddened, from his hate. He told also how he had wandered across the sea, though of England he said nothing, and been saved from misery and death by myself, a very great person in my own country. Still, since I had suffered wrong there, as he Kari, had in his, he had persuaded me to accompany him back to his own land, that there my wisdom might shine upon its darkness, and owing to my divine and magical gifts hither we had come in safety. Lastly he asked the assembled priests and lords if they were content to accept him as the Inca to be, and to stand by him in any war that Urco might wage against him.

To this they answered that they were content and would stand by him.

Then followed many other rites such as the informing of the dead Incas, one by one, of this solemn declaration, through the mouth of the high-priest, and the offering of many prayers to them and to the Sun their father. So long were these prayers with the chants from choirs hidden in side chapels by which they were interspersed, that the day drew towards its close before all was done.

Thus it came about that the dusk was gathering when the Inca, followed by Kari, myself, the priests and all the congregation, left the temple to present Kari as the heir to the throne to the vast crowd which waited upon the open square outside its doors.

Here the ceremony went on. The Inca and most of us, for there was not space for all, although we were packed as closely together as Hastings herrings in a basket, took our stand upon a platform that was surrounded by a marvellous cable made of links of solid gold which, it was said, needed fifty men to lift it from the ground. Then Upanqui, whose strength seemed restored to him, perhaps because of some drug that he had eaten, or under the spur of this great event, stepped forward to the edge of the low platform and addressed the multitude in eloquent words, setting out the matter as he had done in the temple. He ended his speech by asking the formal question,

"Do you, Children of the Sun, accept the Prince Kari, my firstborn, to be Inca after me?"

There was a roar of assent, and as it died away

Upanqui turned to call Kari to him that he might present him to the people.

At this very moment in the gathering twilight I saw a great fierce-faced man with a bandaged head, whom I knew to be Urco, leap over the golden chain. He sprang upon the platform and with a shout of "*I* do not accept him, and thus I pay back treachery," plunged a gleaming copper knife or sword into the Inca's breast.

In an instant, before any could stir in that packed crowd, Urco had leapt back over the golden chain, and from the edge of the platform, to vanish amongst those beneath, who doubtless were men of his following disguised as citizens or peasants.

Indeed all who beheld seemed frozen with horror. One great sigh went up and then there was silence, since no such deed as this was known in the annals of that Empire. For a moment the aged Upanqui stood upon his feet, the blood pouring down his white beard and jewelled robe. Then he turned a little and said in a clear and gentle voice:

"Kari, you will be Inca sooner than I thought. Receive me, O God my Father, and pardon this murderer who, I think, can be no true son of mine."

Then he fell forward on his face and when we lifted him he was dead.

Still the silence hung; it was as though the tongues of men were smitten with dumbness. At length Kari stepped forward and cried:

"The Inca is dead, but I, the Inca, live on to avenge him. I declare war upon Urco the murderer and all who cling to Urco!"

Now the spell was lifted and from those dim hordes there went up a yell of hate against Urco the butcher and parricide, while men rushed to and fro searching for him. In vain! for he had escaped in the darkness.

On the following day with more ceremonies, though many of these were omitted because of the terror and trouble of the times, Kari was crowned Inca, exchanging the yellow for the crimson Fringe and taking the throne name of Upanqui after his father. In Cuzco there was none to say him nay for the whole city was horror-struck because of the sacrilege that had been committed. Also those who clung to Urco had fled away with him to a town named Huarina on the borders of the great lake called Titicaca, where was an island with marvellous temples full of gold, which town lay at a distance from Cuzco.

Then the civil war began and raged for three whole months, though of all that happened in that time because of the labour of it, I set down little, who would get forward with my story.

In this war I played a great part. The fear of Kari was that the Chancas, seeing the Inca realm thus rent in two, would once more attack Cuzco. This it became my business to prevent. As the ambassador of Kari I visited the camp of Huaracha, bearing offers of peace which gave to him more than he could ever hope to win by strength of arms. I found the old warrior-king still sick and wasted because of the hurt from Urco's club, though now he could walk upon crutches, and set out the case. He answered that he had no wish to fight against Kari who had offered him such honourable terms, especially when he was waging war against Urco whom he, Huaracha, hated, because he had striven to poison his daughter and dealt him a blow which he was sure would end in his death. Therefore he was ready to make a firm peace with the new Inca, if in addition to what he offered, he would surrender to him Quilla who was his heiress and would be Queen of the Chancas after him.

With these words I went back to Kari, only to find that on this matter he was hard as a rock of the mountains. In vain did I plead with him, and in vain did the high-priest, Larico, by subtle hints and arguments strive to gentle his mind.

"My brother," said Kari in that soft even voice of his, when he had heard me patiently to the end, "forgive me if I tell you that in advancing this prayer, for one word you say on behalf of King Huaracha, you say two for yourself, who having unhappily been bewitched by her, desire this Virgin of the Sun, the Lady Quilla, to be your wife. My brother, take everything else that I have to give, but leave this lady alone. If I handed her over to Huaracha or to you, as I have told you before, I should bring upon myself and upon my people the curse of my father the Sun, and of Pachacamac, the Spirit who is above the Sun. It was because Upanqui, my father according to the flesh, dared to look upon her after she had entered the House of the Sun, as I have learned he did, that a bloody and a cruel death came upon him, for so the magicians and the wise men have assured me that the oracles declare. Therefore, rather than do this crime of crimes, I would choose that Huaracha should renew the war against us and that you should join yourself to him, or even to Urco and strive to tear me from the Throne, for then even if I were slain, I should die with honour."

"That I could never do," I answered sadly.

"No, my brother Hubert" (for now often he called me by my English name again), "that you could never do, being what you are, as I know well. So like the rest of us you must bear your burden. Mayhap it may please my gods, or your gods in the end and in some way that I cannot foresee, to give you this woman whom you seek. But of my free-will I will never give her to you.

To me the deed would be as though in your land of England the King commanded the consecrated bread and cups of wine to be snatched from the hands of the priests of your temples and cast to the dogs, or given to cheer the infidels within your gates, or dragged away the nuns from your convents to become their lemans. What would you think of such a king in your own country? And what," he added with meaning, "would you have thought of me if there I had stolen one of these nuns because she was beautiful and I desired her as a wife?"

Now although Kari's words stung me because of the truth that was in them, I answered that to me this matter wore another face. Also that Quilla had become a Virgin of the Sun, not of her own free will, but to escape from Urco.

"Yes, my brother," he answered, "because you believe my religion to be idolatry and do not understand that the Sun to me is the symbol and garment of God, and that when we of the Inca blood, or those of us who have the inner knowledge, talk of him as our Father, we mean that we are the children of God, though the common people are taught otherwise. For the rest, this lady took her vows of her own free will and of her secret reasons I know nothing, any more than I know why she offered herself in marriage to Urco before she found you upon the island. For you I grieve, and for her also; yet I would have you remember that as your own priests teach, in every life that is not brutal there must be loss, sorrow and sacrifice, since by these steps only man can climb towards the things of the spirit. Pluck then such flowers as you will from the garden that Fate gives you, but leave this one white bloom alone."

In such words as these he preached at me, till at length I could bear no more, and said roughly,

"To me it is a very evil thing, O Inca, to separate those who love each other, and one that cannot be pleasing to Heaven. Therefore great as you are, and friend of mine as you are, I tell you to your face that if I can take the Lady Quilla out of that golden grave of hers I shall do so."

"I know it, my brother," he answered, "and therefore were I as some Incas have been, I should cause this holy Spouse to travel more quickly to the skies than Nature will take her. But this I will not do because I know also that Destiny is above all things and that which Destiny decrees will happen unhelped by man. Still I tell you that I will thwart you if I can and that should you succeed in your ends, I will kill you if I can and the lady also, because you have committed sacrilege. Yes, although I love you better than any other man, I will kill you. And if King Huaracha should be able to snatch her away by force I will make war on him until either I and my people, or he and his people are destroyed. And now let us talk no more of this matter, but rather of our plans against Urco, since in these at least, where no woman is concerned, I know that you will be faithful to me and I sorely need your help."

So with a heavy heart I went back to the camp of Huaracha and told him Kari's words. He was very wroth when he heard them, since his gods were different to those of the Incas and he thought nothing of the holiness of the Virgins of the Sun, and once again talked of renewing the war. Still it came to nothing for sundry reasons of which the greatest was that his sickness increased on him as the days went by. Also I told him that much as I desired Quilla, I could not fight upon his side since I was sworn to aid Kari against Urco and my word might not be broken. Moreover the Yuncas who had been our allies, wearying of their long absence from home and satisfied with the gentle forgiveness and the redress of their grievances which the new Inca had promised them, were gone, having departed on their long march to the coast, while many of the Chancas themselves were slipping back to their own country. Therefore Huaracha's hour had passed by.

So at length we agreed that it would be foolish to attack Cuzco in order to try to rescue Quilla, since even if Huaracha won in face of a desperate defence, probably it would be only to find that his daughter was dead or had vanished away to some unknown and distant convent. All that we could do was to trust to fortune to deliver her into our hands. We agreed further that, having obtained an honourable peace and all else that he desired, it would be well for Huaracha to return to his own land, leaving me a body of five thousand picked men who were willing to serve under me, to assist in the war against Urco, to be my guard and that of Quilla, if perchance I could deliver her from the House of the Sun.

When this was known five thousand of the best and bravest of the Chancas, young soldiers who sought adventure and battle and whom I had trained, stepped forward at once and swore themselves to my service. Bidding farewell to Huaracha, with these troops I returned to Cuzco, sending messengers ahead to explain the reason of their coming to Kari, who welcomed them well and gave them quarters round the palace which was allotted to me.

A few days later we advanced on the town Huarina, a great host of us, and outside of it met the yet greater host of Urco in a mighty battle that endured for a day and a night, and yet, like that of the Field of Blood, remained neither lost nor won. When the thousands of the dead had been buried and the wounded sent back to Cuzco, we attacked the city of Huarina, I leading the van with my Chancas, and stormed the place, driving Urco and his forces out on the further side.

They retreated to the mountains and there followed a long and tedious war without great battles. At length, although the Inca's armies had suffered sorely, we forced those of Urco to the shores of the Lake Titicaca, where most of them melted away into the swamps and certain tree-clad, low-lying valleys. Urco himself, however, with a number of followers escaped in boats to the holy island in the lake.

We built a fleet of *balsas* with reeds and blown-out sheepskins, and followed him. Landing on the isle we stormed the city of Temples which were more wondrous and even fuller of gold and precious things than those of Cuzco. Here the men of Urco fought desperately, but driving them from street to street, at length we penned them in one of the largest of the temples of which by some mischance a reed roof was set on fire, so that there they perished miserably. It was a dreadful scene such as I never wish to behold again. Also, after all Urco and some of his captains, breaking out of the burning temple under cover of the smoke escaped, either in *balsas* or as many declare, by swimming the lake. At least they were gone nor search as we might on the mainland could they be found.

So all being finished, except for the escape of Urco, we returned to Cuzco which Kari entered in triumph, I marching at his side, wearied out with war and bloodshed.

CHAPTER XI

THE HOUSE OF DEATH

NOW at one time during this long war against Urco victory smiled upon him, though afterwards the scale went down against him. Kari was defeated in a pitched battle and I who commanded another army was almost surrounded in a valley. When everything seemed lost, afterwards I escaped by leading my soldiers round up the slope of a mountain and surprising Urco in the rear, but as it ended well for us I need not speak of that matter.

It was while all was at its blackest for us that a certain officer was brought to me who was captured while striving to desert, or at least to pass our outposts. As it happened I knew this man again having, unseen myself, noted him on the previous day talking earnestly to the High Priest Larico who, with other priests, accompanied my army, perhaps to keep a watch on me. I took this Captain apart and questioned him alone, threatening him with death by torment if he did not reveal his errand to me.

In the end, being very much afraid, he spoke. From him I learned that he was a messenger from Larico to Urco. Believing that our defeat was almost certain, Larico had sent him to make his peace with Urco by betraying all Kari's and my own plans to him and revealing how he might most easily destroy us. He said also that he, Larico, had only joined the party of Upanqui, and of Kari after him, under threats of death and that always in his heart he had been true to Urco, whom he acknowledged as his Lord and as the rightful Inca whom he would help to restore to the Throne with all the power of the Priesthood of the Sun. Further he sent by this spy a secret message by means of little cords cunningly knotted, which knots served these people as writing, since they could read them as we read a book.

Now, being always desirous of knowledge, I had caused myself to be instructed in the plan of this knot-writing which by this time I could read well enough. Therefore I was able to spell out this message. It said, shortly but plainly, that knowing he still desired her, he, Larico, as High Priest would hand over to Urco the Lady Quilla, daughter to the King of the Chancas, who unlawfully had been hidden away among the Virgins of the Sun, also that he would betray me, the White-God-from-the-Sea who sought to steal her away, into Urco's hands, that he might kill me if he could.

When I had mastered all this I was filled with rage and bethought me that I would cause Larico to be taken and suffer the fate of traitors. Soon, however, I changed this mind of mine and placing the spy in close keeping where none could come at him, I set a watch on Larico but said nothing to him or to Kari of all that I had learned.

A few days later our fortunes changed and Urco, defeated, was in full flight to the shores of Lake Titicaca. After this I knew we had nothing more to fear from this fox-hearted High Priest who above everything desired to be on the winning side and to continue in his place and power. So knowing that I held him fast I bided my time, because through him alone I could hope to come at Quilla. That time came after the war was over and we had returned to Cuzco in triumph. As soon as the rejoicings were over and Kari was firmly seated on his throne, I sent for Larico, which, as the greatest man in the kingdom after the Inca, I was able to do.

He appeared in answer to my summons and we bowed to each other, after which he began to praise me for my generalship, saying that had it not been for me, Urco would have won the war and that the Inca had done well to name me his Brother before the people and to say that to me he owed his throne.

" Yes, that is true," I answered, " and now, since through me, you, Larico, are the third greatest man in the kingdom and remain High Priest of the Sun and Whisperer in the Inca's ear, I would put you in mind of a certain bargain that we made when I promised you all these things, Larico."

" What bargain, Lord-from-the-Sea."

" That you would bring me and a Virgin of the Sun who while she was of the earth was named Quilla, together, Larico, and enable her to return from those of the sun to my arms, Larico."

Now his face grew troubled and he answered,

" Lord, I have thought much of this matter, desiring above all things to fulfil my word and I grieve to tell you that it is impossible."

" Why, Larico ? "

" Because I find that the law of my faith is against it, Lord."

" Is that all, Larico ? " I asked with a smile.

" No, Lord. Because I find that the Inca would not suffer it and swears to kill all who attempt to touch the Lady Quilla."

" Is that all, Larico ? "

" No, Lord. Because I find that a woman who has been betrothed to one of the royal Blood may never pass to another man."

" Now perhaps we come nearer to it, Larico. You

mean that if this happened and perchance after all Urco should come to the throne, as he might do if Kari his brother died—as any man may die—he would hold you to account."

" Yes, Lord, if that chanced, as chance it may, since Urco still lives and I hear is gathering new armies among the mountains, certainly he would hold me to account for I have heard as much. Also our father the Sun would hold me to account and so would the Inca who wields his sceptre upon earth."

I asked him why he did not think of all these things before when he had much to gain, instead of now when he had gained them through me, and he answered because he had not considered them enough. Then I pretended to grow angry and exclaimed :

" You are a rogue, Larico! You promise and take your pay and you do not perform. Henceforth I am your enemy and one to whom the Inca hearkens."

" He hearkens still more to his god the Sun and to me who am the voice of God, White Man," he answered, adding insolently, " You would strike too late ; your power over me and my fortunes is gone, White Man."

" I fear it is so," I replied pretending to be frightened, " so let us say no more of the matter. After all there are other women in Cuzco besides this fair bride of the Sun. Now before you go, High Priest, will you who are so learned, help me who am ignorant ? I have been striving to master your method of conveying thoughts by means of knots. Here I have a bundle of strings which I cannot altogether understand. Be pleased to interpret them to me, O most holy and upright High Priest."

Then from my robe I drew out those knotted fibres that I had taken from his messenger and held them before Larico's eyes.

He stared at them and turned pale. His hand groped

for his dagger till he saw that mine was on the hilt of Wave-Flame, whereon he let it fall. Next the thought took him that in truth I could not read the knots which he began to interpret falsely.

"Have done, Traitor," I laughed, "for I know them all. So Urco may wed Quilla and I may not. Also cease to fret as to that messenger of yours for whom you seek far and near, since he is safe in my keeping. To-morrow I take him to deliver his message not to Urco, but to Kari—and then, Traitor?"

Now Larico who notwithstanding his stern face and proud manner, was a coward at heart, fell upon his knees before me trembling, and prayed me to spare his life which lay in my hand. Well he knew that if once it came to Kari's ears, even a High Priest of the Sun could not hope to escape the reward of such treachery as his.

"If I pardon you, what will you give me?" I asked.

"The only thing that you will take, Lord—the Lady Quilla herself. Hearken, Lord. Outside the city is the palace of Upanqui whom Urco slew. There in the great hall the divine Inca sits embalmed and into that holy presence none dare enter save the Virgins of the Sun whose office it is to wait upon the mighty dead. To-morrow one hour before the dawn when all men sleep, I will lead you to this hall disguised in the robes of a priest of the Sun, so that on the way thither none can know you. There you will find but one Virgin of the Sun, the lady whom you seek. Take her and begone. The rest I leave to you."

"How do I know that you will not set some trap for me, Larico?"

"Thus, Lord, that I shall be with you and share your sacrilege. Also my life will be in your hand."

"Aye, Larico," I answered grimly, "and if aught

of ill befalls me, remember that this," and I touched the knotted cords, " will find its way to Kari, and with it the man who was your messenger."

He nodded and answered,

" Be sure that I have but one desire, to know you, Lord, and this woman whom, being mad, you seek so madly, far from Cuzco and never to look upon your face again."

Then we made our plans as to when and where we should meet and other matters, after which he departed, bowing himself away with many smiles.

I thought to myself that there went as big a rogue as I had ever known, in London or elsewhere, and fell to wondering what snare he would set for me, since that he planned some snare I was sure. Why then did I prepare to fall into it ? I asked myself. The answer was, for a double reason. First, although my whole heart was sick with longing for the sight of her, now, after months of seeking, I was no nearer to Quilla than when we had parted in the city of the Chancas, nor ever should be without Larico's aid. Secondly, some voice within me told me to go forward taking all hazards, since if I did not, our parting would be for always in this world. Yes, the voice warned me that unless I saved her soon, Quilla would be no more. As Huaracha had said, there was more poison in Cuzco, and murderers were not far to seek. Or despair might do its work with her. Or she might kill herself as once she had proposed to do. So I would go forward even though the path I walked should lead me to my doom.

That day I did many things. Now, being so great a general and man—or god—among these people, I had those about me who were sworn to my service and whom I could trust. For one of these, a prince of the Inca Blood, of the House of Kari's mother, I sent and gave to him those knotted cords that were the proof of Larico's treachery, bidding him if aught of evil overtook me, or if I could not be found, to deliver them to the Inca on my behalf and with them the prisoned messenger who was in his keeping, but meanwhile to show them to no man. He bowed and swore by the Sun to do my bidding, thinking doubtless that, my work finished in this land, I purposed to return into the sea out of which I had risen, as doubtless a god could do.

Next I summoned the captains of the Chancas who had fought under me throughout the civil war, of whom about half remained alive, and bade them gather their men upon the ridge where I had stood at the beginning of the battle of the Field of Blood, and wait until I joined them there. If it chanced, however, that I did not appear within six days I commanded that they should march back to their own country and make report to King Huaracha that I had "returned into the sea" for reasons that he would guess. Also I commanded that eight famous warriors whom I named, men of my own bodyguard who had fought with me in all our battles and would have followed me through fire or water or the gates of Hell themselves, should come to the courtyard of my palace after nightfall, bringing a litter and disguised as its bearers, but having their arms hidden beneath their cloaks.

These matters settled, I waited upon the Inca Kari and craved of him leave to take a journey. I told him that I was weary with so much fighting and desired to rest amidst my friends the Chancas.

He gazed at me awhile, then stretched out his sceptre to me in token that my request was granted, and said in a sad voice :

"So you would leave me, my brother, because I cannot give you that which you desire. Bethink you. You will be no nearer to the Moon (by which he meant

Quilla) at Chanca than you are at Cuzco and here, next to the Inca, you are the greatest in the Empire who by decree are named his brother and the general of his armies."

Now, though my gorge rose at it, I lied to him, saying,

"The Moon is set for me, so let her sleep whom I shall see no more. For the rest, learn, O Kari, that Huaracha has sworn to me that I shall be, not his brother but his son, and Huaracha is sick—they say to death."

"You mean that you would choose to be king over the Chancas rather than stand next to the throne among the Quichuas?" he said scanning me sharply.

"Aye, Kari," I replied still lying. "Since I must dwell in this strange land, I would do so as a king—no less."

"To that you have a right, Brother, who are far above us all. But when you are a king, what is your plan? Do you purpose to strive to conquer me and rule over Tavantisuyu, as perchance you could do?"

"Nay, I shall never make war upon you, Kari, unless you break your treaty with the Chancas and strive to subdue them."

"Which *I* shall never do, Brother."

Then he paused a while and spoke again with more passion than I had ever known in him, saying,

"Would that this woman who comes between us were dead. Would that she had never been born. In truth I am minded to pray to my father, the Sun, that he will be pleased to take her to himself, for then perchance we too might be as we were in the old time yonder in your England, and when we faced perils side by side upon the ocean and in the forests. A curse on Woman the Divider, and all the curses of all the gods upon this woman whom I may not give to you

Had she been of my Household I would have bidden you to take her, yes, even if she were my wife, but she is the wife of the god and therefore I may not—alas! I may not," and he hid his face in his robe and groaned.

Now when I heard these words I grew afraid who knew well that she of whom the Inca prays the Sun that she may die, does die, and swiftly.

"Do not add to this lady's wrongs by robbing her of life as well as of sight and liberty, Kari," I said.

"Have no fear, Brother," he answered, "she is safe from me. No word shall pass my lips though it is true that in my heart I wish that she would die. Go your ways, Brother and Friend, and when you grow weary of kingship if it comes to you, as to tell truth already I grow weary, return to me. Perchance, forgetting that we had been kings, we might journey hence together over the world's edge."

Then he stood up on his throne and bowed towards me, kissing the air as though to a god, and taking the royal chain that every Inca wore, from about his neck, set it upon mine. This done, turning he left me without another word.

With a heavy heart I returned to my palace where I dwelt. At sundown I ate according to my custom, and dismissed those who waited upon me to the servants' quarters. There were but two of them for my private life was simple. Then I slept till past midnight and rising, went into the courtyard where I found the eight Chanca Captains disguised as litter-bearers and with them the litter. I led them to an empty guard-house and bade them stay there in silence. After this I returned to my chamber and waited.

About two hours before the dawn Larico came, knocking on the side-door as we had planned. I opened to him and he entered disguised in a hooded cloak of sheep's wool which covered his robes and his face, such as priests wear when the weather is cold. He gave to me the garments of a priest of the Sun which he had brought with him in a cloth. I clothed myself in them though because of the fashion of them, to do this I must be rid of my armour which would have betrayed me. Larico desired that I should take off the sword Wave-Flame also, but, mistrusting him, this I would not do, but made shift to hide it and my dagger beneath the priest's cloak. The armour I wrapped in a bundle and took with me.

Presently we went out, having spoken few words since the time for speech had gone by and peril or some fear of what might befall weighed upon our tongues. In the guard-house I found the Chancas at whom Larico looked curiously but said nothing. To them I gave the bundle of armour to be hidden in the litter and with it my long bow, having first revealed myself to them by lifting the hood of my cloak. Then I bade them follow me.

Larico and I walked in front and after us came the eight men, four of them bearing the empty litter, and the other four marching behind. This was well planned since if any saw us or if we met guards as once or twice we did, these thought that we were priests taking one who was sick or dead to be tended or to be made ready for burial. Once, however, we were challenged, but Larico spoke some word and we passed on without question.

At length in the darkness before the dawn we came to the private palace of dead Yupanqui. At its garden gate Larico would have had me leave the litter with the eight Chanca warriors disguised as bearers. I refused, saying that they must come to the doors of the palace, and when he grew urgent, tapped my sword, whispering to him fiercely that he had best beware lest it should be he who stayed at the garden gate. Then he gave way and we advanced all of us across the garden to the door of the palace. Larico unlocked the door with a key and we entered, he and I alone, for here I bade the Chancas await my return.

We crept down a short passage that was curtained at its end. Passing the curtains I found myself in Upanqui's banqueting-hall. This hall was dimly lit with one hanging golden lamp. By its light I saw something more wondrous and of its sort more awful than ever I had seen in that strange land.

There, on a dais, in his chair of gold sat dead Upanqui arrayed in all his gorgeous Inca robes and so marvellously preserved that he might have been a man asleep. With arms crossed and his sceptre at his side, he sat staring down the hall with fixed and empty eyes, a dreadful figure of life in death. About him and around the dais were set all his riches, vases and furniture of gold, and jewels piled in heaps, there to remain till the roof fell in and buried them, since on this hallowed wealth the boldest dare not lay a hand. In the centre of the hall, also, was a table prepared as though for feasters, for amid jewelled cups and platters stood the meats and wines which day by day were brought afresh by the Virgins of the Sun. Doubtless there were more wonders, but these I could not see because the light did not reach them, or to the doorways of the chambers that opened from the hall. Moreover there was something else which caught my eye.

At the foot of the dais crouched a figure which at first I took to be that of some dead one also embalmed, perhaps a wife or a daughter of the dead Inca who had been set with him in this place. While I stared at it the figure stirred, having heard our footsteps, rose and turned, standing so that the light from the hanging lamp fell full upon it. It was Quilla clad in white and purple with a golden likeness of the sun blazoned upon her breast!

So beauteous did she look searching the darkness with great blind eyes and her rich hair flowing from beneath her jewelled headdress, a diadem fashioned to resemble the sun's rays, that my breath failed me and my heart stood still.

"There stands she whom you seek," muttered Larico in a mocking whisper, for here even he did not seem to dare to talk aloud. "Go take her, you whom men call a god, but I call a drunken fool ready to risk all for a woman's lips. Go take her and ask the blessing upon your kisses of yonder dead king whose holy rest you break."

"Be silent," I whispered back and passed round the table till I came face to face with Quilla. Then a strange dumbness fell upon me like a spell or dead Upanqui's curse, so that I could not speak.

I stood there staring at those beautiful blind eyes and the blind eyes stared back at me. Presently a look of understanding gathered on the face and Quilla spoke, or rather murmured to herself,

"Strange—but I could have sworn! Strange, but I seemed to feel! Oh! I slept in my vigils upon that dead old man who in life was so foolish and in death appears to have become so wise, and sleeping I dreamed. I dreamed I heard a step I shall never hear again. I dreamed one was near me whom I shall never touch again. I will sleep once more, for in my darkness what are left to me save sleep and—death?"

Then at last I found my tongue and said hoarsely,

"Love is left, Quilla, and—life."

She heard and straightened herself. Her whole body seemed to become rigid as though with an agony of joy.

Her blind eyes flashed, her lips quivered. She stretched out her hand, feeling at the darkness. Her fingers touched my forehead, and thence she ran them swiftly over my face.

"It is—dead or living—it is——," and she opened her arms.

Oh! was there ever anything more beautiful on the earth than this sight of the blind Quilla thus opening her arms to me, there in the gorgeous house of death?

We clung and kissed. Then I thrust her away, saying,

"Come swiftly from this ill-omened place. All is ready. The Chancas wait."

She slipped her hand into mine and I turned to lead her away.

Then it was that I heard a low, mocking laugh, Larico's, I thought, heard also a sound of creeping footsteps around me. I looked. Out of the darkness that hid the doors of the chamber on the right, appeared a giant form which I knew for that of Urco, and behind him others. I looked to the left and there were more of them, while in front beyond the gold-laid board, stood the traitor, Larico, laughing.

"You have had the first fruits, but it seems that another will reap the harvest, Lord-from-the-Sea," he jeered.

"Seize her," cried Urco in his guttural voice, pointing to Quilla with his mace, "and brain that white thief."

I drew Wave-Flame and strove to get at him, but from both sides men rushed in on me. One I cut down, but the others snatched Quilla away. I was surrounded with no room to wield my sword, and already weapons flashed over me. A thought came to me. The Chancas were at the door. I must reach them, for perhaps so Quilla might be saved. In front was the table spread for the death feast. With a bound I leapt on to it, shouting aloud and scattering its golden furnishings this way and that. Beyond stood the traitor, Larico who had trapped me—I sprang at him and lifting Wave-Flame with both hands I smote with all my strength. He fell, as it seemed to me, cloven to the middle. Then some spear cast at me, struck the lamp.

It shattered and went out !

CHAPTER XII

THE FIGHT TO THE DEATH

THERE was tumult in the hall; shoutings, groans from him whom I had first struck down, the sound of vases and vessels overthrown, and above all those of a woman's shrieks echoing from the walls and roof, so that I could not tell whence they came.

Through the gross darkness I went on towards the curtains, or so I hoped. Presently they were torn open and by the faint light of the breaking dawn I saw my eight Chancas rushing towards me.

"Follow!" I cried, and at the head of them groped my way back up the hall, seeking for Quilla. I stumbled over the dead body of Larico and felt a path round the table. Then suddenly a door at the back of the hall was thrown open and by the grey light which came through the doorway, I perceived the last of the ravishers departing. We scrambled across the dais where the golden chair was overthrown and the embalmed Upanqui lay, a stiff and huddled heap upon his back, staring at me with jewelled eyes.

We gained the door which, happily, none had remembered to close, and passed out into the park-like grounds beyond. A hundred paces or more ahead of us, by the growing light, I saw a litter passing between the trees surrounded by armed men, and knew that in it was Quilla being borne to captivity and shame.

After it we sped. It passed the gate of the park wall, but when we reached that gate it was shut and barred and we must waste time breaking it down, which we did by help of a felled tree that lay at hand. We were through it, and now the rim of the sun had appeared so that through the morning mist, which clung to the hillside beyond the town, we could see the litter, the full half of a mile away. On we went up the hill, gaining as we ran, for we had no litter to bear, nor aught else save the sack of armour which one of the Chancas had thought to bring with him when he rushed into the hall, and with it my long bow and shafts.

Now, at a certain place between this hill and another there was a gorge such as are common in that country, a gorge so deep and narrow that in places the light of day scarcely struggles to the pathway at its bottom. Into this tunnel the litter vanished and when we drew near I saw that its mouth was held by armed men, six of them or more. Taking my bow from the Chanca I strung it and shot swiftly. The man at whom I aimed, went down. Again I shot and another fell, whereon the rest of them took cover behind stones.

Throwing back the bow to the Chanca, for now it was useless, we charged. That business was soon over, for presently all those of Urco's men who remained there, were dead, save one who, being cut off, fled down hill towards the city, taking with him the news of what had passed in the palace of dead Upanqui.

We entered the mouth of the gorge, plunging through the gloom, though as it chanced this place faced towards the east, so that the low sun, which now was fully up, shone down it and gave us light that later would have been lacking.

I, who was very swift of foot and to whom rage and fear gave wings, outran my companions. Swinging myself round a rock which lay in the pathway, I saw the litter again not a hundred yards ahead. It halted because, as it seemed to me, one or more of the bearers stumbled and fell among the stones. I rushed at them, roaring. Perchance it had been wiser to wait for my companions, but I was mad and feared nothing. They saw me and a cry went up of

"The White god! The terrible White god!"

Then fear took hold of them and they fled, leaving the litter on the ground. Yes, all of them fled save one, Urco himself.

He stood there rolling his eyes and gnashing his teeth, looking huge and awful in those shadows, looking like a devil from hell. Suddenly a thought seemed to take him, and leaping at the litter he tore aside its curtains and dragged out Quilla, who fell prone upon the ground.

"If I may not have her, you shall not, White thief. See! I give back his bride to the Sun," he shouted and lifted his copper sword to pierce her through.

Now I was still ten paces or so away and saw that before I could reach him that sword would be in her heart. What could I do? Oh! St. Hubert must have helped me then for I knew in an instant. In my hand was Wave-Flame and with all my strength I hurled it at his head.

The great blade hurtled hissing through the air. I saw the sunlight shine on it. He strove to leap clear, but too late, for it caught him on the hand that he had lifted to protect his head, and shore off two of his fingers so that he dropped his sword. Next instant, still roaring, as doubtless old Thorgrimmer my forefather used to do when he fought to the death, for blood is very strong, I leapt on the giant, who like myself was swordless. There in the gulf we wrestled. He was a mighty man, but now my strength was as that of ten. I threw him to the ground by a Sussex trick I knew and there we rolled over and over each other. Once he had me undermost and I think would have choked me, had it not been that his right hand lacked two fingers.

With a mighty heave I lifted him so that now we lay side by side. He was groping for a knife—I did not see, but knew it. Near his head a sharp-edged stone rose in the path to the height of a man's hand or more. I saw it and bethought me what to do if I could. Again I heaved and as at length he found the knife and stabbed at me, scratching my face, I got his bull's neck upon that stone. Then I loosed my hand and caught him by the hair. Back I pressed his great head, back and back with all my might till something snapped.

Urco's neck was broken. Urco quivered and was dead!

I lay by his side panting. A voice came from the white heap upon the ground by whom and for whom this dreadful combat had been fought, the voice of Quilla.

"One died, but who lives?" asked the voice.

I could not answer because I had no breath. All my strength was gone. Still I sat up, supporting myself with my hand and hoping that it would come back. Quilla turned her face towards me, or rather towards the sound that I had made in moving, and I thought to myself how sad it was that she should be blind. Presently she spoke again and now her voice quavered:

"I *see* who it is that lives," she said. "Something has broken in my eyes and, Lord and Love, I see that it is *you* who live. You, you, and oh! you bleed."

Then the Chancas came bounding down the gorge and found us.

They looked at the dead giant and saw how he had died, killed by strength, not by the sword; they looked and bent the knee and praised me, saying that I was indeed a god, since no man could have done this deed, killing the huge Urco with his naked hands. Then they placed Quilla back in her litter and six of them bore her down that black gorge. The two who remained, for in that fight none of them had been hurt, supported me till my strength came back, for the cut in the face that I had received from Urco's dagger was but slight. We reached the mouth of the gorge and took counsel.

To return to Cuzco after what I had done, would be to seek death. So we bore away to the right and, making a round, came about ten o'clock of the morning unmolested by any, to that ridge on which I had stood at the beginning of the battle of the Field of Blood. There I found the Chancas camped, some three thousand of them, as I had commanded. When they saw me, living and but little hurt, they shouted for joy, and when they learned who was in that litter they went wellnigh mad.

Then the eight warriors with me told them all the tale of the saving of Quilla and the death of the giant Urco at my hands, whereon their captains came and kissed my feet, saying that I was in truth a god, though heretofore some of them had held me to be but a man.

"God or man," I answered, "I must rest. Let the women tend the Lady Quilla, and give me food and drink, after which I will sleep. At sunset we march home to Huaracha, your king and mine, to give him back his daughter. Till then there is naught to fear, since Kari has no troops at hand with which to attack us. Still, set outposts."

So I ate and drank, but little of the former and much of the latter, I fear, and after that I slept as soundly as one who is dead, for I was outworn.

When the sun was within an hour of setting, captains awakened me and said that an embassy from Cuzco, ten men only, waited outside our lines, seeking speech with me. So I rose and my face and wound having been dressed, caused water to be poured over my body, and was rubbed with oil; after which, clothed in the robes of a Chanca noble, but wearing no armour, I went out with nine Chanca captains to receive the embassy on the plain at the foot of the hill, at that very spot where first I had fought with Urco.

When we drew near, from out of the group of nobles advanced one man. I looked and saw that he was Kari; yes, the Inca himself.

I went forward to meet him and we spoke together just out of earshot of our followers.

"My brother," said Kari, "I have learned all that has passed and I give you praise who are the most daring among men and the first among warriors; you who slew the giant Urco with your naked hands."

"And thus made your throne safe for you, Kari."

"And thus made my throne safe for me. You also who clove Larico to the breast in the death-house of Upanqui, my father—"

"And thus delivered you from a traitor, Kari."

"And thus delivered me from a traitor, as I have learned also from your messenger who handed to me the knotted cord, and from the spy whom you had in your keeping. I repeat that you are the most daring among men and the first among warriors; almost a god as my people name you."

I bowed and after a little silence he went on:

"Would that this were all that I have to say. But alas! it is not. You have committed the great sacrilege against the Sun, my father, of which I warned you, having robbed him of his bride, and, my brother, you have lied to me, who told me but yesterday that you had put all thought of her from your mind."

"To me that was no sacrilege, Kari, but rather a righteous deed, to free one from the bonds of a faith in which neither she nor I believe, and to lead her from a living tomb back to life and love."

"And was the lie righteous also, brother?"

"Aye," I answered boldly, "if ever a lie can be. Bethink you. You prayed that this lady might die because she came between you and me, and those that kings pray may die, do die, if not with their knowledge or by their express command. Therefore I said that I had put her from my mind in order that she might go on living."

"To cherish you in her arms, Brother. Now hearken. Because of this deed of yours, we who were more than friends, have become more than foes. You have declared war upon my god and me; therefore I declare war upon you. Yet hearken again. I do not wish that thousands of men should perish because of our quarrel. Therefore I make an offer to you. It is that you should fight me here and now, man to man, and let the Sun, or Pachacamac beyond the Sun, decide the matter as may be decreed."

"Fight *you!* Fight *you*, Kari, the Inca," I gasped.

"Aye, fight me to the death, since between us all is over and done. In England you nurtured me. Here in the land of Tavantinsuyu, which I rule to-day, I have nurtured you and in my shadow you have grown great, though it is true that had it not been for your generalship, perchance I should no longer be here to throw the shadow. Let us therefore set the one thing against the other and, forgetting all between us that is past, stand face to face as foes. Mayhap you will conquer me, being so mighty a man of war. Mayhap also, if that chances, my people who look upon you as half a god, will raise you up to be Inca after me, should such be your desire."

"It is not," I broke in.

"I believe you," he answered, bowing his head, "but will it not be the desire of that fair-faced harlot who has betrayed our Lord the Sun?"

At this word I started and bit my lip.

"Ah! that stings you," he went on, "as the truth always stings, and it is well. Understand, White Lord who were once my brother, that either you must fight me to the death, or I declare war upon you and upon the Chanca people, which war I will wage from month to month and from year to year until you are all destroyed, as destroyed you shall be. But should you fight and should the Sun give me the victory, then justice will be accomplished and I will keep the peace that I have sworn with the Chanca people. Further, should you conquer me, in the name of my people I swear that there shall still be peace between them and the Chancas, since I shall have atoned your sacrilege with my blood. Now summon those lords of yours and I will summon mine, and set out the matter to them."

So I turned and beckoned to my captains, and Kari beckoned to his. They came, and in the hearing of all, very clearly and quietly as was his fashion, he repeated every word that he had said to me, adding to them others of like meaning. While he spoke I thought, not listening over much.

This thing was hateful to me, yet I was in a snare, since according to the customs of all these peoples I could not refuse such a challenge and remain unshamed. Moreover, it was to the advantage of the Chancas, aye and of the Quichuas also, that I should not refuse it seeing that whether I lived or died, peace would then reign between them who otherwise must both be destroyed in war. I remembered how once

Quilla had sacrificed herself to prevent such a war, though in the end that war had come; and what Quilla had done, should I not do also? Weary though I was I did not fear Kari, brave and swift as he might be, indeed I thought that I could kill him and perhaps take his throne, since the Quichuas worshipped me, who so often had led their armies to triumph, almost as much as did the Chancas. But—I could not kill Kari. As soon would I kill one born of my own mother. Was there then no escape?

The answer rose in my mind. There was an escape. I could suffer Kari to kill me. Only if I did this, what of Quilla! After all that had come and gone, must I lose Quilla thus, and must Quilla lose me? Surely she would break her heart and die. My plight was desperate. I knew not what to do. Then of a sudden while I wavered, some voice seemed to whisper in my ear; I thought it must be that of St. Hubert. It seemed to say to me, 'Kari trusts to his god, cannot you trust to yours, Hubert of Hastings, you who are a Christian man? Go forward, and trust to yours, Hubert of Hastings.'"

Kari's gentle voice died away; he had finished his speech and all men looked at me.

"What word?" I said roughly to my captains.

"Only this, Lord," answered their spokesman. "Fight you must, of that there can be no doubt, but we would fight with you, the ten of the Chancas against the ten of the Quichuas."

"Aye, that is good," replied the first of Kari's nobles. "This business is too great to set upon one man's skill and strength."

"Have done!" I said. "It lies between the Inca and myself," while Kari nodded, and repeated "Have done!" after me.

Then I sent one of the captains back to the camp

for my sword and Kari commanded that his should be brought to him, since according to the custom of these people when ambassadors meet, neither of us was armed. Presently, the captain holding my sword returned, and with him servants who brought my armour. Also after them streamed all the army of the Chancas among whom the news had spread like wind-driven fire, and lined themselves upon the ridge to watch. As he came, too, I noticed that this captain sharpened Wave-Flame with a certain kind of stone that was used to give a keen edge to weapons.

He brought the ancient sword and handed it to me on his knee. The Inca's man also brought his sword and handed it to him, as he did so, bowing his forehead to the dust. Well I knew that weapon, since once before I had faced it in desperate battle for my life. It was the ivory-handled sword of the Lord Deleroy which Kari had taken from his dead hand after I slew him in the Solar of my house in the Cheap at London. Then the servant came to me with the armour, but I sent him away, saying that as the Inca had none, I would not wear it, at which my people murmured.

Kari saw and heard.

"Noble as ever," he said aloud, "Oh! that such bright honour should have been tarnished by a woman's breath."

Our lords discussed the manner of our fighting, but to them I paid little heed.

At length all was ready and we stepped forward to face each other at a given word, clad much alike. I had thrown off my outer garment and stood bareheaded in a jerkin of soft sheepskin. Kari too was stripped of his splendid dress and clad in a tunic of sheepskin. Also, that we might be quite equal he had taken off his turban-like headgear and even the royal

Fringe, whereat his lords stared at each other for they thought this a bad omen.

It was just then I heard a sound behind me, and turning my head I saw Quilla stumbling towards us down the stony slope as best her half-blind eyes would let her, and crying as she came:

"Oh! my Lord, fight not. O Inca, I will return to the House of the Sun!"

"Silence, accursed woman!" said Kari frowning. "Does the Sun take back such as you? Silence until the woe that you have wrought is finished, and then wail on for ever."

She shrank at his bitter, unjust words, and guided by the women who had followed her, sank upon a stone, where she sat still as a statue or as dead Upanqui in his hall.

Now one called aloud the pledges of the fight which were as Kari had spoken them. He listened and added:

"Be it known also that this battle is to the death of one or both of us, since if we live I take back my oaths and I will burn yonder witch as a sacrifice to the Sun whom she has betrayed, and destroy her people and her city according to the ancient law of Vengeance on the House of those who have deceived the Sun."

I heard but made no answer, who did not wish to waste my breath in bandying words with a great man, whose brain had been turned by bigotry and woman-hatred.

A moment later the signal was given and we were at it. Kari leapt at me like the tree-lion of his own forests, but I avoided and parried. Thrice he leapt and thrice I did this; yes, even when I saw an opening and might have cut him down. Almost I struck, then could not. The Chancas watched me, wondering what game I played who was not wont to fight in this fashion, and I also wondered, who still knew not what to do. Something I must do, or presently I should be slain, since soon my guard would fail and Deleroy's sword get home at last.

I think that Kari grew perplexed at this patient defence of mine and never a blow struck back. At least he withdrew a little, then came for me with a rush, holding his sword high above his head with the purpose of striking me above that guard, or so I supposed. Then, of a sudden, I knew what to do. Wheeling Wave-Flame with all my strength in both hands, I smote, not at Kari but at the ivory handle of his sword. The keen and ancient steel that might well have been some of that which as legend told, was forged by the dwarfs in Norseland, fell upon the ivory between his hand-grip and the cross-piece and shore through it as I had hoped that it would do, so that the blade of Kari's sword, severed just above the hilt, fell to the ground and the hilt itself was jarred from his hand.

His nobles saw and groaned while the Chancas shouted with joy, for now Kari was defenceless and save for the death itself, this fight to the death was ended.

Kari folded his arms upon his breast and bent his head.

" It is the decree of my god," he said, " and I did ill to trust to the sword of a villain whom you slew. Strike, Conqueror, and make an end."

I rested myself upon Wave-Flame and answered :

" If I strike not, O Inca, will you take back your words and let peace reign between your people and the Chancas ? "

" Nay," he answered. " What I have said, I have said. If yonder false woman is given up to suffer the fate of those who have betrayed the Sun, then there shall be peace between the Peoples, but not otherwise, since while I live I will wage war upon her and you, and upon the Chancas who shelter both of you."

Now rage took hold of me, who remembered that while this woman-hater lived blood must flow in streams, but that if he died there would be peace and Quilla would be safe. I lifted my sword a little, and as I did so Quilla rose from her stone and stumbled forward, crying :

" O Lord, shed not the Inca's holy blood for me. Let me be given up ! Let me be given up ! "

Then some spirit entered into me and I spoke saying :

" Lady, half of your prayer I grant and half I deny. I will not shed the Inca's blood ; as soon would I shed yours. Nor will I suffer you to be given up who have done no wrong, since it was I who took you away by force, as Urco would have done. Kari, hearken to me. Not once only when we were in danger together in past days, have you said to me that we must put our faith in the gods we worship, and thus we did. Now again I hearken to that counsel of yours and put my faith in the God I worship. You threaten to gather all the strength of your mighty empire and because of what I hold to be your superstitions, to destroy the Chanca People to the last babe and to level their city to the last stone. I do not believe that the God I worship will suffer this to come about, though how he will stay your vengeance I do not know. Kari, great Inca of Tavantinsuyu, Lord of all this strange new world, I the White Wanderer from the Sea, give you your life and save you as once before I saved you in a far land, and with your life I give you my blessing in all matters but this one alone. Kari, my brother, look your last on me and go in peace."

The Inca heard and raising his head, stared at me with his fine, melancholy eyes. Then suddenly from those eyes there came a gush of tears. More, he knelt before me and kissed the ground, as the humblest of his slaves might do before his own majesty.

"Most noble of men," he said, lifting himself up again, "I worship you. Yes, I, the Inca, worship you. Would that I might take back my oath, but this I cannot do because my god hardens my heart and then would decree destruction on my people. Mayhap He whom you serve will bring things to pass as you foretell, as it would seem He has brought it to pass that I should eat the dust before you. I hope that it may be so who love not the sight of blood, but who like the shot arrow must yet follow my course, driven by the strength that loosed me. Brother honoured and beloved, fare you well! May happiness be yours in life and death, and there in death may we meet again and once more be brothers where no women come to part us."

Then Kari turned and went with bowed head, together with his nobles, who followed him as sadly as those who surround a corpse, but not until they had given to me that royal salute which is only rendered to the Inca in his glory.

CHAPTER XIII

THE KISS OF QUILLA

HER women bore Quilla swooning from that ill-fated field, and sick and sad she remained until once more we saw the City of the Chancas. Yet all this while strength and sight were returning to her eyes, so that in the end she could see as well as ever she had done, for which I thanked Heaven.

Messengers had gone before us, so that when we drew near all the People of the Chancas came out to meet us, a mighty multitude, who spread flowers before us and sang songs of joy. On the same evening I was summoned by Huaracha and found him dying. There in the presence of his chief captains Quilla and I told him all our story, to which he listened, answering nothing. When it was finished he said :

" I thank you, Lord-from-the-Sea, who through great perils have saved my daughter and brought her home to bid farewell to me, untarnished as she went. I understand now that it was an evil policy which led me to promise her in marriage to the Prince Urco. Through your valour it has come to naught and I am glad. Great dangers still lie ahead of you and of my people. Deal with them as you will and can, for henceforward, Lord-from-the-Sea, they are your people, yours and my daughter's together, since it is my desire and command that you two should wed so soon as I am laid with my fathers. Perchance it had been better if you had slain the Inca when he was in your hand, but man goes where his spirit leads him. My blessing and the blessing of my gods be on you both and on your children. Leave me, for I can say no more."

That night King Huaracha died.

Three days later he was buried with great pomp beneath the floor of the Temple of the Moon, not being preserved and kept above ground after the fashion of the Incas.

On the last day of the mourning a Council was summoned of all the great ones in the country to the number of several hundreds, to which I was bidden. This was done in the name of Quilla, who was now named by a title which meant, "High Lady," or "Queen." I went to it eagerly enough who had seen nothing of her since that night of her father's death, for, according to the custom of this people, she had spent the time of mourning alone with her women.

To my surprise I was led by an officer, not into the great hall where I knew the notables were assembling, but to that same little chamber where first I had talked with Huaracha, Quilla's father. Here the officer left me wondering. Presently I heard a sound and looking up, saw Quilla herself standing between the curtains, like to a picture in its frame. She was royally arrayed and wore upon her brow and breast the emblem of the moon, so that she seemed to glitter in that dusky place, though nothing about her shone with such a light as did her large and doe-like eyes.

"Greeting, my Lord," she said in her soft voice, curtsying to me as she spoke. "Has my Lord aught to say to me? If so it must be quick, since the Great Council waits."

Now I grew foolish and tongue-tied, but at length stammered out:

"Nothing, except what I have said before—that I love you."

She smiled a little in her slow fashion, then asked:

"Is there naught to add?"

"What can there be to add to love, Quilla?"

"I know not," she answered, still smiling. "Yet in what does the love of man and woman end?"

I shook my head and answered:

"In many things, all of them different. In hell sometimes, and more rarely in heaven."

"And on earth which lies between the two, should those who love escape death and separation?"

"Well, on earth—in marriage."

She looked at me again and this time a new light shone in her eyes which I could not misinterpret.

"Do you mean that you will marry me, Quilla?" I muttered.

"Such was my father's wish, Lord, but what is yours? Oh! have done," she went on in a changed voice. "For what have we suffered all these things and gone through such long parting and dangers so dreadful? Was it not that if Fate should spare us we might come together at last? And has not Fate spared us—for a while? What said the prophecy of me in the Temple of Rimac? Was it not that the Sun should be my refuge and—I forget the rest."

"I remember it," I said. "That in the beloved arms you should sleep at last."

"Yes," she went on, the blood mounting to her cheeks, "that in the beloved arms I should sleep at last. So, the first part of the prophecy has come true."

"As the rest shall come true," I broke in, awaking, and swept her to my breast.

"Are you sure," she murmured presently, "that you love me, a woman whom you think savage, well enough to wed me?"

"Aye, more than sure," I answered.

"Hearken, Lord. I knew it always, but being woman I desired to hear it from your own lips. Of this be certain that though I am but what I am, a maiden, wild-hearted and untaught, no man shall ever have a truer and more loving wife. It is my hope, even that my love will be such that in it at last you may learn to forget that other lady far away who once was yours, if only for an hour."

Now I shrank as from a sword prick, since first loves, whatever the tale of them, as Quilla guessed or Nature taught her, are not easily forgot and even when they are dead their ghosts will rise and haunt us.

"And my hope, most dear, is that you will be mine, not for an hour but for all our life's days," I answered.

"Aye," she said, sighing, "but who knows how many these will be? Therefore let us pluck the flowers before they wither. I hear steps. The lords come to summon us. Be pleased to enter the Council at my side and holding me by the hand. There I have somewhat to say to the people. The shadow of the Inca Kari, whom you spared, still lies cold upon us and them."

Before I could ask her meaning the lords entered, three of them, and glancing at us curiously, said that all were gathered. Then they turned and went before us to the great hall where every place was filled. Hand in hand we mounted the dais and as we came all the audience rose and greeted us with a roar of welcome.

Quilla seated herself upon a throne and motioned to me to take my place upon another throne at her side, which I noted stood a little higher than that on which she sat, and this, as I learned afterwards, not by chance. It was planned so to tell the people of the

Chancas that henceforth I was their king while she was but my wife.

When the shouting had died away Quilla rose from her throne and began to speak, which like many of the higher class of this people, she could do well enough.

" Lords and Captains of the Chanca nation," she said, " my father, the King Huaracha, being dead and leaving no lawful son, I have succeeded to his dignities, and summoned you here to take counsel with me.

" First, learn this, that I, your Queen and Lady, have been chosen as wife by him who sits at my side."

Here the company shouted again, thus announcing that this tidings pleased them. For though by now only the common people still believed me to be a god risen from the sea, all held that I was a great general and a great man, one who knew much that they did not know, and who could both lead and fight better than the best of them. Indeed, since I had slain Urco with my hands and overcome Kari, who as Inca was believed to be clothed with the strength of the Sun and therefore unconquerable, I was held to be unmatched throughout Tavantinsuyu. Moreover, the army that had fought under my command loved me as though I were their father as well as their general. Therefore all greeted this tidings well although without astonishment, for they knew it was their dead king's wish that I should wed his daughter and that to win her I had gone through much.

In answer to their shoutings I too rose from my seat, and drawing the sword Wave-Flame, which I wore girt about my dinted armour, with it I saluted first Quilla and then the gathered nobles, saying:

" Lords of the Chancas, when my eyes fell upon

this lady who to-day is your queen, on an island in the sea, I loved her and swore that I would wed her if I might. Between that day and this much has befallen. She was snatched away to be made the wife of Urco, heir to the Inca throne, and afterwards, to escape him, whom she hated, she took refuge in the House of the Inca god. Then, people of the Chancas, came the great war which we shared together, and in the end I rescued her from that house of bondage, and slew Urco while he strove to snatch her away. This done, I conquered Kari the Inca, who was as my brother, yet because I had saved your Lady from his god the Sun, became my enemy, and together she and I returned to this, her land. Now it is her will to wed me, as it has always been mine to wed her, and here in front of all of you I take her to wife, as she takes me to husband, hoping that for many years it may be given to us to rule over you, and to our children after us. Yet I warn you that although in the great war that has been, if with much loss, we have held our own against all the hosts of Cuzco and won an honourable peace, by this marriage of ours, which robs the Inca god of one of a thousand brides, that peace is broken. Therefore in the future as in the past, there will be war between the Quichua and the Chanca Peoples."

"We know it," shouted the nobles. "War is decreed, let war come!"

"What would you have had me do?" I went on. "Leave your Queen to languish in the House of the Sun, wed to nothingness, or suffer her to be dragged away to be one of Urco's women, or hand her back to Kari to be slain as a sacrifice to a god whom you do not accept?"

"Nay!" they cried. "We would have her wed you, White-Lord-from-the-Sea, that she may become a mother of kings."

"So I thought, Chancas. Yet I warn you that there is trouble near. The storm gathers and soon it will burst, since Kari is not one who breaks his oaths."

"Why did you not kill him when he was in your hand, and take his throne?" asked one.

"Because I could not. Because it would not have been pleasing to Heaven that I should slay a man, who for years had been as my brother. Because in this way or in that the deed would have fallen back upon my head, upon the head of the Lady Quilla, and upon your heads also, O people of the Chancas, because——"

At this moment there was disturbance at the end of the hall, and a herald cried:

"An embassy! An embassy from Kari, the Inca."

"Let it be admitted," said Quilla.

Presently up the central passage marched the embassy with pomp, great lords and "ear men," every man of them, and bowed before us.

"Your words?" said Quilla quietly.

"They are these, Lady," answered the spokesman of the party. "For the last time the Inca demands that you should surrender yourself to be sacrificed as one who has betrayed the Sun. He asks it of you since he has learned that your father Huaracha is no more."

"And if I refuse to surrender myself, what then, O Ambassador?"

"Then in the name of the Empire and in his own name the Inca declares war upon you, war to the end, until not one of Chanca blood is left living beneath the sun and not one stone marks where your city stood. It may be that a while will pass before this sword of war falls upon your head, since the Inca must gather his armies and give a breathing space to his peoples after all the troubles that have been. Yet if not this year, then next year, and if not next year, then the year after, that sword shall fall."

Quilla listened and turned pale, though more, I think, with wrath than fear. Then she said :

" You have heard, Chancas, and know how stands this case. If I surrender myself to be sacrificed, the Inca in his mercy will spare you ; if I do not surrender myself, soon or late he will destroy you—if he can. Say then, shall I surrender myself ? "

Now every man in that great hall leapt up and from every throat there arose a shout of

" Never ! "

When it had died away an aged chief and councillor an uncle of Huaracha, the dead King, came forward and stared at the envoys with his horny eyes.

" Go back to the Inca," he said, " and tell him that the threats of the mouth are one thing and the deeds of the hand are another. In the late war that has been he has learned something of our quality, both as foes and friends, and perchance more remains for him to learn. Yonder is one "—and he pointed to myself—" who is about to become our King and the husband of our Queen. By the help of that one and of some of us the Inca won his throne. From the mercy of that one, also, but a little while ago the Inca won his life. Let him be careful lest through the might of that one, behind whom stands every Chanca that breathes, the Inca Kari Upanqui should yet lose both throne and life, and with them the ancient empire of the Sun. Thus say we all."

" Thus say we all ! " repeated the great company with a roar that shook the walls.

In the silence that followed Quilla asked :

" Have you aught to add, O Ambassadors ? "

" Aye, this," said the first of them.

"The Chanca tree is about to be cut down, but the Inca still offers a refuge to the Lion that hides among its branches because he has loved that Lion from of old. Let the White-Lord-from-the-Sea over whom you have cast the net of your witcheries, return with us and he shall be saved and given place and power, and with them a brother's love."

Now Quilla looked at me and I rose to speak, but could not, since all that came from my lips was laughter. At length I said:

"But the other day when I gave him his life, the Inca named me noble. What would he think of me if I said yes to this his offer? Would he call me noble then and the Lion that dwells in the Chanca tree? Or, whatever his lips might speak, would not his heart name me the basest of all slaves and no lion of the tree, but rather a snake that creeps at its roots? Get you gone, my lords, and say that here I bide happy with her whom I have won, and that the ancient sword Wave-Flame, on which Kari has looked of late, is still sharp and the arm that wields it is still strong, and that he will do well now that it has served his turn, to look on it no more," and again I drew the great blade and flashed it before their eyes there in that dusky hall.

Then they bowed courteously, for every man of them knew me and some of them loved me well, turned and went. That was the last that ever I, Hubert of Hastings, saw of nobles of the Inca blood, though perchance, ere long, I shall meet them again in war.

"Let them be escorted safely from the city," commanded Quilla, and soldiers went to do her bidding.

When they had gone she issued another order, that the door should be closed and watchmen set about the hall, so that none could approach it unseen. Then after a pause she rose and spoke:

"My Lord," she said, "who soon, as I trust, will be my husband and my king, and you, the chosen of my people, hearken to me for I have a matter to lay before you. You have heard the Inca's message and you know that his words are not vain. He, who is great in many ways, in one is small and narrow. He sets his god before his honour, and to satisfy his god, whom he thinks that I have outraged, is prepared to sacrifice his honour, and even to kill one to whom he owes all," and she touched me with her hand. "Moreover these things he can do, not at once but in time to come, because for every man of ours, he is able to gather ten. Therefore we stand thus; death and destruction stare us in the face."

She paused and that old chief of whom I have spoken, asked in the midst of a silence, as I think it was planned that he should ask,

"You have set our teeth in the bitter rind of truth. Is there no sweet fruit within? Can you not show us a way of escape, O Quilla, Daughter of the Moon, whose heart is fed with the wisdom of the Moon?"

"I believe that I can show you such a way," she answered. "You know the legend of our people—that in the old days, a thousand years ago—we came to this country out of the forests.

"You know, too, the legend tells that once far away, beyond the forest, there was a mighty empire of which the king sat in a City of Gold hidden within a ring of mountains. That king, it is said, had two sons, and when he died these sons made war upon each other, and one of them, my forefather, was defeated and driven away into the forests, with those who clung to him. By boats he descended the river that runs through the forest, and at length with those who remained to him, came to this land and there once more grew to be a king. Is it not so?"

"It is so," answered the aged chief. "The tale has come down to me through ten generations, and with it the prophecy, that in a day to come the Chancas would return to that City of Gold whence they came and be welcomed of its people."

"I have heard that prophecy," said Quilla. "Moreover of it I have something to tell you. While I sat in despair and blindness in the Convent of the Sun at Cuzco, it came into my mind and I brooded upon it much, who was always sure that the war between the Chancas and the armies of the Incas was but begun. In my darkness and misery I prayed to my Mother, the Moon, for light and help. Long and often I prayed and at length an answer came. One night the Spirit of the Moon appeared to my soul as a beautiful and shining goddess, and spoke to me.

"'Be brave, Daughter,' she said, 'for all that seems to be lost shall yet be found again, and the light of a certain flashing sword shall pierce the blackness and give back vision to your eyes.' This indeed happened, my people, since it was when the sword of my Lord saved me from death at the hands of Urco that the first gleam of light returned to my darkened eyes.

"'Be not afraid, moreover, for the Children of the Chancas who bow to me,' went on the shining Spirit of the Moon, 'since in the day of their danger I will show them a path towards my place of resting in the west. Yea, I will lead them far from wars and tyrannies back to that ancient City whence they came, and there they shall sleep in peace till all things are accomplished. Moreover, you shall be their ruler during your appointed days, you and another whom I led to you out of the deeps of the sea and showed to you sleeping in my beams.'

"Thus that Spirit spoke to me, Councillors, though at the time I did not know whether the vision were more than a happy dream. But now I do know that it was no dream, but the truth.

"For did not my sight begin to return to me in the flashing of the sword that is named Flame-of-the-Wave? And if this were true, why should not the rest be true also? People of the Chancas, I am your Queen to-day and my counsel to you is that we flee from this land before the Inca's net closes round us and the Inca's spears pierce our heart, to seek our ancient home far in the depths of the western forest where, as I trust, his armies cannot come. Is that your will, my People? If so, by the tongues of your Lords and Captains declare it here and now before it be too late."

Back thundered the answer,

"It is our will, O Daughter of the Moon!"

When its echoes had died away Quilla turned to me, lovely to look on as the evening star and with eyes that shone like stars, and asked:

"Is it your will also, Lord-from-the-Sea?"

"Your will is my will, Quilla," I answered, "and your heart is my home. Lead on; where you go I follow, even to the edge of the world and beyond the world."

"So be it!" she cried in a triumphant voice. "Now the evil past is finished with its fears and battles and before our feet, lit by moonbeams, stretches the Future's shining road leading us to the mystery in which all roads begin and for an hour are lost again. Now, too, our separations end in a perfect unity that perchance we have known before and shall know again in ages to be born and lands unvisited. Now, Lord-from-the-Sea, at whose coming my sleeping heart awoke to love and whose sword saved me from shame and death giving me back to life and light, here, before this company of our people, I, the Daughter of the Moon, defying the Sun, who held me captive, and all his servants, take you to husband with this kiss," and leaning forward Quilla pressed her lips upon my own. . . . .

The remaining parchment sheets of the ancient Manuscript are rotted with the damp of the tomb in which it lay for centuries and quite undecipherable.—EDITOR.

PRINTED IN ENGLAND BY CASSELL & COMPANY, LIMITED, LONDON, E.C.4.
F.110 1121